BROKEN FIGHTER

MAFIA WARS - BOOK TWO

MAGGIE COLE

PULSE PRESS

PROLOGUE

Boris Ivanov

THE FIRST TIME I MADE A DEAL WITH THE DEVIL, IT WAS TO save my mother. In the end, it didn't matter. Satan still won.

The second time, I tried to buy my brothers' and my freedom. All the agreement did was create a mirage about our lives, who we were deep down, and who still owns us.

After that chain of events, you would think my conscience would have disappeared. That all reason not to take whatever or whoever I wanted would no longer exist.

But the voice in my head still told me not to make her mine. From the first time I saw her as anything but my best friend Killian's sister, that voice has screamed at me to stay far away from her.

But how do you stay away from the girl you've always known? The one whose face you can't escape all day, who seems to be the only person on earth who can look into your soul? The one who never denies what you're capable of but still doesn't run?

We had a conversation once. I caught her in a weak moment. She drank too much at her older brother Sean's funeral. Killian and his other brothers were too distraught to notice she went off. I followed her, worried. She told me she could see the killer in my eyes and not from the boxing ring. "You've killed men. I saw the change in you years ago. You were seventeen."

I stood in shock then tried to cover it up. "You don't know what you're talking about. You're drunk."

She sadly laughed, and through tears, said, "I'm an O'Malley. I see all the males in my family morph from boys to men and what that means. And no matter what you do, Boris Ivanov, I see you. The real you."

To this day, I'm unsure why I did what I did next. Touching her opened Pandora's box. It was a dip into the well of pleasure I craved but couldn't have. I tucked her silky red hair behind her ear and possessively cupped her porcelain cheeks, as if she were mine, wiping her tears with my thumbs. "Then you should want to stay away from me."

More tears fell as her green eyes pierced mine. "Why?"

"You know why."

"I've tried. You keep coming in to see me." It was an intoxicated admission. She wouldn't have ever said it if she weren't. But there it was, out in the open. I wasn't imagining things. She wanted me as much as I was dying to have her. And she knew I wasn't only coming to see Killian.

If she hadn't been drunk, I wouldn't have stopped myself. The craving I had for her deepened with the unhidden truth. I would have put my mouth over her hot, juicy one and tasted everything I had been obsessing over.

I was still fighting the lust within me when the sound of the metal door shutting, followed by my brother clearing his throat, pulled me out of my dilemma. I released her and spun.

"Killian's looking for you," Dmitri said. I avoided his "what the hell are you doing expression" and went inside. But the damage was done. I had gotten too close to everything I had banned myself from having. I told myself to stay away from her. I couldn't even last twenty-four hours. The next day, I went straight back to Nora's pub, pretending to look for Killian, knowing he wouldn't be there but she would.

Time did nothing to quench our attraction. Anything with her was taboo in too many ways. Our families shouldn't mix, besides Killian and my friendship. It doesn't matter if she and her brothers try to stay out of the O'Malley crime family business. It's in their blood. No matter how hard they try to escape it, I see what's coming.

And while my brothers may think our legitimate businesses don't make us a crime family, how different is what we do compared to the mob? Zamir Petrov may rule the Russian mafia, but we're the Ivanovs. No one, except Zamir, messes with us, or there are consequences.

But the hands of fate shouldn't mix an Irish angel and a Russian killer. So I told myself over and over to stay away from her.

It did no good.

Almost every night, I went to her pub to meet up with Killian. He might as well have been another brother to me. While I played the charade I was there to hang out with him, both Nora and I knew the truth. Never once did I miss the faint blush when she saw me. Or her quiet, breathy gasps when I touched her when no one else was looking. God help me when I caught her green eyes sneaking a glance my way.

I'm an expert at torturing men, but Nora could have had a black belt in tormenting me. We were in a constant state of purgatory, and I couldn't climb out. Every morning, I'd wake up and tell myself, today is the day to forget about her. Then I'd go right back into the Garden of Eden, where she might as well have been holding the apple to my mouth.

I never bit into it. I somehow found the strength not to press my lips on her creamy white skin or lush mouth I'd imagined doing every inappropriate thing possible with.

But Nora watched me. Closer than I ever realized. The one night a year, and days after it, I always stayed away from her and everyone else was for a reason.

Patience is a gift I've always used to my advantage. If you can't trust yourself to stay in control, you shouldn't step in front of temptation, especially one you've obsessed over for years.

Nora O'Malley found my weak spot, took my restraint, and broke it in two. She's a virus that won't leave my body, no matter how much she or I attempted to distance ourselves.

Sometimes, what you think you're doing for the right reasons leads to consequences you never imagined. I shouldn't have ever allowed her to try and stay away from me after that night. The moment Cormac Byrne stepped foot in her pub and set his eyes on her, I saw it. I took him outside and warned him she was off-limits. Nora and I might not have been able to be with each other, but nothing about Cormac was good enough to even be near her.

Men like him never listen though. His eyes revealed everything I needed to know. Why Killian and his brothers never saw it, I don't understand. They should have. Their blood boils with rage the way mine does. Men have taken their last breath under their hands. So why they encouraged Cormac to be with Nora and never saw what I did still baffles me.

The only reason I see is he's Irish. Or I should say he was.

One thing you should never do is look the devil in the eye and try to take what's his. If Satan tells you something, you listen. Any attempt to overthrow him better be ironclad. Cormac was too arrogant to understand this.

I'd always lived by this rule until recently. My brothers and I started a war between the two largest crime families. There were many reasons to do it. But taking down Zamir Petrov, the man who made me into the sinner I am, might not have been the best idea I ever had.

Bad things happen when you lose patience and act with emotions. Nora O'Malley makes my head spin so fast, I struggle to breathe most days. Mixing it with the hatred I have for Zamir might be my downfall.

Every man I've ever killed on Zamir's orders, he made me brand while they were still alive. Not their skin but their bones. A symbol of Satanism, a five-pointed star with a circle around it. I never told my brothers. The less they know about what happens when Zamir calls on me his one time a year, the better.

5

Now, there's no hiding it. All the proof of my skills is in the city lot my brothers and I bought. I didn't know. A dated newspaper from several months ago is in a plastic bag. It's from my last kill. And it's proof Zamir planted them. He's intentionally sending me a message.

There are only three reasons Zamir would bury those bones for the land cleanup crew to find. First, he wants to change the deal on our debt and pull my brothers and me back into his control.

Or, he could know we killed his son, Wes.

But the last possibility might mean I made the biggest mistake of my life. It could be far worse than living the rest of our lives under his dictatorship.

The only other explanation is he knows we started the war. One thing Zamir doesn't have is a heart. Greed rules his soul. Messing with his empire was a risk we knew going in but one I don't want to see the consequences of.

No matter which reason it is, everyone my brothers and I love is in more danger than ever before. No one and no form of sadistic punishment is off-limits to Zamir. My gut says the first person he would go after is Nora. She's also carrying my child. The things he would do to her burn in my mind all day long.

I need to kill him before he's able to get to her. But the problem with Zamir is he's a ghost. He appears and vanishes when he chooses.

As much as I've tried to not let the devil consume me, I'm going to have to. The only way to overpower evil is to pour more gasoline on the fire. Zamir taught me that.

But how do you become more sadistic than the devil himself without harming the person you love the most? Can you really keep everything good in your life when you morph into everything you despise?

Chills dig into my bones. I gaze over at Nora, curled up in my arms, sleeping peacefully, and I can't help wonder if part of Zamir's plan is to not only destroy my brothers and me but torture us in a different way. If I tap into the monster existing within me, the one I've never fully let loose, how will it be possible for Nora to still love me?

1

Nora O'Malley

Two Years Ago

"WE'RE OUT OF WHISKEY. THE GUINNESS IS RUNNING LOW, too," my brother Declan informs me.

I squeeze my eyes shut. "How is this possible? I ordered double."

Declan grunts. "It's an O'Malley funeral. Next time order triple."

I open my eyes. His smirk only makes me want to smack him. "What am I supposed to do? They're all drunk and going to be pissed."

"I'll run down to the Kellys and see if they have a keg and a few cases we can buy off them for the night." Declan pulls his keys out of his pocket.

I sigh. "Thanks."

He leaves out the back door.

I stare at the peeling paint on the hallway wall, trying to convince myself everything will be okay. My grandmother passed in the middle of the week. I inherited her pub, which I've worked in my entire life. There's no reason I should be in this situation. But the first major decision I had to make, which only included ordering enough alcohol for her wake, I failed at.

An Irish pub out of whiskey and Guinness.

Sorry, Nana. You're probably rolling over in your grave.

She's dead. I'm never going to see her or hear her voice again.

I wipe my face, grateful I'm in the hallway, turned toward the wall. I haven't cried once today. I pulled it together and got this far.

And now I'm breaking down over whiskey and Guinness.

I'm in the midst of my pity party when my body hums against his hard frame. Flutters erupt from his hand, pressing into the curve of my waist. His other fingers push my hair to the side, and he drags one down my neck. He leans into my ear. His deep, gruff voice sends delicious chills down my spine. "Serve them vodka. Time for everyone to understand what real men drink."

My heart hammers. I freeze for several seconds, leaning into him, wishing I didn't want him and also at the same time, praying I could have him.

He continues, "I'll go make a bet with everyone in the bar they can't handle vodka, which will naturally make them attempt it."

I spin into his chest, inhaling the smell that's driven me crazy since we were kids. No matter what I do, I can't seem to stop the throbbing of my body every time it wafts into my nose.

Everything about him makes the hairs on my arms stand up. He towers over me and has tattoos all over, including one that says "unscarred" over his abdomen. Every time I see that tattoo, I want to hold him and never let go. He got it on his twenty-first birthday, as if to prove a point. To whom, I don't know. The outside world may see him as he wants them to, but I know there's no way he could ever be unaffected by what he does.

He kills people. I saw his eyes change from innocence to darkness. I knew what it meant the moment I saw those cold, self-loathing, "don't mess with me" eyes. It didn't matter I was only a young girl, barely thirteen.

My brothers are all boxers. Most of my cousins who take part in the O'Malley mob business are, too. They all have the same fighter's eyes Boris does. Each of their gazes changed at some point or another to include something deeper and colder. It happens when you become someone you didn't think you were. My grandmother explained it to me. I don't know what the circumstances were or how Boris got involved in whatever it is he can't seem to get out of, but nothing will ever make me believe what's inked on his body.

I wish I knew who the holder of his demons was. Once a year, I see the self-loathing escalate. A few times he's gotten a text or call. I've seen him close his eyes as his face hardens.

Within seconds, he leaves. I don't know who's on the other end or where he goes, but for a few days, he'll disappear. When he comes back, there's always more darkness in his expression.

Somehow, the piercing of his gaze only drew me in further. Even at thirteen, I pined for him. He hardly acknowledged my existence then, other than being Killian's younger sister. But I watched him withdraw and change even though no one else did. Then suddenly, when I hit my twenties, Boris's interest in me grew. My nana saw it. To this day, no one else in my family knows about our attraction or flirtatious behavior, but she somehow knew. Years passed before she sat me down in one of the booths, pointed to the game room where Boris and Killian were playing pool, and said, "You are an O'Malley. You do not have Russian in your blood. It is not meant to be, Nora. Do not taint the purity of our bloodline. Nothing good can come out of anything with him."

"I haven't—"

"Not yet. But you are nearing your thirties now. I have witnessed this building between the two of you. I cannot ignore it any longer. I thought it would wither and fade, but it hasn't. If anything, it's getting stronger. And if your brothers find out, they will kill him."

My pulse beat so hard in my neck, I put my hand over it. "We aren't doing anything."

She raised her eyebrows and took my hand. "It's time you married. You're meant to have Irish babies, like your sisters. You cannot fulfill your role in our family with him."

I opened my mouth to speak then shut it. Denying my attraction to Boris would only insult my nana. The next words flew out of my mouth and shocked me but didn't seem to surprise her. "I love him." My chest tightened at the realization and the fact I just admitted to my nana something I hadn't to myself. And I had never even kissed Boris.

Her eyes turned to slits. It was blasphemy in her world. "It doesn't matter. You need to find someone Irish."

That was a few years ago. I still haven't kissed Boris. The closest I ever got was a few months ago at my brother, Sean's, funeral. I was drunk, and my liquid courage made me admit to him I knew he wanted me. It was an unspoken attraction between us until that point—something we danced around for over a decade. I thought he was going to kiss me, but his brother interrupted us.

Since then, the magnetic pull toward each other has only gotten more powerful. Every chance he gets to touch me, he does. And unless my brothers are around, he no longer hides his obsession with me. He tortures me with every look and touch. He's made me into a quivering mess of pent-up frustration. I'm not sure how much more I can take, but there doesn't seem to be an end in sight.

He glances to the side quickly, making sure no one else is in the hall, then moves his hand to my ass and tugs me into him.

I gasp. He's never touched my ass before or been so close. My head barely reaches his chest. The heat in my face grows.

He squeezes my ass, as if it's his, and tilts my chin with his other hand. "This is easily solved. How much vodka do you have?" His words sound innocent as his hot breath merges into mine.

Vodka? Why are we discussing vodka?

There's a bar full of Irish people.

"I..."

Oh, Jesus, Mary, and Joseph!

His lips inch closer. I shudder against him, which is another thing I can't seem to control lately. Every time he touches me, it's an electric shock to my cells.

He cocks an eyebrow. In a firm voice, he says, "How much vodka, *moya dusha?*"

That's the other thing he started doing after Sean's funeral. In private, he started calling me *moya dusha.* I searched online and it says it means *my soul.* It's another thing adding to the constant state of flutters inside me when I'm around him.

My gaze roams to his lips. They're full, with a bit of roughness, surrounded by his black mustache and beard. It matches his longer dark hair, which is the opposite of his short, well-trimmed beard. I've never even dated anyone with facial hair; they've all been clean-cut. But something about his twists my panties. It adds to his dangerous flair. His hair is messy, and all I can think of doing is running my hands in it to steady myself just from being around him.

"Enough it would take them years to drink it," I mutter.

He grunts. "We'll see about that." He releases me, and I want to grab his hand and put it back on my ass cheek where it doesn't belong.

It can't. He's not Irish. Everything my nana said was right. My brothers will kill him. My sisters' husbands would jump right in, too. Or Boris would kill them, fighting back. Either way, I don't want to see, or be the cause of, it. I can't even go to the fights where Killian and Boris are in the ring with a referee. Any other match, I can watch them. But not when they box against each other.

And there's no reason to mix our blood with his. My gut tells me if we ever gave in to our temptation, there will be no way to go back. I'm going to want more and more and never be able to walk away.

"Are your cases in the basement?" he asks.

"Yes."

He puts his hand on my cheek, swiping his thumb over my lips and staring at me with his dark, lust-filled eyes. "Stop worrying. I'll take care of this." He pulls away and turns, but I grab his arm.

"Boris."

He spins back and licks his lips, waiting for me to speak.

I'm unsure what to say. My mind is a concoction of my desire for him, grief over my nana, and the failure of my first attempt to run her business, which is now mine.

And all the O'Malleys, including my sisters, are here to witness it.

My sisters, Erin and Nessa, are twins. They are eighteen years older than me. Their children and I are closer in age. I consider my nieces and nephews more like siblings. When they had babies, I felt like an aunt but never before. Their children even call me Auntie.

Sean was a year older than Killian. Sean and I were the closest before his death. Killian, Nolan, and Declan have always been protective of me and are even more so since Sean passed.

Erin and Nessa aren't happy my nana left me the pub. Even though they rarely come in anymore, nor do they work here, they thought it would be theirs. They've gone as far as to try and convince me to sign over part of it to them. My brothers have stood up for me and insisted they drop it. They all agree I'm the one who earned it. Nana wouldn't have left it to me if she wanted them to have it. But my sisters won't even look at me without glaring.

It's not even been a week since Nana passed, but I feel the rift in my relationship with their children, whom I've been close with my entire life. They took their mothers' sides. I feel like I've lost more siblings. It's made Killian, Nolan, and Declan even more vigilant toward me.

Not ordering enough whiskey and Guinness is something they will all use to berate me. It's an Irish sin and considered a rookie mistake. The decades I've spent in the bar should have prepared me for this, and Erin and Nessa will use it to point out I'm incapable of continuing my nana's legacy.

I look away, my eyes suddenly fill with tears, and I'm unable to control anything.

Boris steps forward, pulls me against him, and doesn't say a word.

I sob in his arms until I hear my brother Killian's stern voice. "Nora, what's wrong?"

Boris doesn't let me go. "She's upset."

"Yeah, I can see. What happened?"

"Do I need to answer that?"

Killian sighs and slightly slurs his words. "We're all going to miss her, but she was old. She had a good run."

I push out of Boris's arms and glare at Killian. "Stop saying that."

"It's—"

"Killian, I need you to go to the basement with me," Boris says and opens the stairwell door.

"Why?"

"We need to bring vodka up."

He snorts. "You're joking, right?"

"Nope. I bet you a thousand bucks the O'Malleys can't get three shots each down. Ladies excluded, of course."

"Of vodka?"

"Yep."

"Why would they want to?"

"I just bought these cases from Nora in your nana's honor. Are you going to refuse to toast her?"

Bought them off me? "You don't—"

"Killian, let's go," Boris growls and points to the basement.

"Did you have to buy vodka? You know we're Irish, right?"

"Don't trip on the way down. It won't be fair when we fight next," Boris orders, following him down the steps.

"Where are they going?" my other brother, Nolan, asks, coming into the hall.

"To get a few cases of vodka."

He scrunches his face. "Why would we need those?"

I wince and admit my failure. "Declan went to see if we can get a keg and few cases of whiskey off the Kellys. We're out. Boris is going to make a toast to Nana to try and delay."

"Vodka in Nana's name." Nolan whistles. "She's going to roll over in her grave."

"Stop it!"

"Guess it could be worse."

If he only knew the half of it.

2

Boris

BLOOD DRIPS DOWN MY CHEEK. I GLANCE UP, GASPING FOR AIR, trying to focus. The referee holds Killian's arm up, and the tiny gym my brothers and I own erupts in cheers.

Killian's face is bloody like mine. It's already swelling, and I can feel mine doing the same. He bends and holds out his hand, and I take it. He yanks me up. With a heavy breath, he proclaims, "Whiskey rounds on you all night." It's a long-standing tradition we have. Whoever loses buys the bar drinks until closing time. We've always done it in his grand-mother's pub. Now Nora owns it, so I'm even happier to drop my money in it.

I grunt. "You got lucky."

He wipes the blood off his nose. "Was a good left hook you gave me."

"I'm multitalented," I boast.

Our brothers surround us. We slowly make our way to the locker room, shower, and change. When I finish, Sergey is waiting.

"Are you coming with me?" I ask in Russian.

He hesitates then converses back in Russian. "Yeah. I'm going."

My stomach drops. *Not this again.* "Are you babysitting me now?"

His face hardens. "I never claimed that."

My pulse increases. "You do this every year. Nothing's changed. He sent me the text, and now I wait. He'll call. I'll go. End of story until next year."

Sergey stays quiet a moment then says, "I've been thinking."

"About what?"

"It's the one time of the year we can find him."

The hairs on the back of my neck stand up. "Sergey, what are you getting at?"

"We should follow you, take his guys out, then finish him off."

"It's not possible. You know this."

"If we—"

"No. I will hold up our end of the deal. It's once a year he owns me. The rest of the year, I'm free. You are free. Accept it and get this crazy thought out of your head."

"But—"

I step up to him so we're eye to eye. "Enough, little brother. I made the deal. It's my issue. I don't want to discuss this any further. And you can't hang with me every night, waiting it out. You and I both know he might not contact me for weeks."

He crosses his arms. "So, I can't go with you and hang out?"

"Of course you can. But I'm telling you not to put your life on hold for this."

He clenches his jaw.

I pat his cheek. "Get ready to drink whiskey all night."

He groans. "I can't believe you let him take you out with a jab."

"Thanks for reminding me. I'm sure I'll hear it all night from everyone now."

"Except Nora."

I freeze. The mention of her name heats my blood again.

"What are you doing with her?" Sergey asks.

"Nothing."

Sergey raises his eyebrows. "You're going to lie to me?"

I spin to my locker and grab my bag out of it. "Nope. I've not done anything with her."

"I'm not blind, Boris."

"Not sure what you think you see, but nothing is going on between Nora and me." It sounds confident, but my blood is already heating at the thought of her beautiful face.

Sergey shakes his head. "Killian is going to kill you."

I grunt. "Let him try. If he wants to go head-to-head without a referee between us, I guarantee you I'm not ending up on the floor."

"Boris—"

"Back to the original question. Are you coming to babysit me all night or hangout?"

He walks toward the door. "Let's go."

It doesn't take long to get to the pub. As soon as I walk in, I scan the pub for Nora. She's at the cash register, closing out a tab. Her long red hair is curled. It hangs to the middle of her back. Her O'Malley T-shirt is formfitting and barely over her belt. And her juicy ass curves perfectly in her skinny jeans.

When she turns, she sees me. Her cheeks don't flush how they usually do when I walk in. Instead, her face turns to horror.

I beeline to the bar. "What's wrong?"

"Your face. Oh my..." She puts her hand over her mouth, and her eyes glisten. She glances behind me and says, "Why do you two have to do this to each other every year?"

I had forgotten my face is a mangled mess.

"You ask the same question all the time. Our answer hasn't changed. It's fun," Killian says and plops down on a barstool.

I sit next to him. "We're fine."

Her angry green eyes could be lasers. Every year she gives Killian and me a lecture. Our faces could be bruised from any other fight and she wouldn't say a word about it. In fact, she would come watch. But she doesn't like Killian and my matches against each other.

She opens a cabinet under the bar, pulls out clean towels, then opens the ice chest.

"Aren't you going to ask who won?" Killian boasts.

She gives us the look of death. Her voice turns stern. "No, I am not going to ask."

Sergey sits in the seat next to me. "Don't encourage him, Nora. It's criminal how he took Boris out."

I elbow my brother, and Killian chuckles.

Nora's cheeks turn red. She slams an ice pack in front of me. "Your face is swelling."

Fuck, I wish no one else was here. I'd bend her over this bar right now and make her forget all about my swelling face and concentrate on my swelling cock.

These exact types of thoughts are going to get me in trouble.

While the ice cools my face, everything about Nora's pissed-off attitude and glare makes my pants tighter. She's always been a spitfire. It's a combination of her grandmother's Irish blood and having to stick up for herself amongst her four brothers. Well, three, now that Sean is dead.

She has two older sisters who have always disliked my relationship with Killian and his brothers. It all has to do with me being Russian. I think they're bitches, not just to me but to Nora. I would never disrespect them to the O'Malleys, but I've had to bite my tongue on numerous occasions. When they make comments about Nora, I'm never able to keep quiet. It's gotten me in trouble more than once with Declan, who tries to keep the peace in the family. The ironic part is until Nora inherited the pub, their children were always around and I'd had a good relationship with each of them. But now, everything is strained, and they haven't stepped foot inside since the day of the funeral. And they've held their children away from Nora, which is killing her. She considers them first nieces and nephews, not second generation.

Killian jumps up and whistles. The pub goes quiet. "Whiskeys for everyone. Thank Boris for going down tonight."

The bar erupts in cheers. Nora's green eyes could match a lightning bug glowing on a dark night. "You didn't make a stupid bet again."

Killian groans. "What's gotten into you tonight? You're not normally this upset."

"Have you seen your faces? All for who's buying drinks?"

"Chill out," Killian says, goes behind the bar, and pours shots of whiskey. He sets them in front of Sergey and me and puts down a glass in front of Nora and himself. "Have one."

She angrily shakes her head and steps aside. She sets a tray on top of the bar, fills it with shot glasses, then pours whiskey in each.

"Killian!" Someone calls out, and he takes a tumbler and bottle of whiskey and goes into the game room.

Nora picks up the tray and walks around the bar. She sets it on a table. The patrons race to grab it, and she returns behind the bar, avoiding me but also glaring at me whenever she does gaze my way.

"Darts?" Sergey asks.

I stare at Nora. "I'll meet you in a few minutes."

Sergey lets out a frustrated breath then leans into my ear. "Only a man who's a fool or desperate for ass would stay around to deal with her attitude tonight."

"Shut up," I mutter and elbow him. I almost slap the shit out of him for insinuating Nora is a piece of ass.

He pats me on the back as he walks past.

A customer comes in and sits at the corner of the bar. Nora approaches him and takes his order. She stands in front of me, filling a pint with Guinness for him.

I pull the ice pack off my face. "You're rather fired up right now."

She doesn't say anything.

I double-check no one is behind me. "You look nice tonight." I take my time, checking out every inch of what I can see.

Her face flushes, and her chest rises and falls faster.

Yep, come back to Daddy.

She takes the lager to the man and comes back, puts his cash in the register, and spins. "Why?"

"Why what?"

"You could pick anyone in the world to fight. Why do you have to beat up each other?"

"We always have. It's a sport. Why would we stop?"

"Some things are meant to change when you get older."

I stare at her lips. They're pale pink, full, and suckable. Indecent thoughts once again ruin me. "Maybe you're right, and they are." I slowly lock eyes with her.

She puts her hands on the counter, as if she needs to steady herself. In a low, almost whisper, she closes her eyes and says, "I can't do this anymore."

My chest tightens. "Do what?"

She meets my gaze. I want to get back in the ring and have Killian punch me several more times. The look in her eyes is an agonizing twist of hurt.

"Moya dusha—"

"Boris, you fought well. Surprised you went down on a jab though." Clyde, one of the bar patrons I've known forever, takes the seat next to me.

I groan inside, and Nora spins and walks into the back.

"Excuse me. Duty calls." I leave Clyde and go into the hall. Instead of going into the restroom, I go into her office and quietly shut and lock the door behind me.

The room isn't large. There's only a desk, two chairs, and a window. It overlooks the back alley. Nora stands in front of it, her hands on the ledge and her eyes shut. She's taking deep breaths.

I take the two steps to get to her and put my arms around her waist. It's a stupid move. I know I shouldn't touch her. The control I've maintained over the years is unraveling quickly, and I can't seem to get it back.

She inhales sharply but doesn't push me away.

"Want to tell me what's upsetting you so much tonight?"

"You know what's wrong."

"No, I don't. You aren't normally this agitated about Killian and me fighting."

"Don't blame this on your fight."

A chill runs down my spine. "If this isn't about the fight, then what's it about?"

She pinches her fingers over her eyelids. Her lip trembles. She whispers, "Is this a game for you? Like another fun hobby?"

My pulse beats harder. "Moya dusha, what do you mean?"

"You know what I mean." Tears slip from her eyes, and her chest heaves.

There are many things I can handle in life. Pain is something I've learned to tolerate. Watching Nora cry is worse than getting punched in the ring. I spin her into me. "I don't. Tell me."

She stares at my chest.

I hold her cheeks and tilt her head up. "What have I done to hurt you like this?"

"Stop coming around. I don't want you here anymore. I can't handle it."

The air in my chest thickens, suffocating me. A sharp pain stabs at my heart. "You don't want to see me anymore?"

"We will never be. And you're torturing me. Every day I see you, all you do is torment me. I can't handle it anymore. So please..."

If they had a master's degree in torture, I could teach the class. I'm an expert at it. I can extend a person's pain for longer than they ever thought possible. But I've never done it to a woman or anyone I love.

I love her. It slaps me in the face. As much as I've tried to avoid admitting it, I can't anymore.

"Nora, I—"

My phone rings, loud and clear, with the ringtone I've set for only one person. A chill, as shrill as the sound coming from my cell, climbs down my spine.

This is not happening right now.

I look at the ceiling, squeezing my eyes shut, and pull it out of my pocket. I put the phone to my ear. In Russian, I say, "Hello."

Zamir's voice is low. It's a sinister tone he's perfected. He replies in Russian, "I'm texting you an address. You have thirty minutes to get there. It's on the outskirts of the city. Don't be late."

My stomach flips. I don't dare look at Nora. It's the one time of the year he owns me. I dial my driver. He'll drop off the car and I'll go myself.

"Boris, I was just about to call you. We've got two flats," Kirill says.

"How did that happen?"

"Nails in both. There's only one spare. I won't be able to get this fixed until tomorrow."

No, no, no!

I can't have anyone drive me. I need to go myself.

"There's got to—" I glance out the window. Nora's SUV is parked in the alley. I hang up and hate myself even more. "I have to go. I'm sorry, but I have no choice."

Her eyebrows pierce together. "Why?"

"Please don't ask. I need your car. Mine has two flats."

In a worried voice, she demands, "Boris, tell me what's going on. Something is wrong. I see it."

I don't wait for her to give me permission—there isn't time. If I'm late, there will be consequences. I open her purse and rifle through it.

"Boris!"

"I'm sorry. I'll drop it off when I'm done."

"Done with what?"

I pull the keys out and avoid looking at her. "Tell Sergey I had to go. Have him call his driver and take you home after you close."

"Boris!" She grabs my arm.

I shake it off and go out into the back alley. I adjust the seat so I can get in.

Nora follows me. She gets into the passenger's side.

"What are you doing? Get out," I growl as I slide onto the driver's seat.

"Tell me what is going on."

I finally look at her. *Stay calm.* "Nora, I need you to get out. I will drop your car off when I'm done. I need to go."

"Done doing what?"

I lose every ounce of control I usually can exhibit. I bark, "Nora, get out."

Her eyes widen. I've never yelled at her before. Everything in me hates myself at this moment, but time is ticking. It's a game Zamir likes to play with me. I was late once. It resulted in me staying with him for a week instead of the regular two to three days.

I lock eyes with her, lower my voice, and repeat, "Please get out and go inside so I can leave. If you don't, there will be consequences for me."

She opens her mouth to speak, but I say, "Please."

More pain crosses her expression, but she obeys. The second she steps inside the bar and the door closes, I leave.

I glance at the address on my phone and groan. As usual, it comes from a burner phone. The location is on the outskirts of Chicago, and it's going to take me every second to get there on time even though it's not rush hour.

I speed as much as I can, conscious about not getting pulled over by the police. When I pull into the abandoned warehouse, I only have a minute to spare. I run inside. When I get into one of the backrooms, Zamir's guys pat me down.

He steps out of the shadows. The voice that haunts my dreams says in Russian, "You were almost late."

"I wasn't."

His thugs finish patting me down and hand me the knife I carry when Zamir sends me his annual text. It was a present from him after we made our deal and a requirement I bring it with me. It's another way he controls me. Once a year, I take it out of my drawer. The rest of the year, I only carry the knife my father gave me. Each of my brothers got one from my father, but he would roll over in his grave if he knew how we use those knives.

Zamir steps forward. He's not as tall as me but isn't too much shorter. His dark hair is now full of gray streaks. The expensive black suit he wears is tailor-made and impeccable. A blend of musk, specially made for him, flares in my nostrils, making my stomach pitch. He studies me, his evil eyes piercing mine. "I'm surprised you went down with a jab."

How does he know the details about the fight?

Because he knows everything.

Stay calm.

I don't respond. The more Zamir assesses me, the antsier I get, but I don't give him the satisfaction of flinching.

His glare turns into a sinister smile. "Time for fun." He steps back and goes into a different room.

I follow him without question. I've done this too many times. I know how Zamir works, what he expects, and the role I need to play. Every step I take, I reach for the devil inside me.

When we get to the room, I freeze. Ulan Drozdov, one of the foremen who's worked for us for as long as my brothers and I have been in business, sits tied to a chair, naked, with a gag in his mouth. His eyes widen in fear when he sees Zamir and turns to confused shock when he sees me.

Zamir walks over to him and strokes his head. "Ah. Yes. You didn't know I owned Boris, did you?"

I cringe from the truth. I hate Zamir owns me, even if it's only once a year.

Ulan shakes, his chest heaving harder, his eyes darting between Zamir and me.

How long has he been involved with Zamir?

Has he been spying on my brothers and me all this time?

Why is he here?

Zamir's never had me torture and kill any man I knew. They've all been men he had a vendetta against for some reason or another. Ulan is one of our most trusted employees. He runs a crew of guys who all love him. My brothers and I consider our employees like family. Ulan is no exception.

Zamir's expression turns colder. "When you take my money and don't follow through, there are consequences."

Ulan closes his eyes tight.

Zamir leans closer to his ear. "When you freely come to my house and sample my whores but don't give me what I ask for, I take it personally."

Ulan's wife and four children come into my mind. The disgust in my stomach builds. Zamir threatened to put my mother in his whorehouse. Any man who utilizes it deserves a special seat in hell. It's common knowledge all the women are forced to be there and do the things men make them do.

Zamir pulls the gag off him. "It's time to tell me what I want to know."

"Please," he begs, and tears fall.

Staring at him, watching him shake in fear, and knowing he's been working for Zamir, my skin crawls. It doesn't make me sympathetic toward him.

Over the next two days, Zamir has me do everything to Ulan he's taught me over the years. While he's alive, Zamir has me brand his femur with the symbol of Satanism, a five-pointed star with a circle around it.

I piece together parts of what Ulan was doing, and the devil in me only grows.

He was paid to recruit more men for Zamir, which means we may have guys on our crew who are working for Zamir. Questions spiral the entire time. How much spying did Ulan do on my brothers and me? What does Zamir know about us he wouldn't if Ulan hadn't been one of our closest employees? What is Zamir planning on doing with the information he has on us?

When Ulan is dead, his remains are cut up and packed for Zamir's thugs to dispose of. They take me into the back room, hose me down, and burn my clothes in the metal container. I put on the black shorts and T-shirt his men give me.

It's the middle of the night. The cold air barely registers on my skin when I step outside. I go to Nora's car and drive several blocks before I pull over.

I should be exhausted, but I'm more awake than ever. We've had a traitor among us. I don't know how deep his betrayal goes. And I can't get his cries or eyes out of my mind.

After every event with Zamir, I need space to get the smell of death, cries of pain, and visions of torture out of my mind. Torturing and killing Ulan takes me to a different place.

We trusted him with not only our business but our men. *Our* people. *His* people. For years, I've known Ulan's face and voice, so unlike a stranger, it snaps something inside me.

It's personal.

I drive into the city, heading to Nora's. The plan is to give her keys back to her and leave. But when I see her, everything is more intense. And the need to make her mine and unravel her completely has never been so strong.

When her green eyes blaze into mine, full of so many things I've seen before but never in the state of mind I'm in, a new beast steps into the devil's lair.

And what the devil wants, he takes.

3

MC

Nora

THE CURLING IN MY GUT NEVER ENDS. MY HANDS SHAKE SO badly at work, I keep spilling lager.

Where is he?

It's been too long.

No, it hasn't.

He always disappears like this for several days. One time, it was over a week. On the tenth day, he showed up, acting like nothing was wrong.

I asked where he was, but he nonchalantly focused on the big screen TV and replied, "Nowhere exciting."

"What does that mean?"

He continued to avoid looking at me.

Killian told me to drop it. "A man's business is his business, not yours, Nora. Let's go play pool."

That was the end of the conversation. But it was years ago. Every other time is four to five days before he appears.

It's been forty-eight hours. How am I going to last another two to three days minimum?

As soon as Boris left, I pulled Sergey into the office and told him what happened. His eyes went cold. I had never seen Sergey with an expression so hard. He has the warmest eyes out of all the Ivanov brothers. Something tells me I've been underestimating him.

"Please, tell me where he is," I begged.

He shook his head. "I can't. I don't know."

"You don't know?" I asked in disbelief.

"No."

"Then who is he with?"

Sergey's jaw spasmed. The ticking didn't stop the rest of our conversation. "I can't tell you."

"Please."

"I'm sorry, Nora, I can't."

Sergey took me home then sent Boris's driver to transport me to and from work the rest of the time Boris had my car. That was days ago.

At the end of the night, I lock up the pub and go home. Boris's driver escorts me into my house, and before he leaves, I spin in the doorframe. "Do you know where he is?"

The driver's eyes widen. "No, ma'am."

I nod and shut the door. I shower and put on the only thing I have of Boris's. It's a T-shirt I won in a bet with Boris years ago. Part of me thinks he intentionally lost and wanted me to have his shirt, since it involved a football game. Boris rarely loses bets and especially not on games. He has some sick sense where he knows the odds. Years ago, he and Killian went to Vegas. Boris won millions of dollars. It's how he and his brothers started their real estate business.

I wear the shirt almost every night to bed. It doesn't smell like him anymore, since I've washed it so many times. Nor does it help me get over my obsession with him.

It's around three thirty in the morning. I should try to sleep, but all I can do is pace.

I told him to stop coming around me.

I told him I didn't want to see him.

It's only been two days, and I'm flipping out from not seeing him.

He's somewhere bad. It isn't the same thing.

It doesn't matter. I can't handle not seeing him either way.

Where is he?

What if he's dead?

I go into my bathroom and dry my hair, just to have something to do. At first, I think I'm hearing things. I turn off the dryer, and there's another loud knock.

My heart beats faster. I check the peephole. Boris is in a black T-shirt. The darkness in his eyes when he left the pub is still in them. His bruised face from his fight with Killian is a mix of purple and yellow.

I yank the door open. My voice cracks. "Boris."

He stares at me for a brief moment, almost as if he's debating whether I'm real or not. Then his eyes slowly travel down my body and back up. His chest rises and falls faster, and his eyes lock onto mine.

He steps toward me, and I step back. The door shuts and locks, and he continues moving until I'm up against the wall.

I'm not sure why I retreat. My heart races, and flutters fill my stomach. The hum I only feel around him increases until my entire body feels electric.

"Bor—"

I can't finish. His hands possessively grip my cheeks. The lips I've dreamed about for hours, finally, are on mine. He doesn't wait for me to open my mouth. His tongue roughly slides through my lips and circles my mouth quick and deep. The air becomes thick. His hot breath becomes my oxygen.

My body throbs, and I run my hands through his hair, pressing him to me, as if his face could somehow get closer.

His erection grows, pushing into my stomach. A trail of tingles bursts on my skin as he drags his fingers down the side of my torso and bunches the T-shirt. He palms my naked ass, groaning, then inching his long fingers between my legs and wet heat.

"Jesus, Mar—"

His tongue consumes mine again. He picks me up by my ass, his large palm holding me up, while he pumps his fingers in and out of my sex.

I frantically release his shorts and wrap my legs around his waist. Then his shaft rubs against my clit while his finger fucks me.

"Oh fuck," I scream, shaking. Unexpected pleasure pools everywhere as adrenaline bursts in every cell.

He doesn't stop his fingers or cock ravishing me and nibbles on my neck, mumbling something in Russian.

I tremble, sandwiched between the wall and him, gripping his hair and squeezing his shoulders with my arms.

He slides his fingers out of me, tugs the T-shirt over my head, then sucks on my breasts so hard, a mix of endorphins and pain goes straight to my pussy. I'm still reeling when he drops to his knees. It's quick, and he effortlessly throws my thighs over his shoulders, as if I'm weightless.

His tongue, teeth, and lips instantly make me dizzy. He's a sprinter running a marathon and brings me to a peak then slows me back down, grunting and groaning.

I can't stop yelling, "Jesus, Mary, and Joseph." Sometimes, I get the entire phrase out. Sometimes, I can't finish. But I'm desperately riding his face, pushed against the wall.

He takes the hand he finger fucked me with and slides it up my chest and holds the bottom of my chin so my head tilts to the ceiling. Then he shoves his fingers in my mouth.

He's an unfed animal. I'm his prey, and he tears me to shreds with his mouth. It feels like it goes on forever. Sweat pellets on my skin. I orgasm, come down only a little, then he sends me back up.

My body hangs over his head, unable to hold myself up any longer. He shimmies up my torso, palms the back of my thighs, and yanks my legs around his waist.

There's no thinking or stopping. It's only Boris and me and all the years of denying each other our bodies. His large frame traps me against the wall, warm, full of muscle, and better than anything I've ever felt. His intoxicating scent flares in my nostrils.

His tongue goes back in my mouth, tasting me, hungrily flicking against mine. His groans become louder while thrusting, inching in me but quickly until I'm so full of him, I can hardly breathe.

"You're so goddam tight, moya dusha," he mumbles. "Fuck."

The hum in my nerves turns to a full-on buzz. My senses are overloaded and vibrating from every sizzling touch. I grip his slippery skin tighter, digging my nails into his shoulders.

His cheek touches mine, his breath hits my ear, and he growls, "You're mine, moya dusha."

"Yes." Rational thought has gone out the window. It's not possible for me to be his. But at this moment, I am.

His fingers press into my hips, and his thrusts become faster. He buries his face in the curve of my neck, biting and sucking on it, pounding into me harder.

"Jesus, Mar...oh... Boris!" I yell as he hits something inside me, creating a tornado of addicting chaos, unlike anything I've ever felt.

His cock swells, pushing against my inner walls, hitting me deeper, extending my adrenaline buzz until I see white.

A low, throaty groan echoes in my ear. His hot seed fills me. We stay against the wall, breathing hard, with sweat dripping down our bodies.

When he pulls his face away from me, we stare at each other. The demons in his eyes almost kill me. I put my hands on his bruised cheeks. "Where have you been?"

He closes his eyes then steps back and releases me. "I shouldn't be here right now."

"Don't do this, Boris." I stroke my thumbs over his lips. "Please. Don't leave me right now."

He glances at the ceiling, his jaw clenched. "I'm not in the right frame of mind to be around you."

I pull his face so he has to look at me. "Come to bed."

Whatever happened the last few days broke him. I see it. I want to know where he's been and what he did, but something tells me not to push him right now.

He doesn't move and swallows hard.

"Come to bed," I repeat sternly.

"Nora—"

"If you fuck me and leave me right now, I won't forgive you. My wrath will be much worse than anything Killian will do to you."

It hangs in the air. What we did. Who we are. The reasons we shouldn't ever touch each other again swirled with the undeniable need I have to keep him as mine.

He takes a deep breath and nods. I lead him to my room, and we get into bed. We say nothing. I fall asleep, curled into his chest, inhaling every part of him I can.

When I wake up, he's gone. My keys are on the nightstand. A note is on the pillow.

MOYA DUSHA,

I need a few days. I'm not good like this and shouldn't be around anyone, especially you.

Boris

IF THE NOTE AND KEYS WEREN'T HERE, I'D THINK I MADE THE entire thing up. I hug the pillow, inhaling his scent and wondering what happened while he was gone. And what does this mean between us, now we've crossed the line?

Nothing has changed. He still isn't Irish. My family will kill him.

Or he will kill them.

Neither option sits well with me. I don't know where he was or what he did. But his haunted expression fills my mind, and chills run down my spine.

I almost text him but re-read the note. So I decide to hold off. I text him after a few days pass, thinking he's had enough space. But he never replies.

Days turn into almost three weeks and my anxiety grows. When he comes into the pub, he acts like nothing has changed. Most of his time is spent focused on Killian or my other brothers.

Every time he meets my eye, he looks away.

His dismissive actions cut me. I replay our night together, over and over. The only conclusion I come to is he didn't enjoy me. That it was good for me and not him. And I've never been so embarrassed or hurt.

In private, I cry. At the pub, I avoid him at all costs. When he does speak to me, I'm short with him and get out of the conversation as soon as possible.

Nothing I do helps me get over him. Our night only showed me how good we were together. But then I curse myself. I was the only one who enjoyed it. It only meant something to me. He doesn't feel what I do. If he did, he wouldn't be ignoring me.

A web of pain weaves inside me, growing, suffocating my heart. I need to get over him, but I don't know how. Nothing I do seems to make my suffering diminish.

One day, my brothers Declan and Nolan come into the pub with their rugby team. A new guy, Cormac Byrne, I've never met is with them. He takes interest in me. I'm not super attracted to him. He's the opposite of everything Boris is, with his stereotypical red Irish hair and green eyes. But he's Irish, so my brothers approve. When he gets their blessing to ask me out, Boris is sitting a few seats away.

I focus all my attention on Cormac, feeling Boris's piercing stare and resisting the urge to look at him. I want Boris to claim me and demand I not go out with Cormac. But he never does.

So I agree to a date with Cormac and tell myself it's the right thing to do. My nana was right. Nothing good can come of Boris and me. It doesn't matter I love him. He's not Irish. And he doesn't even want me. So it's time I get over him.

4

Boris

NOT ONCE HAVE I EVER SPOKEN TO MY BROTHERS ABOUT MY time with Zamir. I text them I'm home, and they give me my required space. They don't pressure me to discuss it. They make it clear they're here for me if needed but never push. And I prefer it like that. I don't want to discuss anything to do with Zamir or what happens the few days a year I'm with him. I file it away in the back of my mind and try to forget about every moment I spent with him.

But there's never been anyone I knew. Their wives and children weren't faces etched in my mind. I never gave a paycheck to any of my victims or discussed confidential upcoming business developments or attended their parent's funeral. And I never worried about who they were associated with or if they might also be connected to my brothers and me.

Unlike in the past, I can't hide. I look down at Nora, an angel sleeping peacefully, and my self-loathing grows.

She deserves so much more. A man who isn't full of demons. One who doesn't make her worry for days and can't give her answers. Someone who she can bring home to her family and not apologize for.

I'm aware of how the O'Malleys feel about Nora marrying an Irishman. While my brothers nor I care about keeping our Russian bloodlines pure, we do try to keep our money in the Russian community. It's not the same thing, but it's a cultural issue, so I can't fault the O'Malleys for having their own racial bias. And I know it's nothing personal against me.

Her grandmother, however, did have a personal stance against me not dating Nora. She took me aside once. It was several years ago. I had come into the pub, knowing Killian and his brothers wouldn't be there and Nora would. But her grandmother sent her down to the basement to sort stock the minute I walked in. Then she sat me down in a booth.

She warned me to stay away from Nora. I tried to deny my attraction for her, but her nana wasn't dumb. She ignored my every attempt to dissuade her from the truth. "I know you have secrets. Dark, evil, take-to-your-grave secrets. They are not O'Malley issues. Nothing good can come by involving my Nora in your life. She's a good girl. She deserves more."

I couldn't disagree with her. She was right. Nora did deserve more. She *still* deserves more.

The smell of Ulan's death and the sound of his cries mix with her grandmother's words. His eyes and her nana's haunt me.

What am I doing with her?

There's a reason I stayed away from her.

I need her. She makes me a better man.

And that right there is why I'm a selfish bastard.

I need to get out of here, clear my head, and do what is right for Nora.

It's glass cutting into my heart when I leave her. But I text my driver, struggle to figure out what to write her so she doesn't hate me for leaving, and reluctantly go.

I get home, change into workout clothes, and go to the gym. When I walk in, my brothers look up in surprise.

"We have a big problem."

Maksim puts his hand on my back. "Boris, are you okay?"

I ignore answering his question. How can I ever answer honestly after I've spent days tapping into everything evil that dwells inside me? Instead, I change the subject. "Zamir's victim for me was Ulan."

The blood drains from each of my brothers' faces.

I wait several moments for the shock to settle. "Ulan was a regular at Zamir's whorehouse. His job was to recruit. I'm not sure how long he was spying on us. It didn't come out, but there's no way he'd be on Zamir's payroll without Zamir wanting details about us."

"Which of our guys are with Petrov?" Sergey's jaw twitches.

"Jesus," Dmitri mutters.

Nora screaming, "Jesus, Mary, and Joseph," with her cheeks flushed, while digging her nails into my shoulders and gyrating on my face comes to my mind. I shake out of the memory, trying to keep my cock from going hard.

"We need to find out," I state.

"Damn it." Maksim scowls and rubs his hand over his face.

Sergey cracks his neck. "I'll visit the sites. See if I can dig up anything."

"I'll go with you," I volunteer.

Dmitri asks, "Boris, did you just get back?"

"Yes."

"Take a day or two."

"I'm fine."

"Boris—"

"There's no time. Who knows how long Ulan was on Zamir's payroll? It's impossible for no one else on our crew not to be involved."

"A day or two—"

"Is another day or two we put money into Petrov pockets," I bark.

Maksim and Dmitri exchange a glance.

I start stretching out my arm. "It's going to take all four of us to figure this out. Our crew is too large. We don't have time to waste. And any projects we discussed with anyone outside of this room, we need to forget about. If Zamir knows anything about our future plans, they're in jeopardy."

"From now on, no one is in any discussions, except the four of us. No one on the crew is to be trusted right now," Maksim says.

"There's something else," I say.

My brothers all raise their eyebrows.

"Zamir knew Killian beat me with a jab."

Sergey's eyes turn to slits. "There's a Petrov in the gym?"

"There were lots of guests. And the Irish would have been boasting," Maksim points out.

"I'll talk to Leo. Everyone got past him," Dmitri says. Leo is the man we entrust to keep the riffraff out of our gym.

"Assuming we can trust him," I state.

Maksim shakes his head. "Leo hates the Petrovs maybe more than we do."

"Still, we need to be cautious. We never would have thought Ulan would get wrapped up with Zamir," Sergey replies.

Dmitri blows out a big breath of air. "I'll be careful, even with Leo."

"Best if we proceed with caution." I go into the locker room, throw my bag on a bench, and go back out. I jump on a treadmill, and my brothers hop on ones next to mine.

I warm up quickly, put it on a five incline, and move the speed up until it's at an eight, trying to forget about the last few days.

Well, everything except my night with Nora. I push everything to the back of my mind, except her and how perfect she was. She's always been. But the way she felt in my arms after all these years of wondering and waiting was more intense than anything I imagined.

Watching Nora unravel was better than kicking Killian's ass in the ring. Nothing's ever riled my blood up more than boxing. And it's another reason I can't let it happen again.

I hit the speed another notch higher, but no amount of working out gets Nora out of my system. It didn't work before I tasted her, and it sure as hell isn't working now.

And there's a reason I stay away from everyone, including my brothers, after my yearly dealings with Zamir. It usually takes me a few days to adjust back to normal life. If my brothers and I torture or kill a man, I don't have any issues. Something about being in Zamir's presence for days on end makes it harder to release the devil within me. Or maybe hide him is a better word, because once you pay your dues to Satan, there's no escaping him. There's always another moment in time where he will be needed. And once you know how to call upon him, there's no way to stop yourself from tapping into his power.

I should have never driven to Nora's house last night. Zamir knows how to break me until there's nothing left. He does it every year, and only then does he allow me to leave.

Nora told me to stay away from her. But I couldn't. I was weak from Zamir, and instead of doing what was best for her, I brought her into my pit of hell.

I can't touch her ever again. It's not in her best interest.

I jump off the treadmill, spend an hour lifting weights with my brothers, then shower. Sergey and I spend the next few weeks engrossed in talking to every member of our crew.

Maksim and Dmitri look over all our plans and who's been involved in what, trying to see if there were any links Ulan was involved with Zamir we missed. But they find none.

After a few days, Nora had sent me a text.

Nora: *Are you okay? I miss you.*

I spend hours every night looking at it, wanting to tell her how much I can't stand not being near her. I'm dying to see her, but I don't go near the pub. Killian texts and calls me, but I blow him off. I increase my time at the gym and with my trainer, trying to beat all the desire I have to be with her out of me.

Killian walks into my gym one night. "Boris, where the hell have you been?"

I stop punching the bag and turn, breathing hard. I grab a towel and wipe my face.

"Well?" Killian asks.

"I needed a few days."

Killian's face hardens. He doesn't know where I go or why, but he knows I have a debt to pay once a year. He doesn't know it's to Zamir. His voice lowers. "It's been weeks. You all right?"

"Yeah." I grab my water bottle and chug half of it down.

"Get in the shower. The game is on in an hour."

I should tell him no. Make up some excuse why I can't go.

I can't avoid her forever.

God, I want to see her.

"Give me a few minutes." I shower, change, and go to the pub with Killian. The minute I see her, my heart squeezes and stomach flips.

Her green eyes fill with hope and concern.

The devil doesn't belong around her. She needs someone without all my secrets.

"Nora." I nod and focus again on Killian.

"Boris, who'd you bet on?" he asks.

"Michigan State."

"Thank God. Go green," Killian cheers.

The bar erupts in a mix of shouts.

"Beer or vodka, Boris?" Killian asks.

"Beer." I avoid Nora's piercing gaze. I'm hurting her. I know I am. But the sooner she gets past us, the better.

"Jack's got a pitcher in the game room," Killian says.

I don't look at Nora. I follow Killian, sneaking glances at her throughout the night.

It's torture. I want to take her into the back room and kiss her until her lips swell.

It's not what is best for her.

I should never have crossed the line with her.

Killian hands me a pool stick. I go through the motions and tell myself this is the last night I'm coming into the pub. Killian and I will have to hang somewhere else.

But the next night, I'm pacing my penthouse, counting down the minutes until I can leave for the pub and see her.

The same thing happens every night. Each time I see her, she seems to hate me more.

I should be happy she's losing interest in me. It's what's best for her. But it only makes my obsession with her grow.

One night, Nolan and Declan bring a new guy into the pub. His name's Cormac Byrne. The minute he walks in, I get a bad feeling about him. Within minutes, he sets his sights on Nora.

Jealousy ignites and grows when she shows interest in him. I can't tell if she's doing it to piss me off or is really into the guy. And I hate every minute of watching it.

We're in the game room the next night, playing pool. Cormac walks in and takes Declan aside.

"You good if I ask Nora out?"

My chest tightens, but I expect Declan to tell Cormac to fuck himself. He's not good enough for Nora, and something about the guy is off. Surely, Declan can see it.

Declan pauses. "Are you going to be a gentleman with my sister?"

"Of course. My intentions are good."

Bullshit. You're a snake.

Declan glances out toward the bar where Nora is and nods. "Okay. You have my permission to ask her out. It would be good for her to get a life outside of this place."

My gut drops. *You have to be kidding me.*

Cormac pats Declan on the back. "Thanks."

To my surprise, Nolan and Killian are both on board, too. I don't get it. I can smell his danger a mile away. They should be able to as well.

But I'm Russian. He's Irish. And it tells me how blind the O'Malleys are when it comes to their own people.

Then Ulan comes into my mind and how my brothers and I made the same mistake, never seeing the truth about the kind of person he was.

"Wish me luck." He arrogantly strolls to the bar.

"I'm going to get another beer." I follow him.

Cormac is already asking Nora out when I get there. I stare at her, willing her to look at me and tell him no. But she acts like I'm not there, flirts with him, and agrees to go on a date.

When Cormac steps outside to pee in the alley, I follow him.

"She's off-limits," I say as he's mid-stream.

He turns his head, and amusement crosses his face. "Oh?"

"Find another woman. It's not her."

He snorts and zips his pants. He steps up to me. He's only a few inches shorter than I am, but I'm confident I'd take him out in one punch.

"Last I checked, you weren't with her. Is there something I'm not aware of?"

I want to inform him she's mine. Every part of me wants to go into the pub and tell all of Nora's brothers they can fuck themselves over their Irish bullshit because she's mine now and forever. But it isn't fair to her. So I don't.

Arrogance fills Cormac's face. "I thought so." He walks past me.

Right as he gets to the door, I warn him, "If you harm her in any way, I will come after you. I will skin you, carve my name into your bones, and scalp you all while you are alive. After I cut your tongue out, only then will I kill you."

He turns. His green eyes glow in the darkness. "If you think you scare me, you don't."

His first mistake was asking Nora out. His second one, he just made. He should heed my warning and be terrified of me. But that's the thing about arrogance. It makes you believe you're stronger than you are. It gives you the illusion you can do whatever you want without consequences.

One thing he should learn about an Ivanov is you should never disregard our warnings. I don't repeat myself. I don't give second chances. And I certainly won't show any mercy upon anyone who does anything to hurt Nora.

5

M C

Nora

ALL DAY, I'VE TALKED AND RE-TALKED MYSELF INTO GOING ON a date with Cormac. The only person I think about is Boris. I try to get the visions of our night together, the way he made me feel, and how I still love him, out of my head. Nothing works.

I can't look anywhere in my house or the pub without seeing him. And every night he walks into my bar, it only destroys me further.

Since Cormac's been coming in, Boris suddenly is watching me closely. He doesn't like Cormac or his interest in me. He hasn't said anything, but I see it in his expression.

It's cruel.

Boris doesn't want me to be with anyone, but yet, he doesn't want me for himself. It confuses me. The pain spirals with every jealous expression I see on his face.

I don't know how we would have survived together. I'm still an O'Malley, and he's an Ivanov. But my heart wants to believe we would have figured it out.

This is why I'm a fool. Nana warned me about this. Our worlds are too far apart.

Maybe Boris did the right thing.

I need to stop living in dreamland.

It smacks me in the face when I'm cashing out a customer. I'm an O'Malley. There are expectations. Boris and I cannot be.

It's time you married. You're meant to have Irish babies. You cannot fulfill your role in our family with him, Nana's voice says in my head.

I count out the change and spin then hold my breath. Cormac's cocky grin is on his face. His red hair is disheveled. Any Irish girl would think he's perfect.

He's not Boris.

He checks every box of who an O'Malley should be with.

His eyes glance at my chest, lingering for a moment, and my skin crawls.

Why did I wear this shirt?

I forced myself to put effort into getting ready for our date. Most days, I wear jeans and my O'Malley's T-shirt, since I work almost every day at the pub.

It's rare for me to dress in anything fancier, but I pulled several outfits out of my closet, debating what to wear. I finally decided on a pair of chocolate-brown leather pants and a gold, V-neck top. It's mesh and formfitting.

Cormac wanted to pick me up at my house, but I didn't want him to. Something about the pub gave me a layer of security. From what, I don't know, but my gut is telling me not to trust him. I know it's my head messing with me due to my feelings for Boris.

When I walked into the pub, Boris was there. It's like he was waiting for me. Flames licked across my skin when his eyes traveled across my body. I ignored his attention and walked right past him. But the way Cormac's eyes assess me makes me regret not sticking to my jeans and T-shirt.

I need to get over Boris. Cormac's a nice guy, Irish, and my family approves.

"You look beautiful, lass."

Many men in my family utilize Irish terms even though they were born and bred in America, including my brothers. It's from listening to our older generation who lived in Ireland speak. Something about Cormac using Irish dialect irritates me. Maybe it's the reminder he's Irish, and so am I, so we're supposed to fit together. But everything about it sounds wrong.

Boris murmured Russian in my ear when we were together. He's always spoken it, as it's his first language. I don't understand a word of it. But anytime Russian flies out of his mouth, my temperature rises.

It doesn't bother me when my brothers call a girl lass, but being on the receiving end of Cormac's lass feels fake.

"Nora, can I get a vodka?"

Boris's deep voice makes my heart rate increase. I ignore Cormac's compliment and slowly meet Boris's gaze. His jaw clenches, eyes drill into mine, and guilt crashes through me.

It shouldn't. He is only paying attention to me again since Cormac's shown his interest. I'm a game to Boris, and he clearly showed his cards.

"Aren't you off duty now?" Cormac inserts. "It's time for our date."

My pulse increases at the thought of being alone with Cormac. And my anger at Boris and how he's treated me boils. I grab a fifth of vodka and a glass and slam them on the bar top. "Help yourself. No one around here wants what you want anyway."

Boris's face hardens. He shifts in his seat.

I turn to Cormac and smile. "I'm ready if you are."

An arrogant expression fills Cormac's face. He glances at Boris and then back at me. "Drop your car off at your house, Nora. I'll follow you."

It's the exact opposite of my plan. But since Boris dislikes me with Cormac, I nod. "Okay."

I get in my car. Against my better judgment, I drive to my house. I leave my car and get into Cormac's.

"You really are smoking, lass."

I ignore the flip in my gut. "Thanks. Where are we going?"

His smug expression grows. "I made reservations at The Rush."

The Rush is a new restaurant all of Chicago is raving over. It is supposed to be extremely intimate.

I force a smile. "Wow. How did you get a reservation?"

"I've got connections," he says, as if I should be impressed.

I don't reply and stare out the window.

"What's the deal with you and the Russian thug?"

I quickly glance at him. Heat rises in my face. "What?"

He arches an eyebrow. "I'm not blind."

"I don't know what you're talking about."

"No?"

My heart hammers harder. "No. He's best friends with Killian."

"He's a thug. I'm surprised Killian hangs with him."

"He's not a thug." I'm not sure why I'm defending Boris to Cormac. But I can't stop myself.

Cormac grunts. "He is. But he's got his eye on you. Something tells me you two have a past."

"I've known him forever. Like I said, he's Killian's best friend."

"So, I don't have anything to worry about?"

"No," I sternly say. "And don't be starting rumors about me with my brothers."

He steers the vehicle into the other lane then glances at me. "I won't. But I don't play games with my women, Nora. So if anything is going on with you and him, tell me now."

"There isn't," I assure him and ignore the comment about me being his woman.

"Good. I like you, Nora. I think we have a lot in common, too, don't you?"

I don't know anything about Cormac, except he plays rugby with my two older brothers, drinks whiskey and Guinness, and is Irish. But the last point is all a lot of people who visit my pub, and even in my family, consider enough to make a perfect match.

I don't answer him right away. Giving him the satisfaction of acknowledging we're a perfect Irish pairing seems wrong to me. "Maybe you should tell me more about yourself before I answer your question."

He grunts in amusement. "Okay. I'm an investment banker, moved here a few months ago from Raleigh, North Carolina, and have a huge family." He wiggles his eyebrows. "Just like you."

"Why did you move? Don't you miss your family?"

He shrugs. "My career. There's more money to make in Chicago."

"But what about your family?"

"I can visit. Or they can come here."

I focus on the passing buildings.

"You've never left Chicago, have you?"

"No. My family means everything to me."

He pulls into the parking garage and finds a spot. He leans closer to my face. "I guess it's good I have no plans of leaving Chicago, then. Don't worry, I won't make you leave your family."

My nerves flip in my stomach. I've dated before but not a lot. My obsession with Boris has always kept me from accepting a lot of offers. I'm not sure if his behavior is normal or not, but Cormac's confidence around me, as if we're going to be together and it's already decided, makes me uneasy.

This is a date. I should be flattered. Any other girl would be.

"Good to know. Should we go in?"

His eyes travel to my lips. I reach for the door and jump out. He meets me near the trunk and puts his arms around my waist so I'm trapped. "Nora."

I release a breath and look up.

He furrows his eyebrows. "Did I do something wrong?"

"No."

"You seem freaked out."

"Sorry. I-I'm kind of nervous," I blurt out. It's not a lie. I am. But not for the reasons I should be.

He smiles. "Me, too."

I move my head back in surprise. "You are?"

"Yeah. I like you. A lot."

A lump grows in my throat. I swallow it.

He smiles. "I have an idea."

"What?"

"Why don't we go have a nice dinner, forget we're on a first date, and take the pressure off."

I take a deep breath. "Okay."

"Good." He releases me, grabs my hand, and leads me into the restaurant. It's dimly lit, oozes romance, and is extremely private. The hostess leads us to a table enclosed by three walls. The only two chairs are next to each other.

After the waitress comes and takes our drink orders, Cormac pulls out his phone. "Want to see my family?"

"Sure."

He pulls up a photo of his mom, dad, three sisters, and two brothers.

I relax a bit. I tease, "Wow. You've all got the Irish ginger look down."

"My father's from Ireland. He moved when he was sixteen. My mother's grandparents emigrated. What about your family?"

"You're not up on the O'Malleys? Everyone in Chicago seems to know about my family."

"I'm new. Fill me in."

I skip the crime family information. I find it hard to believe he doesn't already know it. I also don't tell him my parents are dead or how they died. I would have to explain how my father got sucked into the O'Malleys' issues and how my mother drowned the year following his death during a Fourth of July party on a nearby lake. My grandparents were integral in raising Nolan, Killian, Sean, and me. Declan and my sisters were already out of the house. My mom worked at the pub with my nana, and my father was gone a lot. "My grandparents were from Ireland."

"Have you ever gone?"

"No."

Cormac's eyes light up. "My parents took us when I was fourteen. It's a beautiful place and like a different world. You should experience it."

"It's hard to leave the pub. A lot can go wrong."

"Declan said you inherited it from your nana?"

"Yes."

The waitress sets down our drinks. "Are you ready to order?"

"Nora?"

I scan the menu. "I'll have the salmon, please."

"Same." Cormac hands our menus to her.

I don't miss his cocky grin or her flirty smile. It should make me feel jealous, but it doesn't. But it does make me more cautious of him. I take a sip of my rosé.

"Is the house dressing okay on your salads?" the waitress asks, staring at Cormac.

"Sure," I reply.

She doesn't even glance at me. "And you, sir?"

"Sounds good." Cormac impatiently taps his whiskey tumbler.

"Can I get you anything else?" she asks.

"We're good," he replies and winks.

My stomach flips.

She smiles and leaves.

Cormac turns to me. "I have an idea."

"You seem to be full of ideas."

He grins. "Is that a good thing?"

I force a smile. "Maybe."

"Why don't you have your brothers watch the pub, and I'll take you to Ireland for a few weeks."

I gape at him, realize my mouth is hanging open, and shut it.

He chuckles. "Why do you seem so surprised? You're Irish. You need to experience the motherland."

"Sorry, but do you ask all your first dates to go to Ireland with you? Is this a thing I wasn't aware of?"

He leans closer. "I thought we weren't on a first date?"

Is he crazy?

His lips twitch.

"You're teasing me, aren't you?" I ask.

"About Ireland?"

"Yes."

His face falls. "Not at all. Tell you what, why don't we revisit this conversation in a month."

"A month?"

"Yeah. And if I hadn't made my intentions clear before, let me eliminate any confusion. I'm not planning on anything being short term with you, Nora."

My chest tightens. I like Cormac more than I did a few hours ago, but he's a flirt. It doesn't make me trust him. Plus, I still don't have any feelings toward him.

His face falls. "You're unsure about me. I can see it."

"No... I...umm... I..." My face scorches. *What am I trying to say?*

His cocky expression appears. "I'll give you time to get used to me. But I'll warn you now, Nora. I go after what I want."

I should feel excited a successful guy my family approves of is so into me. It makes all the dynamics of my life easier if I just allow myself to fall for him. But all I can think is "Why can't Boris want me?"

6

Boris

WATCHING CORMAC DO WHATEVER HE CAN TO WIN OVER Nora is a new type of slow-motion torture. Every move he makes repulses me. Any attention she gives him makes the patience I usually have, wear thin.

His day is coming. I don't know what the catalyst will be, but my gut says his time to face me is getting closer.

Killian, Declan, and Nolan all think the guy is perfect. Everything he does seems to increase their respect for him. I begin to wonder if it's just my infatuation with Nora, making me hate him.

After several weeks of watching him flirt with her, I bring Sergey to the pub with me. It's the day after their first date. I don't tell him about Cormac. If anyone can smell a rat, it's my brother.

Sergey and I sit at the bar. Nora is hostile, which seems to be her new way of dealing with me. She's nice to Sergey, but as soon as she's out of earshot, Sergey mutters, "What did you do to Nora?"

"Nothing," I lie.

His eyes harden. He knows I'm not telling the truth, but there's no way I'm telling anyone what happened between Nora and me.

Cormac walks in. Nora's distributing drinks to a booth of regulars. He sneaks up behind her and sticks his hand in her pants and squeezes her ass.

She jumps and drops a tray of drinks.

"I'm so sorry," she frets to the customers.

Sergey and I both rise out of our seat, and within seconds, I have Cormac against the wall. My hand squeezes his throat, and his cheeks turn as red as his hair.

"Boris, no!" Nora cries out.

"Easy there," Sergey warns, standing next to me but not stopping me from whatever I'm going to do next.

It's not like me. I never lose my cool. Every move I make is typically calculated. But everything about Nora makes me unhinged.

"Boris, what the hell," Killian barks and runs over and pulls me off Cormac.

Cormac slightly bends, choking and scowling at me.

"What's going on?" Declan asks behind us.

I spin. "Your friend needs to learn where to keep his hands."

Killian's eyes turn to slits. "What are you talking about?"

I point to Nora, who's shaking next to the spilled drinks. "His hand doesn't belong in your sister's pants while she's working."

Rage fills the O'Malleys' eyes. Declan steps toward Cormac. "Did you disrespect my sister?"

He straightens. "No. And you should be asking your Russian thug friend why he's so interested in Nora."

"Cormac!" Nora reprimands, her face turning red.

"What did you call my brother?" Sergey seethes, stepping between Declan and Cormac.

Cormac sniffs deeply. Arrogance and disgust mar his countenance. "I called him the same thing I'll call you—a Russian thug."

At the same moment Killian grabs both my arms to hold me back, Sergey reaches for Cormac's neck, turns and pushes it up, then punches him in the gut.

"Cool it!" Declan grabs Sergey by the shoulders and yanks him away.

"He wants to see thug? I'll show him thug," Sergey growls in Russian.

Cormac drops to the ground holding his stomach, coughing.

Nora yells, "Stop it. All of you right now."

"He had it coming," I claim.

69

Nora's eyes glisten. She closes them and yells, "Out. All of you."

Killian says, "Nora, I want to know—"

"What part of out don't you understand? All of you go," she screams. She points to Cormac. "And take him with you."

Cormac looks up at her in surprise. "Nora—"

"No. All of you. Go. This is *my pub. My business.* Get out and don't come back until you can behave." She turns and starts walking away.

Cormac rises, takes two steps, and reaches for her arm. He yanks her toward him, and she slips on the spilled drinks. "What are you—"

Nora comes down hard on her knee and cries out in pain.

Killian releases me, and we both pounce on Cormac at the same time.

Sergey and Declan try to pull us off him while Nora's pain-filled cries get louder. Nolan comes into the pub with a few other rugby guys, and they help break us apart.

I glance at the floor in horror. Nora's crying. Her knee has glass embedded in it. Sue, a regular customer, helps Nora off the floor.

"Nora, let me take you to the hospital," I say.

"Stay away from me. All of you, just stay away." She sobs into Sue's arms.

Sue glares at us.

Nolan wipes the blood from his hand onto his pants. I'm not sure if it's mine, Killian's, or Cormac's. He picks Nora up. "You need to get the glass out of your knee. I'll take you."

She sobs into his chest.

I text my driver then say, "Kirill is pulling into the alley."

Nolan gives all of us a disgusted look and carries her out the back door.

Two guys from the rugby team stand next to Cormac. Killian points to him. "Get him out of here."

Cormac's face fills with surprise. "Me? I'm not the—"

"Get out before I tear you to pieces," Killian yells, his face red and eyes flaring with rage.

The bar goes quiet.

Cormac points to me. "You're choosing a Russian over me?"

Killian steps forward, and Declan puts his arm out to stop him from going any closer. "If you ever touch my sister again, I'll find you."

Cormac sarcastically laughs. "And do what?"

Declan spins in front of Killian and pushes him back. "Let him go." He looks over his shoulder and growls to the rugby guys, "Get him out of here, now."

I don't take my eyes off Cormac until he's out of the bar. As soon as the door shuts, Killian barks, "Boris, office, now."

Sergey pats me on the back. He shouts, "We're sorry for the scene. Drinks are on Boris and me the rest of the night."

Half the patrons in the bar erupt in cheers. Most of the regulars are scowling at all of us.

Sergey starts organizing the rugby guys to clean up. Killian, Declan, and I go to the office.

"What the hell happened?" Killian growls.

"He shoved his hand in her pants. Not even just over her ass but in her pants. He scared the shit out of her and she dropped her tray of drinks. What I should be asking you two is, why the hell are you pushing him on Nora?"

Declan shifts and steps closer to me. He avoids my question. "Why did Cormac insinuate something was going on between you and Nora?"

My pulse increases. I've never lied to them before, but it flows out of my mouth easily. "Not sure. But I've always looked out for Nora, and you've never had a problem with it in the past."

Declan's face softens. "You're right."

I point at both of them. "Your friend may be Irish, but he's bad news."

"What's he done before today?" Killian asks.

"I'm not sure, but I'm going to find out. Something isn't sitting right with me about him."

"You're overreacting now because of what just happened," Declan said.

"Were we in the same room?" I snap. "Nora's on the way to the hospital with shards of glass in her knee."

Declan defends him. "Yeah. He's a douchebag and not coming back in here. If he comes near Nora again, he's going to be sorry. I'll personally see to it. But he's as white-collar as they come. What happened doesn't mean there's anything deeper than a surface-level dumbass."

I snort. "I'm telling you there's more to him than you see."

"As long as he stays away from Nora, I don't care what he does," Killian states.

But nothing about Killian or Declan's inability to see past Cormac's "white-collar" front comforts me.

We go back out to the main area and help clean up the mess. Sergey and I spend the rest of the night serving the patrons and helping Declan and Killian run the bar. The entire time, I try to stop myself from leaving and going to the hospital. Around eleven, Nolan comes back.

"How is she?" I ask.

Anger emanates from him. "They removed several pieces of glass, but there still could be smaller pieces floating around that her X-rays didn't reveal. A CT scan would reveal any remaining pieces, but she wouldn't approve them to do one because of the cost. I told her I would pay for it, but she wouldn't sign the forms. The doctor said to watch for localized inflammation with pimple-like eruptions. Those will push the glass out when it pops. She had to get stitches, and she needs to stay off her feet for the next week. We need to watch her and make sure she doesn't get an infection. They gave her an antibiotic to help prevent it."

"Where is she?" Declan asks.

"At home. She's also on pain medicine. I put her in bed and

told her I'd come back tomorrow at nine. I'm hoping she sleeps through the night."

"Shit," Killian mutters.

Nolan scowls. "Yeah. What the hell were all of you thinking? She could have been trampled or worse."

More guilt crashes through me. All of us stay quiet.

Nolan steps closer to me. "I asked Nora, and she denied it, but I want to know right now. Is something going on between you two?"

"Why would you ask that?" Sergey interjects.

"Answer me first." He raises his eyebrows.

I'm at the point where I have no problem telling them I want Nora as mine. They can take me out back and all three of them beat me for all I care. I only want Nora. As much as I've tried to stop myself from wanting her, I can't. And she deserves better than me, but it's too late to pretend we didn't happen. At least if I'm with her, she can't be with guys like Cormac. But she denied anything was going on between us. So I'm not going to put her in any position she doesn't want to be in with her brothers.

I use the same excuse I told Killian and Declan earlier. "I've always looked out for Nora. Nothing has changed."

"Why are you asking this?" Sergey demands again.

Declan's eyes could be darts. "Cormac texted me something was going on between you two."

"He's trying to come between Killian and Boris's friendship. It's his way of getting back into Nora's good graces," Sergey insists.

I tell Nolan the same thing I told his brothers. "He's bad news. The three of you need to take your Irish blinders off."

"What does that mean?" Nolan barks.

"It means you can't see past the show he puts on because you think he's one of you. And I'm not judging you for it, we've all done it, but you need to look closer. Something isn't right with him, and you let him into your house. So take the blinders off before it's too late."

The O'Malleys glance uncomfortably at each other.

"I'm not wrong about him. What do you even know about him besides he's on your rugby team and Irish?"

More uncomfortable glances.

I throw the bar towel I have on my shoulder onto the pile on the counter. I point to the O'Malleys. "You've known me forever. I may be Russian, but I've never had any issues with any of your people. You've not had any with mine. I don't go looking for trouble. You all know this about me. Get your house in order. Let's go, Sergey."

We leave through the back door and go into the alley where my driver is waiting.

Once the car pulls out, Sergey shakes his head. "You slept with Nora, didn't you?"

I don't respond.

"What were you thinking?"

I glance out the window.

"You need to stay away from her. We don't need trouble with the O'Malleys."

I angrily reply, "You don't think I know that?"

Sergey sighs. "You can't do it, can you?"

I arch an eyebrow.

"Stay away from Nora."

The truth floats in the air. He's stated what I should have been honest about with myself the morning I left her in bed. There's never been any escaping Nora. Why I thought I could have her and there could be any way of keeping my distance after was foolish.

"Dmitri and Maksim are going to go apeshit when they find out," Sergey mutters.

"You're not telling them," I sternly reply.

Sergey shakes his head.

"What?"

"I don't know how the O'Malleys haven't seen it, but it's so obvious I don't need to tell Dmitri and Maksim. Your obsession with Nora's been building for years. They're going to find out. It won't be from me. It'll be from your actions. And now Nora's brothers have a suspicion something is going on, you either need to cut it off for good or figure out how to come clean."

Everything my little brother says is true. There's no denying it. And if it were up to me, I would admit to the O'Malleys

I'm in love with Nora. But after my stupidity of trying to stay away from her for her own good, I don't know if she'll ever forgive me.

I pull out my phone and put it on speaker.

Sergey raises his eyebrows in question.

"Boris," Obrecht answers. He's our cousin and the best tracker we have.

"I need you to get whatever information you can for me on Cormac Byrne. He just moved to Chicago from Raleigh."

"Anything specific I'm looking for?"

"Whatever you can find on the prick."

"Got it."

I hang up.

Sergey cracks his knuckles. "My gut says Cormac's too dumb to stay away. His arrogance won't let him."

"Whatever his game is, Obrecht will find out."

Sergey sniffs hard. "I'd be more than happy to show him what a Russian thug does."

One thing Sergey can't stand is being called a thug. Add Russian in front of it, and you have a recipe for some long-term pain.

"Naw. We have more skills than a thug. Let him experience those and beg for the thug."

Sergey grunts, and the driver pulls up to his building. He reaches for the handle and says, "Figure this shit out with

Nora. We can't be in a war with the O'Malleys." He doesn't wait for me to respond and gets out.

Instead of listening to his warnings, I do the exact opposite of what I should. I redirect my driver to Nora's house. My stomach flips. The decision I made has consequences. It already got Nora into a situation where she's injured. All I wanted to do was protect her, but it did the exact opposite.

I don't knock when I get to her house. I take out her keys I snagged earlier from her purse at the bar.

Everything is quiet when I go inside. It takes me a minute for my eyes to adjust to the darkness. When I open the door to her room, she's lying in bed.

At first, I think she's asleep, but then I realize she's crying.

I race over to her and pull her into my arms.

"What—"

"Shh. It's me."

She relaxes, allows me to hold her, but only for a minute. In a quick move, she pulls out of my embrace. Her green eyes glow in the dark with something I've never seen in them before.

It's hatred.

She pulls back her hand, and as hard as she can, she slaps me.

7

MC

Nora

HE CLENCHES HIS JAW AND TAKES A DEEP BREATH BEFORE turning back to me.

Every second since he left me in this bed, I've thought about him. I wondered if he was okay. I tried to figure out how we could tell my brothers so they wouldn't hate him. I desperately missed his arms around me.

And then he showed up in the pub and spent every day torturing me.

He's only interested in me since Cormac came into the picture. I'm not stupid. I never saw Boris as a man to play games, but I was wrong. I should have known, since he gambles on them. Maybe that's all I was—some sort of twisted bet he had with himself about how easy it would be to make me his and leave me destroyed.

Perhaps part of his plan was to see how much further I could fall.

I can't be positive about anything, except I never thought Boris would be a cruel man. At least, not toward me. But he proved to me he is.

What I hate even more than him right now is myself. Because even though I despise how he's treated me, his intoxicating smell is flaring in my nostrils, making me want him. He's still holding me, even though I put everything I had into my slap. My body hums next to his like always. No matter how much he's hurt me, I don't want him to let me go.

I call upon every ounce of my courage and I squeeze my eyes shut, trying to stop the tears. "Leave."

He pulls me into him, and this time, I don't pull away. I succumb to his arms. His accent sounds thicker. "I'm sorry."

"Go away," I try again, weaker than my first attempt.

His arms tighten around me. He kisses the top of my head. "I'm not going anywhere. And I'm sorry you got hurt."

My senses come back to me. I push out of his arms. New tears fall, and I jab his chest. "It's your fault I got hurt."

"I know."

He knows?

His agreement only makes me angrier. My voice gets louder the more I speak. "You know? Don't sit here and tell me you know. No, on second thought, tell me, what exactly do you think you know, Boris?"

"I fucked up, moya dusha."

"You fucked up?"

"Yes."

My voice cracks, and my insides shake. "You used me, ignored me, then only decided to come back because another man wants me."

"That's not true."

I sarcastically laugh through my tears. "Now you lie to me. Why are you even here? You didn't like being with me. I got it loud and clear. Are you here to hurt me more? Is it fun for you to break me to pieces over and over?"

"Is that what you think?" he asks in a shocked voice.

"Don't pretend you don't know what you're doing. You know you're hurting me."

He firmly grasps my cheeks. "You think I stayed away because I didn't enjoy being with you?"

I don't respond. The embarrassment and hurt is too great. My lip quivers harder, and my tears drip on my shirt, which is his old one. Yep, I'm a sucker for punishment. I still sleep in his shirt to torture myself further. I try to turn away from him, but he won't let me.

His voice is stern. "All I think about is our night together."

"And then you left."

"Moya dusha, I had to clear my head."

"Because of me."

"No. You had nothing to do with it. I shouldn't have dropped your car off that night. I know better than to be around anyone after—" He looks at the ceiling.

My heart pounds harder.

"After what?"

He stays silent. In his lack of answers lies the truth. He's never going to let me in, and I'm always going to be left in the dark, wondering what he refuses to tell me. I've given him all of my trust, and he's given me none of his. I'm no more than a pawn in whatever this messed-up game he's playing with me is. I need to let him go. This isn't a relationship. It's never been and will never be.

"I can't do this anymore. You don't want me. I won't be your challenge to master."

His dark eyes meet mine. "What are you talking about?"

"You know what I'm talking about."

"No, I don't," he sternly says. He pulls me closer to him and palms my head. "You've never been a challenge to me. The only person on earth I want is you."

"Tonight. Tomorrow, you won't."

"You're wrong, Nora," he growls.

"I'm not. I—"

His lips cut me off. His delicious tongue slips into my mouth. He quickly flips me on my back. Everything I've obsessed over since the last time he was here flies at me. His hard, warm body is over mine, creating a buzz so intense, I shudder. Our mouths, hands, and limbs wrap together, desperate and in perfect sync.

I shouldn't kiss him back or let him remove my T-shirt or grip his head to pull him closer. But I do. Any resistance I have to keep him away breaks, and my body lights on fire.

"You're mine, moya dusha," he murmurs in my ear, sliding his fingers between my legs and fisting my hair with his other hand before tugging it back.

"You're cruel," I whisper.

"I'll fix it, what I've done to us." He slowly pumps his fingers in me and circles his thumb on my clit.

"You ca...oh..." I close my eyes, swallowing as his mouth sucks on my throat.

"I will."

"You...oh, Jes..." And then there's no more discussion. It's adrenaline and my heated cries and sweat erupting on every inch of my skin.

I can't blame Boris for what we do next. He doesn't remove his clothes. I'm the one who frantically pulls at them.

"You're knee—"

I shut him up with a frantic kiss and spread my legs wider, shoving his pants over his hard ass, then tugging at his shirt.

His mouth dips to my breasts, licking, nibbling, and sucking until I'm screaming out, "Jesus, Mary, and Joseph!"

I forget about the throbbing pain in my knee. Every cell in my body fills with endorphins. He's an addiction of pleasure I can't escape. His warm, blood pumping flesh is a teaser hit leading up to the plethora of ecstasy I remember too well from the last time he touched me.

His sweat merges with mine. I slide my hands down his muscular back and push his ass. He enters me in one thrust, and I cry out.

The scent of our sex swirls in the air. His grunts and groans are a song I want to play over and over. My walls spasm against his erection, and my body trembles under his.

Russian words fly out of his mouth, getting louder and faster, until my head is spinning, and I'm screaming out on repeat, "Jesus, Mary, and Joseph!"

He deeply groans in my ear, his cock pumping inside me like a machine gun going off.

It tips me past the edge again, and everything becomes blurry.

He scoops his arms under me, holding me tight to his chest as we struggle to find air. He murmurs, "I love you, moya dusha."

I freeze. In the aftermath, reality returns. I've loved Boris too long to remember when I fell for him. For years, I wanted to hear those words. But all the ways he hurt me come racing back. Nolan questioning me at the hospital about my relationship with Boris then his reminders about my role in our family and the importance of the O'Malley bloodline. The fight at the pub—in my nana's business, the one she entrusted me to keep afloat, which most days I feel like I'm failing at—and Boris and my brothers covered in blood, haunts me. The memory of Cormac's hand in my pants on my naked ass, in front of my customers, makes my skin crawl. He was only there because I agreed to go on a date with him. If Boris had never done what he did to me, I wouldn't have gone out with Cormac. I would have shot him down and told my brothers to tell him to leave me alone.

"You don't," I reply in a whisper.

He lifts his head and brushes his lips to mine as he firmly says, "I do. I always have."

"Then tell me why you did what you did."

His eyes darken. "To protect you. I shouldn't be around you when my head isn't clear."

"Why wasn't it clear? Hmm?"

"I can't tell you. And you deserve a man better than me, but I can't stay away from you. I *won't* stay away from you any longer."

"If you love me, you'll tell me where you went and why. You stayed away for weeks, clearing your head. When you came back, you hurt me. I deserve the truth."

"Nora, this isn't about my love for you. I can't tell you. I never will. It's like your nana said, I'll take it to my grave."

The hairs on my arms rise. "You spoke with my nana?"

Guilt crosses his face. "Years ago. She pulled me aside and told me to stay away from you."

I stay silent, processing his admission. I shouldn't be surprised. My nana wasn't one to keep quiet if she thought something was wrong. "You told my nana your secret, but you won't tell me?"

"No. She just knew."

I don't doubt his statement. My nana had a sixth sense about everything. "So this secret of yours, is it over?"

He closes his eyes briefly and swallows hard. "No. It never will be."

"Then tell me."

"I can't. It's to protect you, too."

I laugh. "Protect me? Am I to stay in the dark on who you are and what you do once a year and wonder what the consequences will be the next time you need to clear your head?"

His eyes widen. "How do you know it's once a year?"

Anger cyclones so much, my insides shake. My voice rises. "Have you not been paying attention? I've loved you forever. I've watched every move you make in torturous silence. I've seen everything you do, including your disappearing act once a year."

He rolls off me, sits up, and rubs his hands on his face.

"Tell me," I demand.

His face hardens, and he locks eyes with mine. "I can't."

All the rage I've been holding in since he left me takes over. "Then get out."

"Moya dusha—"

"No! Get out!" I yell louder and point to the door.

He tries to pull me to him, and I slap him again. The sound of my hand hitting his cheek echoes in the room.

He freezes, his face turned to the wall, his chest rising and falling faster with each breath.

Tears stream down my face. "Leave. I will not be your fool any longer. If you can't be honest with me, there is nothing between us."

"Nora—"

"Get out!" I sob.

He inhales deeply, nods, and rises. He grabs his clothes off the floor and walks to the bedroom door then spins back to me. "If I could tell you, I would. Out of all the people in the world, you would be the person I would confess to."

I wipe my face. "Then tell me."

"I'm sorry, I can't."

"Then there's nothing between us. Leave. Don't come back. Stop torturing me. If you have any decency within you, you'll never touch me again."

I've never seen Boris look hurt before. But his expression takes every part of my heart and twists it until I can hardly breathe.

He doesn't say a word, turns, and steps out of my sight.

A few minutes later, I hear the front door shut.

I cry the rest of the night and into the morning. When Nolan comes around at nine, I'm still covered in tears. I blame it on my knee, but nothing could ever be as painful as what Boris does to my heart.

8

Boris

IT TAKES ALL MY WILLPOWER TO STAY AWAY FROM NORA. I don't go into the pub. I spend all my extra time at the gym, but every night, I make sure she gets home okay.

She doesn't know I'm watching her, but Obrecht hasn't given me anything on Cormac yet. I don't trust him. I've added another one of our trackers to follow him. He's slowly getting back into the good graces of the guys on the rugby team. It's away from the eyesight of the O'Malleys, but he's had drinks with several of them, relaying his sob story. He's not going to stay away. And I'll be damned if he gets close to Nora ever again.

It's been a month since I last spoke to her. Her knee seems to have healed. She's walking normally again and back into her daily work routine.

Things are strained between Killian and me. We've only spoken a few times. It's the longest we've ever gone without hanging out. The last conversation we had didn't go well. It was a few weeks after everything happened. He came into the gym, looking for me, and wanted to know when I was coming back into the pub.

"Did you dig up anything on Cormac?" I asked.

"You're grasping at straws, Boris. He's a dick. That's all."

I shook my head and scowled. "When you come to your senses and realize there's more to him, come find me." I turned and went into the locker room. When I came out, Killian was gone.

Every moment away from Nora is torment. I'm used to pain. But this is a soul-gnawing feeling I've not experienced before. It's a thousand times worse than when I was trying to stay away from her for her own good. I'm not sure how to stop it. Nothing I do even helps reduce it. It only seems to grow with time.

My brothers are all I have. We work out every morning like always. We're still trying to find out if we have guys on our payroll who have turned to the Petrovs, but nothing is coming up. True to his word, Sergey hasn't told them about Nora and me, but his premonition comes to fruition.

Maksim comes into the gym, red-faced and glaring at me. "You put Obrecht on an Irish guy?"

"Yep." I bend down and put my lifting shoes on. I've already run six miles before my brothers got here.

"And you didn't tell me?"

I glance up. "You don't own Obrecht. I don't need your permission."

"Since when do we give orders to Obrecht without all of us knowing about it? Hmm?"

Dmitri steps forward. "Why is Obrecht on this guy? Who is he?"

"Tell me you aren't involved in O'Malley business," Maksim barks.

I rise. "No, I'm not involved in any of their business."

"Then why?" Maksim demands.

I don't respond.

"Goddamnit. Tell me this isn't about Nora," Maksim growls.

I glance at Sergey.

"Don't look at me. I'm not a rat."

Dmitri spins toward him. "You knew about this and said nothing?"

"It's not my business."

"Obrecht is our business. The O'Malleys' issues becoming ours is our business," Dmitri seethes.

"The O'Malleys' issues aren't ours," I state.

Maksim steps forward. "It's bad enough the Petrovs are part of our life. We don't need the Rossis coming after us, too." Killian and his brothers are convinced Lorenzo Rossi, the Italian mob boss's son, killed Sean. There's a lot of bad blood between the O'Malleys and Rossis.

"I said I'm not involved in the O'Malleys' issues. Now get off my back."

Dmitri steps forward so he's eye to eye with me. "Are you sleeping with Nora?"

"Not anymore. She doesn't want anything to do with me, so calm down."

"Dammit, Boris," Maksim barks.

"What does Obrecht have to do with the O'Malleys?" Dmitri asks.

"There's a new guy in town. Cormac Byrne. Something is off with him. He's into Nora. And the O'Malleys can't see past him being Irish."

"So we are involved with the O'Malleys' business," Maksim seethes.

I point at Maksim. "I'm getting sick of repeating myself in this conversation."

"The dude is bad news," Sergey says. "What did Obrecht say?"

Maksim angrily shakes his head at Sergey but says, "He's the investment banker for the Baileys. So I want to know what you're involved in."

My gut drops. The Baileys are the other Irish crime family who has had a long-standing war with the O'Malleys. I repeat, "I'm not involved in anything."

"Then what's Killian up to?" Maksim asks.

"Killian would kill the guy if he knew he was working for the Baileys, and he definitely wouldn't push him on Nora," Sergey replies.

"What else did Obrecht find out?" I ask.

Maksim crosses his arms. "That's it. But there's no way he's coincidentally hanging around the O'Malleys. I told Obrecht to keep digging."

I nod. "Thanks." Maksim's pissed, but he's not stupid. And he's not going to let anyone mess with Nora or her family, either. As much as he doesn't want to be involved in their business, they're an extension of our family.

"Next time you call Obrecht, you tell us. We don't give Obrecht orders without all of us informed."

I hold my hands in the air. "Fair enough."

Dmitri shifts on his feet. "Why doesn't Nora want to see you?"

I pick up a weight and put it on the bar to do squats. "Because I'm an idiot and fucked up."

"Killian or her other brothers know?"

I snort. "Nope. And it's going to stay that way. Not because of me but because of Nora."

My brothers don't say anything else. We work out, shower, and part ways. My driver picks me up. I head to a job site for a meeting I have scheduled with one of our foremen when my phone rings.

I glance at the screen, and the hairs on the back of my neck stand up. I have Obrecht's brother following Cormac. Sometimes he's our tracker, sometimes a bodyguard, sometimes he just drives for us. But he's just as lethal as my brothers, Obrecht, or me. I answer in Russian, "Adrian, what's going on?"

"He has Nora. I'm following him. He's headed south."

"What do you mean he has Nora?"

"He went into her house. He carried her out. I couldn't see her face. She's wrapped in a blanket, but it's her. I saw her hair. He put her in the trunk."

The devil awakens in me, but the calm control I usually have is nowhere to be found. "Pull that motherfucker over and take him to the garage. Call me when you have Nora safe in your car and tell me her status."

"Done." Adrian has an undercover police siren he utilizes whenever needed. My guess is someone like Cormac is arrogant enough to pull over without even thinking it could be his worst enemy.

I hang up and throw my phone across the car. "Dammit!"

She better not be dead.

What the fuck has he done to her?

Where is he trying to take her?

He won't kill her. She's an O'Malley. That makes her valuable.

I don't call any of my brothers. I've never gone to the garage without them. It's the building we bought years ago when we needed a place to deal with our enemies.

I tell my driver to pull over and grab my bag out of my trunk. I get into the backseat and change.

A couple of the things Zamir taught my brothers and me were to be prepared and to cover our tracks. I tell the driver to head to the garage.

I stare at the phone, my heart beating out of my chest. I wait to hear from Adrian that he has Nora and she's alive. When the phone finally rings, I shut my eyes and answer. "Tell me she's alive."

"She is. He used chloroform. It was in his backseat. She's next to me but still unconscious."

"Where did you pull him over?"

"Past the tracks on the south side."

"No one saw?"

"No."

"Good. I'll meet you at the garage."

I take deep breaths, trying to calm the devil within me, knowing I need patience to find out what Cormac was going to do with Nora and also extend his pain. He thinks I'm all thug, but he's going to learn the true difference between a thug and a professional.

When I get to the garage, Adrian's car is outside. I have my driver drop me off and I go inside.

There isn't much in the garage, and it's only two concrete rooms and a full bathroom. My brothers and I installed it to clean up after our sessions. The first room has a desk and a couch. The second is covered in plastic from floor to ceiling.

It's where I'll be spending all my time until I get the answers I need.

Adrian is leaning against the desk. Nora is lying on the couch, asleep. When I see her, my heart twists. The air in my lungs gets thicker, and I don't think. All I know is I don't want her anywhere but where I can see her. I crouch down and stroke her cheek. I tell Adrian, "Thanks, I'll call you to clean up when I'm finished."

"You don't want me to take Nora home or to your brothers?"

I lock eyes with Adrian. "No. This all stays between us."

He raises his eyebrows and rises. "All right. Call me when you're done or if you need someone else to filet the prick." He leaves, and I lock the door behind him.

I go back to Nora and pull her into my lap. She's passed out, breathing softly. I kiss her forehead, lay her back on the couch, then tuck the blanket around her. I lean into her ear and whisper, "He's going to pay for ever touching you." I kiss her cheek and tear myself away from her.

I take my knife out of my pocket and open the door to the other room. Cormac is tied to a chair, naked. He's passed out with his head hanging down from whatever Adrian gave him. Besides the plastic, the only other things in the room are a rope hanging from the ceiling and a solution to wake Cormac up.

I pour the solution on the rag, hold it to his nose, and he stirs, coughing. When he regains full consciousness and recognizes me, his eyes widen, and he tries to move his limbs.

No one I've ever tortured has ever been this personal. I

struggle to maintain my composure, wanting to rip him to shreds, piece by piece.

You need to find out what he wanted with her first.

I crouch down, so I'm eye to eye with him. I hold the steel of my blade flat to his cheek. "What was your intention with Nora? Hmm?"

He spits on me.

I wipe it off my face with my forearm. "Didn't the Baileys teach you not to piss off the devil?"

Surprise registers on his face.

I grunt. "Yes. I know all about you and the Baileys." I take the point of my knife and slide it down his face. I begin at the side of his eye and move down his cheek, over the pulse in his neck. It's only the first few layers of his skin, so blood wells at the surface, but it's not deep enough to create a huge loss.

His breathing gets heavier, and he winces.

I lean into his ear. "Did you ever wonder how many days you could go with only small amounts of blood flowing out of you? They say the pain can be worse than a deeper cut."

He shudders.

"Of course, I reward those who cooperate."

I take the knife and move it near his balls. "But maybe, a man like you would prefer to be castrated and sewn back up?"

"Don't," he begs, his voice cracking.

I twirl the tip of the blade on his pelvis. "Why did the Baileys send you to Chicago?"

His jaw clenches.

I move the knife down, and he caves. "To spy on the O'Malleys."

"Why?" I calmly ask.

"I don't know."

"Wrong answer." I quickly slide my knife over his chest, so his nipple slices in half.

"What the fuck!" he screams, his face twisting in horror.

I lean back to his ear. "Let's set some rules. When I ask you a question, you answer. The next time you don't, I take a toe."

A tear slips from his eye, and I wipe it with my gloved finger.

I whisper, "Tears won't help you. Only the truth will."

For hours, I torture him. Every time he doesn't tell me what I want to know, I make him pay. Sometimes, I start to slice through him just to remind him what happens if he doesn't answer my questions.

I fall into my role of the devil. All I can see is the man who drugged my woman and attempted to harm her. He's almost dead, can hardly talk, and I may or may not get anything else out of him. But I'm not here to show him mercy. I continue to torture him and am pulling the skin off his arm when I hear Nora gasp through his low sobs.

It pulls me out of my trance. I spin, and she's standing in the door, her hand over her mouth, with tears in her green eyes.

What was I doing keeping her here? I should have had Adrian take her to my brothers.

I glance at my blood-covered body, then at Cormac, who's unrecognizable. I don't think about what I say next, it just comes out in a ramble. "He's on the Bailey's payroll. He came to Chicago to hurt your family. He kidnapped you to use as leverage."

Nora stays silent, but her lip quivers harder. Tears fall down her porcelain cheeks.

I step toward her, but she retreats.

I freeze. "I would never harm you."

She swallows hard, and her eyes travel the length of my body and back up.

"He knew Sean."

Pain swirls in her expression, and she turns to Cormac.

The rope is tied under his arms so he's standing on his toes. He's a bloody, soon-to-be corpse. He moans in agony.

"He set him up with the Rossis, Nora."

"No," she whispers, and more tears fall.

"I'm sorry, but it's true." I would do anything at this moment to hold her, but I can't with the blood that covers me.

Her face crumples, and I helplessly stare at her. She finally wipes her face. In a shaky but stern voice, she says, "Cut out his heart."

"Go in the other room."

"No."

"Moya dusha—"

"Finish him off, or I will, Boris. So help me God, I will take your knife and do it myself," she cries out.

I stare at her, not wanting to show her anymore evil.

"Please," she whispers.

I finally agree. "Okay." I turn, and in one swift move, I slice open Cormac's chest and remove his beating heart, just like how they killed Sean. I spin and hold it in my hand.

Nora watches it until it stops moving.

I drop it on the ground. "Go back to the other room. I'm going to shower, and then we're leaving."

She says nothing and does what I ask.

I shower, clean my knife, and put on the extra set of clothes we keep at the garage. I text Adrian to come and then my driver.

When I go into the other room, Nora is sitting on the couch, twisting her fingers in her lap.

I sit and tug her to me. She breaks down, and the grief I saw on her face when Sean died seems to grow exponentially.

She's still sobbing when my driver comes. I carry her to the car then take her to my place. For days, she remains in shock, unable to eat or sleep or talk.

I'm not sure how to help her. I don't know how it's going to be possible to stay out of the O'Malleys' war. And I have no clue how to convince her to fully be mine.

The second day she's with me, Sergey comes over. "Why aren't you answering your phone? Killian and his brothers are losing their shit. Nora's missing. And where the hell have you been?"

"No, she's not. She's here."

Sergey's eyebrows crease. "Are you crazy? The entire O'Malley clan has been looking for her for several days."

"Cormac kidnapped her."

Concern fills his face. "Is she okay?"

I shake my head. "No. She's in shock. Cormac confessed he set Sean up. She's...she looks how she did when he died."

Sergey's face hardens. "You can't keep her here."

"She's mine to take care of," I growl.

He crosses his arms and shakes his head. "Is that what Nora wants?"

I walk to the window, staring out into the Chicago skyline, watching the waves from Lake Michigan crash into the shore.

He lowers his voice. "Can you talk to her right now?"

"No."

"So she can't tell you if she wants her family to know about you two?"

My gut drops further. "No."

"Then you have to take her to Killian. You know this."

I don't answer him and stare into the sunlight. It's warm and cheerful, the exact opposite of reality.

"The O'Malleys are searching for her. This won't end well," Sergey asserts.

Several minutes pass and I ignore Sergey, trying to think of how to get around the issue.

Sergey's voice interrupts my thoughts. "Cormac kidnapped Nora. Boris has her. She's at his penthouse."

I spin, anger coursing through my blood, clenching my fists at my side.

Sergey scowls at me. "Yeah, we're here. Come now." He hangs up.

I step in front of him and bark, "What the fuck did you just do?"

"Made the decision you should have. Nora's family is worried sick. You can't keep her here without them knowing."

"It's not your decision to make," I growl.

"Is she in your bedroom?"

I don't answer.

"Get her dressed and out of your bedroom."

"Stay out of my business."

"This isn't only your business. When are you going to realize that? Now get her ready, or I will."

"Don't you dare threaten to touch her."

Sergey's face turns red. "Killian's coming. We don't need a war with the O'Malleys. If Nora can't be part of this decision, you know there's no other choice."

I grind my teeth. He's right. But I don't want to let her go.

"Time's running out."

I point in his face. "What you just did is bullshit."

"No. It's reality, so snap back into it. Killian is coming."

I angrily shake my head and go into the bedroom. Nora's in my T-shirt, sitting in the armchair and hugging her knees, staring out the window.

I kneel next to the chair and stroke her cheek. She doesn't even look at me. "Your brother is coming. They've been worried about you."

She says nothing.

"I want you to stay here, but I need you to give me permission to talk to Killian about us."

She starts to hum an Irish song Sean used to sing. She did it when he died, and she started doing it again yesterday. I haven't heard the song since his funeral.

I put my forehead on her cheek. "Moya dusha, I need you to come back to me. Please."

She just keeps humming. And I wonder if I permanently damaged her. If everything she saw me do was too much. It's not the first time I've thought about it. The last few days, it's gotten harder to push it out of my mind.

"You have five minutes to get her changed," Sergey says.

"Get out,'" I growl.

Nora jumps but keeps humming.

"Boris—"

"Out!"

Sergey leaves and I pick Nora up and carry her to the bed. I dress her in her clothes, sit down, and pull her onto my lap. "I love you. I need you to come back. Give me permission to tell Killian about us and then you can stay here."

She turns and looks at me. For a brief moment, I think she's going to agree. But her eyes return to their lifeless state. She reaches for my cheek and hums louder.

The buzzer cuts through the air and I cringe. Nora only keeps humming. I kiss her softly.

"Boris," Sergey yells.

There's no more time. Sergey's right. I'm in the wrong. I can't keep Nora here. And without her blessing to tell her family about us, they can't know.

I carry her out to the living room, put her on the couch with a blanket, and avoid my brother's stare.

The elevator opens and Killian comes flying in. He freezes when he sees Nora.

"I told you to get your house in order," I accuse, pissed off at my brother for calling him and Killian for not heeding my warning about Cormac.

"What happened and where is he?" he seethes.

"I had a tracker on him. He kidnapped Nora and was going to use her as leverage."

"For who?"

"The Baileys."

The color drains from Killian's face. He glances at Nora again. "How could we have missed this?"

All the rage and frustration I feel over Nora's current mental state and having to hide how I feel about her, I unleash on him. "Easily done. He's Irish, right?"

Killian closes his eyes. When he opens them, he says, "Boris, that wasn't—"

"Bullshit. You didn't listen to me because I'm not Irish. You took that motherfucker's word over mine."

"I didn't."

"You did. So did your brothers."

Killian clenches his jaw. "Where is he?"

"In hell where he belongs."

Killian slowly nods and sits next to Nora. "What did he do to her that she's like this?"

"Besides knocking her out with some chloroform, nothing. But when she woke up, she made me tear out his heart."

Killian's head snaps toward me. "You killed him in front of Nora?"

My voice gets louder. "He set Sean up with the Rossis."

The look on Killian's face could match Nora's.

I step closer. "I told you to take care of your house. The Baileys are coming after you. Why are they interested in you and not your other family members?"

He shakes his head. His eyes fill with worry. "I don't know."

"Don't bullshit me," I bark.

"I'm not. I don't know," Killian claims.

"You better find out."

Nora stops humming. We all turn toward her, but it's only a brief moment before she starts again.

"How long has she been like this?" Killian asks.

"Not long," I lie.

"He's had her this entire time?"

"No. I had him picked up within minutes of kidnapping her."

"And you didn't call me?"

"Why? So you could tell me he's harmless?"

"That's not fair."

Silence fills the air. Killian and I glare at each other.

He asks, "Why are you so pissed off at me?"

"This was avoidable. If you and your brothers hadn't dismissed my warning."

He sighs. "I'm sorry. What else do you want me to say?"

I don't respond.

"So he didn't hurt Nora?"

"No."

Killian breathes a sigh of relief. He nods, rises, and picks her up off the couch. "Thank you for taking care of her."

"Let me know how she's doing."

His remorse-filled eyes lock onto mine. "I'm sorry we didn't listen."

I nod.

He leaves, and I feel as if he's carrying my entire world with him.

9

M̃C

Nora

IT'S SEVERAL DAYS BEFORE I FULLY COME OUT OF SHOCK.

Sean is dead.

Cormac set him up.

The visual of Cormac's unrecognizable body, Boris standing over him with both of them covered in blood, rarely leaves my mind. The scent of death and Cormac's moans haunt me.

Boris is a killer.

I knew he was. But seeing him in action makes it somehow more real. And based on what he did to Cormac, nothing about Boris makes him an ordinary killer.

When I told him to cut out Cormac's heart, he did it within seconds. He knew exactly what to do, as if it weren't the first time he pulled a man's beating heart out of his chest.

Watching Cormac's heart take the last few beats in Boris's hand made everything they did to Sean clear. When I heard what they did to Sean, I only imagined it. Now I can see it.

I don't know why Cormac set my brother up. What did Sean do to get on the Rossi's radar? It's the same question my other brothers and I have been asking ourselves since Sean died. There still aren't any answers. I'm not sure if we will ever get them.

When I come out of it, I'm in Killian's house, sitting in an armchair, looking out the window. I'm humming the Irish song Sean used to sing all the time at the pub. I stop and turn.

Killian is on the phone with his back to me. He says, "She's still humming. If she doesn't come out of it soon, I'm going to take her to the hospital."

I should tell him I'm out of it, but something tells me to listen.

"I still want to know more about what happened. How long was that piece of shit in her house with her? Are you sure he didn't do anything to her?"

He's talking to Boris.

I need to know what he told Killian.

"Why did you take her to your house? You should have brought her to me."

I was at Boris's house?

Oh God. Does Killian know about us?

"Killian," I say, but it's a whisper. I clear my throat. "Killian."

His eyes widen. "Nora." He says into the phone, "I think she's out of it. I'll call you back."

I walk over to him. "How many days have I been here?"

"Two." He studies me. "Are you all right?"

Am I? Have I been since Sean died? Will I ever be, without Boris? I slowly nod.

"Did he hurt you?"

"Boris would never—"

"I meant Cormac."

"Oh, sorry. I'm kind of foggy still."

He leads me to the couch. "Sit down." More worry fills his face.

"I'm fine," I try to assure him.

Guilt replaces his worry. "No, I'm sorry. I should have listened to Boris. We shouldn't have ever let Cormac anywhere near you."

"It's okay."

"No, it's not," he sternly says. "Thank God, Boris had a tracker on Cormac."

Goose bumps pop out on my skin. "Is that how Boris found me?"

"Yes. You were unconscious."

"Cormac walked into my house. It's like he had a key. I know the door was locked, even the bolt. It was morning, and I hadn't gone out of the house yet."

Killian nods. His voice is laced with fear. "Nora, I need to know. Did he assault you in any way before he drugged you?"

"No."

"Are you sure?"

"Yes. Stop worrying. He didn't."

He sighs in relief then in a disgusted voice, he replies, "He was working for the Baileys."

My pulse rises. "I know. But why were the Rossis interested in Sean? I don't understand." I've asked my brother this over a hundred times, and his answer hasn't changed.

"I don't know."

"Boris didn't find out?"

"No. He died too soon."

He means Cormac.

"That's my fault. I told him to kill him when I woke up. If I hadn't told him to do it, he could have found out," I blurt out.

"This isn't your fault, Nora."

I stay silent as new guilt eats at me. I finally ask, "Why are the Baileys interested in us? We've tried so hard to stay out of our family's war. Nana is probably rolling over in her grave."

He sniffs hard. "We don't know." He puts his hand on mine. "Boris said you told him to cut Cormac's heart out?"

I shudder at the memory but firmly say, "Yes. And I would do it again."

Killian pulls me into him. "Are you okay?"

I nod into his chest. "Yes."

He releases me. "Boris said you saw a lot."

"I don't want to talk about it."

"But—"

"Killian, don't push me. I want to forget about it and move on with my life."

His face darkens. "Are you positive Cormac didn't do anything to you? I need to know."

"No. He came in and put the cloth over my nose. I got woozy and passed out. The next thing I knew, I was in the room."

"The room?"

Boris hasn't told him everything?

"Wherever I was with Boris." I rise. "I need a shower. What's been going on with the pub? It's not shut down, is it?"

"No. We've been managing it for you."

"Please tell me you didn't let Erin and Nessa or any of their kids help? I'll never hear the end of how I am not fit to run it."

"Of course we didn't. Declan, Nolan, and I ran it."

Tears well in my eyes. "Thank you. Nana would be so upset if it weren't open."

"Nora, I know she left it to you, and it's yours to do as you see fit, but you've gotta get a better schedule."

"What are you talking about?"

"You're always there. It's not healthy. You should be dating and—"

"Dating! Do you not see what just happened from me dating?"

"That's not normal, and you know it. Nana didn't want you to end up running her pub and alone."

She wanted me to have Irish babies.

Everything from the last few days, along with years of wanting Boris and not being able to have him, the expectations my family has for me, and my brothers pushing one Irish guy after another on me collide.

"You, Nolan, and Declan all need to stop."

"Stop what?"

"Pressuring me."

"How are we doing that?"

I don't answer his question and spend a good minute glaring at him. "Stop giving your blessing to different Irish guys who want to date me. Just because they're Irish doesn't mean they're good men. I'm more than capable of deciding who I should or shouldn't date."

"I know that."

"No, you don't. If I had listened to my gut, I would never have said yes when Cormac asked me out. But all you, Nolan, and Declan do is pressure me. I'm so sick of all the expectations of what my life is supposed to be like."

"Nora, we don't—"

"You do! Don't deny it. I'm supposed to have Irish babies and continue the pure bloodline. I get it. You don't have to keep reminding me."

"Nora—"

"No! You're such hypocrites. All three of you have fucked girls of every nationality. Yet, I'm supposed to only be with someone Irish."

His eyes turn to slits. "Who do you want to date that isn't Irish, Nora?"

My insides quiver.

Killian and Boris will fight, and one of them will end up dead.

"No one. Don't skim over the point where you get to screw whomever you want—"

"So you want to start banging a bunch of dudes—"

"Jesus, Mary, and Joseph! I don't even know why I'm discussing this with you. I'm going to shower."

"Nora, don't walk away pissed."

I ignore him, grab clothes out of the bag in the guest bedroom, which I assume one of my brothers packed, and go into the bathroom to shower.

I stay in the shower until the water turns cold. When I get out, I put on my clothes and grab my bag. I go to the kitchen and ask Killian, "Can you drive me home?"

"Why don't you stay a few more days?"

"No. I'm okay. I want to go home."

He shuts his eyes and says, "I don't mean to be a hypocrite."

"But you are. And since I'm female, I don't get the option to waver."

He opens his eyes and winces. "You're right. I'm sorry. It's not fair."

"No, it's not."

Silence fills the air. He finally gives me his cocky grin and says, "I'll try harder not to be a hypocrite."

I roll my eyes and shake my head. "Can you drive me home now?"

"Yeah." He hugs me again. "I was freaking out when you were missing."

"I wasn't. I was unconscious." I wink. "Well, except for when I told Boris to cut out Cormac's heart."

Killian's face falls. "I miss Sean so much."

Tears fill my eyes so fast, they fall before I can stop them. "I know. It still hurts."

Killian looks at the ceiling and scrunches his face. "I don't know what he got involved in. Anywhere I look leads to a dead end. But now that we know the Baileys were involved..." He licks his lips.

Chills race down my spine. "Killian, do not do anything stupid. Promise me."

He doesn't answer. He puts his hand on my back and leads me to the door. "Let me take you home."

"We promised Nana we wouldn't ever get involved with the O'Malley wars."

He opens the door to his car, and I get in. "I made that promise to Nana before Sean was murdered." He shuts the door, goes around the front of the car, and slides into the driver's seat.

My gut twists. I put my hand on his arm. "Killian. Promise me you aren't going to get involved with everything we've been trying to stay out of."

He turns and locks eyes with me. A new fear fills me. "All I'll promise you is I'll do my best. But whatever I have to do to avenge Sean's death, I will."

I close my eyes and lean my head on the headrest. There's nothing I can do to stop him. And I can't pretend I don't want Sean's killer to get everything and more he did to Sean.

I don't live far from Killian, so the drive isn't long. He carries my bag inside my house. "You sure you're going to be okay?"

"Yeah."

"Why don't you rest another night. We'll handle the pub."

"Okay. Just don't let Erin or Nessa near it."

He grunts. "You seem to forget I don't understand how we're related to those two."

"Good point."

"I'll come check on you—"

"No. Don't," I firmly say.

"Why?"

"I'm fine. I don't want you checking on me. Please take care of the pub for the night. I appreciate it. I'll be in tomorrow."

He hesitates.

"I'm good," I reiterate.

"Okay. I'll see you tomorrow, then?"

I force a smile. "Sure."

He hugs me again and leaves. I go into my room and pull my phone off the charger. I call Boris.

He doesn't answer. I look at the time on my phone.

He'll be boxing at the gym.

I take a few minutes to fix myself up and grab my purse. I get in my car and drive to his gym.

I shouldn't go by myself. It's almost nighttime and dark already. It's a horrible neighborhood. I've only been here with my brothers. I find a space several shops away and park.

When I get out of my SUV, I run the few hundred yards. Leo is at the door.

"Nora, what are you doing here by yourself?" he says in his thick Russian accent.

"Can you let me in and not tell anyone I was here?"

He raises his eyebrows in surprise but says, "I don't talk."

"Thanks."

He opens the door, and I step inside. I take a deep breath.

I'm unsure what's made me come here. Maybe it's because I got kidnapped by an Irish man my brothers gave their blessing to. Or the horror of seeing Boris so expertly kill Cormac and wanting to know how he acquired those skills and if it's linked to where he goes once a year. Perhaps I'm just fed up with not being able to choose who I love. But I don't want to stay away from Boris anymore. I need to figure out how to be with him and deal with my brothers without it destroying their friendship or my relationship with either.

I climb the stairs. When I get to the top, I see Boris in the office. The blinds are drawn, but the slats are slightly open. He's pacing. I ignore the looks from the trainers and boxers and cross the gym.

The door is slightly open, and I'm about to go in when I hear Sergey say, "We have enough issues with the Petrovs. Stay out of the O'Malleys' affairs. Killian can handle his own house."

The Petrovs? What are they doing with them?

Boris snorts. "Lots of good that did. Nora could have been seriously injured or worse."

Sergey's voice drops. "You need to distance yourself from Nora. Nothing good can come of it. You know this."

"Keep your nose out of my business," Boris growls.

"This is our business. Anything you get involved in with the O'Malleys becomes Ivanov business. Use your head."

"Don't insult me, little brother."

"Five of our guys are with the Petrovs. Right under our nose. We have business to take care of. This is what you should be focusing on. We cannot afford any other issues right now. If Maksim and Dmitri find out—"

"Are you telling them?"

"Now who's insulting whom?"

"Then they aren't going to find out. Shut your mouth and—"

Sergey aggressively says something to him in Russian, and they go back and forth.

I stand against the wall.

He's involved with the Petrovs.

They are rumored to be the worst crime family and ten times as bad as anything the O'Malleys have going on. All I've ever thought about is how my family is affected if we're together. It didn't occur to me we would hurt his family, too.

I don't go inside the office. I leave the gym as quickly as possible. Leo follows me to my car. "Please don't say anything to anyone I was here. I-I changed my mind about why I came. No one spoke to me."

He stares at me.

"Please, Leo."

"Okay, Nora. Drive safe, and don't stop anywhere in this neighborhood."

"I won't."

I go straight home. When I get inside, I lock the door and put on Boris's T-shirt. I crawl into bed. My pillow becomes stained with my tears.

It will never be.

I need to get past him.

How?

Lightning and thunder explode in the sky, and I jump. At first, I don't hear the knock. Through the storm, I hear the banging on the door and my name.

I go to the front door, look through the peephole, and open it.

Boris stands there, his clothes soaked through. He steps in, shuts then locks the door without taking his eyes off me.

I should tell him to go. Every moment with him has bad consequences for both his family and mine.

But I don't. Once a storm begins, there's no escaping it. All you can do is hide from it or embrace it.

The buzz of my skin crackles the moment I see him. I don't have a choice in the two options. He's lightning to my veins. And the need for him to strike me over and over has never been greater.

10

MC

Boris

As soon as the door is locked, I cup Nora's cheeks, and she shudders. "You're okay?"

"Yes," she whispers.

"I've been so worried about you."

"I'm better. I just..."

I pull her into my arms and kiss the top of her head. "You scared me. It was worse than the last time. And I know it's my fault. I'm sorry you saw what I did."

She pulls away from me. Her face hardens. "I'm not."

The sound of the rain hitting the roof fills our silence. I finally ask, "Why did you come to the gym?"

She opens her mouth in surprise then shuts it.

"My trainer said you came in but then left. You shouldn't come there by yourself. It's dangerous."

"I know."

"Then why did you? Tell me."

She nervously shifts on her feet. "I heard you and Sergey talking."

Shit.

"What did you hear?"

She bites on her lip and furrows her eyebrows.

I lean closer to her and repeat, "Moya dusha, what did you hear?"

Her voice cracks. "Why are you involved with the Petrovs?"

I want to tell her I'm not, and we only said Petrov because of the five guys we found in our employ who are with him. But enough lies are surrounding Nora's and my relationship. After what she witnessed me do to Cormac, I owe her the truth. "It's not a simple answer. Come sit down."

She doesn't move, and neither do I. Her green eyes glow in the darkness. A bolt of lightning streaks through the sky, lighting up her face. She finally slides her hands up my chest and laces her fingers in my hair, pulling me toward her.

It's all it takes before my lips are on hers, and our tongues are urgently circling the other's. I palm her ass and pick her up. She wraps her legs around my waist and pretzels her arms around me.

Between kisses, she says, "We can't do this anymore."

I kiss her deeper. "You're wrong."

"We're playing with fire."

My arm tightens around her. I hold her head firmly to mine. "You can't put out the flame when the match is already lit."

She freezes. "Then everything burns to the ground."

I can't disagree with her statement. There's truth to it. And the dynamics of both our families aren't straightforward. But I can't let her go. "You're mine, moya dusha. I love you. No amount of potential destruction is keeping me away from you."

She closes her eyes, and her lip quivers.

I carry her to the couch and sit with her straddled over me. "Give me permission to tell Killian about us."

Her eyes fly open. "You can't."

"I'll deal with his backlash."

"Then what? Your family and my family get involved in each other's wars?"

My chest tightens. "What do you know about my family's war?"

She swallows hard. "I don't know what you're involved in with the Petrovs, but I don't want my brothers near them. And your brothers don't need to be involved in the O'Malleys' issues. Sergey is right."

I'm going to kill Sergey when I see him next.

"Don't do that," Nora says.

"What?"

"Get pissed at your brother. He's right. We both know it."

I shake my head. "You're wrong. My issues with the Petrovs are not your brothers' and will never be."

"How? Tell me how you guarantee me that."

I turn and focus on the rain, wondering how I tell her about my past. It's a secret I thought I would take to my grave. But I was wrong and so was her nana. After everything I made her witness with Cormac, I no longer can deny the truth from her. She saw me at my worst, calling upon the devil within me. But my gut still flips when I say, "Do you still want to know where I go once a year?"

She sits back on my knees and nods. "Yes."

I tell her the one thing that scares me the most about disclosing the truth to her. "I'll tell you everything you want to know. But I don't want you to run from me."

She strokes my cheek. "I have already witnessed what you're capable of. You do not scare me, Boris. You never have. Even after you changed."

No matter our circumstances, I know Nora loves me. I don't understand how she still can and isn't petrified of me after what I did to Cormac. It's why I worry this may be the one thing to break her love for me. I try to decipher how to piece together what she needs to know. She already knows so much of my history.

My blood runs cold when I say, "Zamir Petrov kidnapped my mother after my father's death. In order to get her back, my brothers and I had to do what he said."

Compassion and horror fill her face. Her voice lowers. "What did you have to do?"

"Pay off her debt. Well, all of our debt."

"How?"

My mouth goes dry. I swallow the lump forming in my throat. "He would bring men into a room, and my brothers and I would have to torture and kill them."

She stays quiet, and thunder explodes in the sky, shaking the house. She jumps, and I circle my arms around her. "He taught you how to do what you did to Cormac?"

"Yes. I'm a master of torture. I can make men live for days in pain before they take their last breath." My nerves don't stop humming as I let her process it and admit out loud for the first time ever, who I am and what I'm capable of.

"And if I hadn't told you to cut out Cormac's heart, you would have found out why the Rossis wanted Sean dead?"

I lie to her so she doesn't hate herself. There's no way of knowing, but my guess is I would have. But I didn't think about those consequences when Nora told me to cut out his heart. "No. He was too far gone."

She lets out a breath then cups my cheek. "Your mom... She killed herself shortly after Zamir kidnapped her and you got her back?"

I blink hard. The pain of my mother's death never seems to get any easier. My brothers and I all have different view-points on which of us is to blame the most. "Yeah."

"So, Zamir owns you?"

My heart pounds faster. "Only once a year. Do you remember when I won all the money in Vegas?"

"Yes. Of course."

"I paid him ten million for our freedom. The other five I gave to Maksim to start our business. My brothers are free, but once a year, he owns me."

She slides closer. Her voice shakes. "So you're part of the Petrovs?"

"No... Yes..." I heavily sigh. "Only once a year."

A line forms between her eyebrows. "Does Killian know about this?"

"No. He knows I owe a debt. Nothing more. He agreed to stop asking me about it."

"Don't ever tell him or my brothers," she blurts out.

"I won't."

Her eyes fill with worry. "You know my brothers, especially Killian. He will think there is a way to go after Zamir."

"Which is why I've never told him. But you don't need to worry about this. There is no way to go after Zamir. His nickname is the ghost for a reason."

Nora shakes her head. "Killian will try."

"He will never know."

She takes a deep breath. "What did Sergey mean when he said you had five employees with Petrov?"

My blood boils. "Zamir is coming after my brothers and me. He's planted men to spy on us, possibly sabotage our projects."

"Why?"

"We assume it's his way of trapping us so he can fully own us again."

Nora's face turns pale. "The Petrovs are known to be worse than my family."

"Yes."

She scrunches her face. "If it is known you are with me, an O'Malley, won't Zamir come after you ten times harder?"

"No," I quickly say, not wanting her to use it as an excuse for us not to be together.

"Don't lie to me. Not after everything we've been through."

I stare at the ceiling to avoid her gaze.

She makes me look at her, and her eyes glisten. "He will. You will be seen as aligning with the O'Malleys. The most dangerous reason we can't be together isn't because of my brothers or yours. It is because of Zamir."

Chills run down my spine. The truth is a slap in the face with brass knuckles. She's right. And Zamir has no boundary between women and children. If she's mine and an O'Malley, he will stop at nothing to hurt her and her brothers.

This entire time, I thought the biggest hurdle we faced was our Irish/Russian issue. But it's not. It's my past, which is still weaved into my future.

"Tell me I'm wrong," she whispers. "Please."

My voice cracks. "I can't."

A tear drips down her cheek. "So, we will never be."

I fist her hair and pull her so close, there is no more room between us. "No. I will not let him steal anything else from me. I will figure this out."

"How?"

I don't have an answer for her. The only woman I've ever wanted is her. No matter how hard I tried, my obsession for her never went away. The addiction flowing through my blood at all hours of the day, only she can quench. I'm not going to sit back and not fight for her. No matter what I have to do to figure this out, I will. "Give me time. I will. I promise."

"But—"

I quiet her with my lips, hungry and desperate to consume every inch of her body, as if it will somehow solve the ache I always have for her.

"Tell me you want me, moya dusha," I murmur. It's one of the rare times in my life I've felt as if an answer could destroy me.

"You know I do. It's not—"

Every ounce of love I have for her, I pour into our kiss. And I don't take her to the bedroom, ask her permission, or let any of the reasons we should cut off everything right now stop me.

I tear off her T-shirt, flip her onto the couch, and fall on my knees. Before she can catch her breath, I yank off my shirt, throw her thighs around my neck, and demolish every part of her pussy. Any part of me I can use to make her realize she's mine, I do. My fingers, tongue, and lips own her, and she squeezes her thighs while riding my face and crying out, "Jesus, Mary, and Joseph," so many times, I lose track.

My cock is swollen and hurting. It's been too many days since I've been inside her. And I turn her over on the couch, onto her knees, and enter her like an animal in heat.

"Oh God!" she yells.

I lean over her so my chest is on her back. I keep one hand on her hip, and the other I fist in her hair. Cheek to cheek, I thrust into her, rotating between Russian obscenities and English demands.

I need to know she understands we are meant to be. "You're mine, Nora. Tell me you know this."

She shuts her eyes. Her face is flushed, she's breathing hard, and her sweat-coated skin slides against mine.

"Tell me!"

"Yes."

"And you love me?" I ask, slowing my thrusts down as her sex begins to spasm on my shaft.

Her green eyes lock onto mine. She nods. "Yes."

I kiss her. It's rough and possessive. It leaves no room for her to question my desire for her or allow her to back out of us being together.

"We aren't having this conversation again. I will figure this out." I promise her.

Zamir will not win this time. I will not lose Nora over him. No matter what it takes, I'll figure out how to protect her and be with her.

Her whimpers get louder, and her tremors get faster and closer together until she's shaking and squeezing my shaft so hard, I can't handle it anymore.

I detonate inside her. I growl, "We will not deny what is between us anymore."

In the aftermath, I hold her around the waist so her body stays against mine. I steal more of her breath and flick my tongue in her mouth, needing every moment of any body part I can get inside her.

She's mine. I suppose she's always been mine, even before we crossed the line. I pick her up and carry her to her bed. We slide under the covers, and I kiss her some more.

When we finally come up for air, she says, "Boris, we can't—"

I put my finger over her lips. "We'll keep it between us until I figure out how to keep everyone safe from Zamir."

"But how will it ever be possible?"

"I'm not sure, but I'll figure it out."

Worry crosses her face.

"We aren't going to act like this isn't real between us, moya dusha. No more dates. No more flirting with guys your brothers try to push on you. No more."

She cocks an eyebrow. "And you?"

"I don't want anyone else. The same applies to me."

She stares at me so long, I think she might tell me she doesn't agree.

My heart hammers faster.

She finally reaches for my face and pulls me to her. "Okay. Just you and me. But no one can know."

I firmly say, "For now."

A tiny smile appears, but I don't miss the sadness in it. There's doubt we can get to the place we need to be. She quietly replies, "For now."

"Good." I slide my hand between her legs. "Let me see how many times I can get you to yell, Jesus, Mary, and Joseph."

Nora

Several Months Later

BORIS AND I FALL INTO A ROUTINE. WE ACT LIKE WE ALWAYS have when we're at the pub, except his secret touches and glances get more frequent. At night, we're together, either at his place or mine.

I would have thought being with him almost every night would reduce the hum in my veins. It doesn't. When he sneaks behind me at work or gives me his panty-melting stare, it only intensifies until I'm so desperate for him, the moment we're alone we're going at it.

Everything feels back to normal at the pub, minus Boris and my secret life. I'm not sure how we keep everything hidden from the world, but we manage to. The only person who seems to be aware of our relationship is Sergey. He doesn't say anything to me about it, nor does he treat me any differently, but every time I see him, I think about the conversation I overheard at the gym. It's a reminder about why Boris and I shouldn't be together and how we're selfish taking this risk. But I can't stop what's going on between us. Every time I attempt to talk about it with Boris, he promises me he'll find a solution.

Killian won't leave me alone about cutting back on my work hours. He's gotten my brothers and Boris to pressure me, too. One of our long-time employees wants more responsibility, so I talked with her about stepping into a manager role. However, I've never had one before, and it makes me a little nervous not to be at the bar every night.

"Darcey's worked here forever. And it's a pretty high chance one of us will be here when you aren't," Killian states. My brothers have all cornered me, trying to convince me to promote her and take several nights a week off.

"The pub isn't your responsibility."

Nolan crosses his arms and sits back in the booth. His cocky expression appears. "Yes, we all know you were Nana's favorite and inherited it."

"I worked here my entire life. You all have real careers and lives."

Declan snaps his fingers. "That's our point. Time for you to get a life."

"I do have a life," I claim.

Killian snorts. "No offense, but this pub isn't a life. You only see your friends when they come here."

"You're thirty-four and not getting any younger," Nolan points out.

"Meaning, I'm running out of time to have Irish babies," I snap.

Nolan holds up his hands. "Easy there, killer."

"We aren't saying that." Killian locks eyes with me. Since our conversation the day he dropped me off at my house, he's been more cautious about what he says around me. I see it in his expression when he's choosing his words. Part of me wants him to go back to rattling off whatever he wants, without thinking. But I also appreciate he at least listened to me.

My other brothers haven't changed at all.

"This pub is a livelihood. It's not a life. Nana never should have allowed you to be here so much. You should be married by now with a family," Declan states.

"Me?" I cry out. "You're a hypocrite. All of you." I point to Nolan and Declan. "You've sailed into your forties. And you," I point to Killian, "are almost there."

"It's not the same," Declan claims.

"Yeah, I know. I have to worry about my eggs going dry, and you get to keep firing your sperm into any girl who will let you. I get it." I glare, pissed off once again at my brothers' double standard of how they get to live versus me.

"Do you not want a family anymore?" Nolan asks.

I sigh and look at the wall since Declan's sitting next to me, and there is no escaping out of the booth. My insides shake.

When I was a young girl, all I did was play with dolls and pretend I had a big family. Ironically, most of the time, it was in this booth while my grandmother was working. I still do want children. But the pressure put on me about it is getting old. And how can I ever have children if I'm with Boris and we can't tell our families about us or go out somewhere in public?

I turn back to my brothers. "What if I don't?"

Shock appears on their faces.

"You don't mean that," Declan says, as if not having children would be the worst thing on earth.

"Maybe Erin and Nessa are the only ones meant to have children."

"Don't say that," Declan blurts out.

I flip the conversation on my brothers. "What about you?" I point to Declan, Nolan, then Killian. "You're forty-three, forty-one, and thirty-nine. You carry the O'Malley name, as will your children. I don't see your Irish babies running around here. When are you going to marry an Irish lass and stop screwing everyone else who isn't? Hmm?"

"Jeez, Nora, you don't need to be crude," Nolan mutters.

"I'm being crude? Are you listening to yourselves?"

"What's Nora being crude about?" Boris's deep voice fills my ears, and I freeze. The throbbing in my veins begins.

"We're trying to convince her to give Darcey the manager position and get a life outside of the pub," Killian replies.

I lock eyes with Boris. In an angry voice, I hurl, "No. My brothers are worried about my eggs drying up and not popping out Irish babies."

Boris's jaw clenches.

My blood pounds between my ears. Silence fills the air, and I regret saying anything. I elbow Declan. "I need to get back to work."

"Nora—"

"No. I'm glad you all could give me another guilt trip on how I'm disappointing the O'Malley clan."

"We didn't say anything of the sort," Killian claims.

"Didn't you?" I push Declan's shoulder again. "Move. I have a pub to run."

He sighs and gets out. I resist glancing at Boris and go into the back office. Several hours pass. I figure out next week's alcohol and food order. I'm in the middle of placing it when Boris comes in. He doesn't shut the door and sits on the other side of my desk. "Your brothers wonder if it's safe to talk to you again."

"Ha ha. Funny."

He reaches across the desk and puts his hand on mine, stroking my wrist with his thumb.

The humming in my body increases. I take a deep breath. In a low voice, I say, "It's not fair."

"No, it's not."

"But it's true, isn't it?"

135

Boris raises his eyebrows.

"I'm running out of time, but they aren't."

Surprise appears in his expression and then it hardens. His thumb stops moving. Air fills his lungs, and his chest slowly rises. "You have lots of time."

"Do I?"

"Yes."

I look away, our real issues between us hanging in the air. We could never have a child together, at least, not how things currently are. Our baby would be a target for Zamir. The O'Malleys would have a fit. There's no alliance with the Ivanovs. They aren't even a crime family in the O'Malleys' eyes. The only way it could ever be acceptable to my family is if there were a strategic reason for Boris and me to be together.

It happened with my cousin. She had an arranged marriage with a Vietnamese man. My uncle and her husband's father set it up so the two families could work together. It was supposed to bring power to the Vietnamese against the other Asian crime powerhouses in Chicago. It was meant to give the O'Malleys new strength to fight the escalating feud with the Rossis. But her husband ended up dead only a few days after the wedding. Since there were no children, the alliance fell apart.

I don't even know if Boris wants children. But it doesn't matter. A baby between us would only increase the issues we can't solve. Plus, I've been on birth control since I was eighteen. My doctor also mentioned I should be aware many women need to be off it for five years before they can conceive. She said it's not scientifically proven, but she wanted me to understand it could be a possibility and something she was seeing more and more of from women having children later in life.

I would never have thought thirty-four would be considered "later in life."

"Why haven't we ever used a condom?" I blurt out.

Boris glances over his shoulder at the open door. In a low voice, he says, "I'm clean. I didn't even question if you are. And you're on the pill."

"How do you know that?"

He slowly licks his lips. "You're not the type of girl who sleeps around."

My face heats. It's true. I've only been with a few guys. Somehow, the fact Boris knows this embarrasses me. "I meant about the pill."

"Your alarm rings every night at nine o'clock, and you take it. You keep it in your apron pocket."

My cheeks grow hotter. My pills make me nauseous if I take them in the morning. At night, a few hours after I've eaten, they don't affect me. Years ago, I set my routine and kept it. "Does everyone in the bar know?"

"No. You hide it well."

"You noticed."

"Yeah. I'm aware of everything you do. You already know this."

I glance at my laptop screen.

"Moya dusha—"

I rise and pull my hand out from under his. "I better go check on things."

He steps in front of me before I get to the door.

My heart hammers, and I focus on his chest.

A loud thud and the sound of glass breaking explodes in my ear. I rush past Boris, through the pub, and into the game room.

Killian has a guy I've never seen before pinned against the wall. His hand is on his throat, and the man's turning purple. My other brothers each have another man in a similar position.

Molly, one of my servers, is shaking. A tray of drinks is all over the floor. Shards of glass are everywhere.

"Killian!" I cry out. "Declan! Nolan!"

Boris flies past me and pushes me back. He does the same to Molly, and I put my arms around her shoulders.

"You think you can come into our pub and disrespect our women?" Killian seethes.

The man chokes, and his arms flail, but Killian is too strong.

"Killian," Boris calmly says.

The other men my brothers hold against the wall are in no better shape.

Killian leans forward in the man's face. "You're leaving. If I see you in here or within a mile from here, you won't ever walk again. Understand?"

The man can't answer. He's so purple, I'm scared he's going to pass out.

"Killian!" I yell again.

Boris taps Killian's shoulder. Killian glances at Boris then moves his hand from the guy's neck to the back of his shirt. He drags him out the front door, and my brothers follow in his steps. Boris goes with them.

I turn to Molly. "What happened?"

"The guy Killian had against the wall grabbed my ass then cornered me. I'm sorry."

"You don't have anything to be sorry for."

Guilt fills her face.

"What is it?"

She winces. "I know him."

Goose bumps break out on my skin. "Who is he?"

"A guy I met at the club. I went out with him a few times, but he's into bad stuff. I-I told him I couldn't see him anymore."

"What kind of bad stuff?"

She looks over her shoulder, swallows hard, and lowers her voice. "I swear I didn't know who he was."

"Who is he?"

She scrunches her face.

"Molly, who is he?" I repeat in a stern voice.

"He's part of the Rossis."

The blood drains from my face, leaving a wake of chills behind.

My brothers and Boris come back inside.

"Molly, are you okay?" Nolan asks.

"Yes," she quietly replies.

I point to my brothers. "Tell them."

She hesitates.

"Tell us what?" Killian asks.

"They are with the Rossis," I blurt out.

My brothers' and Boris's faces all harden.

"I'm sorry. I didn't know who they were when I met them. I swear!" Molly claims.

Nolan, who's always had a sweet spot for her, assures her, "It's okay. But let's go to the office. Tell us everything you know."

She nods, and my brothers follow her. Boris begins to follow. I grab his arm.

He spins.

I wait until my brothers are out of earshot. "Where are you going?"

"To find out who they are."

"Stay out of this."

He crosses his arms. "They're part of the Rossis. They will be back."

"Don't get involved. This isn't your business."

He stares at the ceiling and then at me. He checks to make sure my brothers aren't listening. In a calm voice, he says, "You're my business, moya dusha. That means this is mine."

"It's not."

His eyes grow cold. "I protect what's mine. We're done discussing this." He spins, and I watch him walk into the office, with new fear filling me.

Boris

MAKSIM HANGS UP THE PHONE. "THE MAYOR AGREED TO SELL us the lot. We have a ninety-day cleanup stipulation. Closing is set for noon tomorrow."

"We got our price?" Dmitri asks.

"Yes."

Sergey grabs the vodka off Maksim's minibar and pours four shots. He hands one to each of us, and we all hold our glass in the air. "Nostrovia!"

"Nostrovia!" I down the liquid in one mouthful. It's smooth and heats my throat to my stomach.

"I'll call Sam and tell him we're ready to start the cleanup as soon as possible," Maksim says.

Sergey puts our glasses in the sink. "That's two years minimum of work for our guys. With the other projects we have going on, we're going to need to hire a few more crews."

"Are we sure we've cleaned house now?" Dmitri asks.

Sergey and I lock eyes. We found a total of seventeen men on our crews whom we linked back to Zamir. Sergey and I took them out, one by one. Our business is legitimate, but we've never had Zamir's men hiding right under our nose. So it's the first time we've ever had to bring force into our business dealings. "It's handled. We took care of it."

Dmitri and Maksim exchange a glance but only nod. They didn't want Sergey and me to do anything illegal but finally agreed there was no other way. Anyone associated with Petrov needed to be eliminated. So Sergey, Adrian, and I spent a lot of time over the past month at the garage. We interrogated them about what they knew regarding the Petrovs. We learned who else on our crew was a part of them before they took their last breath. Maksim and Dmitri dealt with issues on the lots we've been buying and continued to handle our current projects' day-to-day tasks. They also dealt with the mayor to secure the city lot we don't have but need. Without it, we can't create the development in discussion.

Sergey crosses his arms. "I've already spoken with the foremen. They think we're going to have to hire some more Poles."

Maksim raises his eyebrows. "We're tapped out of Russians already?"

"Ones we know aren't connected to the Petrovs, yes."

I step toward the window and stare out at the whitecaps on Lake Michigan. "Zamir's growing again."

"It's why we need this project to start. The more we can keep our men working, the fewer reasons they have to turn to him," Maksim insists.

My chest tightens. "Zamir got to Ulan. We paid Ulan over six figures a year. It wasn't enough."

"Every man has his own reasons to turn to Zamir. All we can do is continue to pay above-average, fair wages and keep expanding," Dmitri claims.

Sergey snorts. "Now that Giovanni Rossi is going to trial for the pension fraud case, the unions are going to be scrutinized closer. It's going to create some opportunities for other builders. We should be able to use it to our advantage." Giovanni is the head of the Rossi family. He's old-school Italian mob. He was recently incarcerated for stealing from the union workers' pension fund. The governor was involved, and it's been a big ordeal in Chicago.

My alarm rings on my phone. I turn it off. "We've gotta go, or I'll be late for my session with Aleksei. Do you want us at the signing tomorrow?"

Maksim shakes his head. "No. I'll take Dmitri. We only need two signatures. I'll text you when it's a done deal."

"Good. You know I hate those meetings."

Sergey grunts. "Better to let the old men handle it."

"Watch it," Maksim growls.

Sergey and I say our goodbyes and leave for the gym. When we get in the car, his phone rings. He smiles and answers, "Eloise. Are you on your flight?"

Sergey's had a casual relationship with Eloise for a while now. They date when she's in town but aren't exclusive. I'm not sure if dating is even the right word. She's an in-demand French model who travels all over the U.S. Besides being beautiful, I'm not sure what he sees in her. I think she's stuck up and not very nice to him, which doesn't sit well with me.

His face falls. "You have five days off."

Oh, little brother. Why are you into this woman?

Sergey's jaw twitches. He stares out the window. "This is getting old, Eloise." He taps his fingers against his thighs. "Yeah. Maybe next time." He hangs up and shakes his head.

"What's going on?" I ask.

"Nothing. Same old shit, different day."

"I don't get it," I say.

"What's that?"

"The city is full of women. Why pick one who's just a pain in the ass?"

Sergey snorts. "That's rich, coming from you."

"Watch your mouth. Don't talk about Nora like that," I growl.

"You're sneaking around behind her brothers' backs. Hell, ours, too."

"It's no one's business."

"Stop lying to yourself. You know it is. How long will it be before you get dragged into O'Malley issues? The last thing we need is to be on any other crime family's radar. It's bad enough we're on Zamir's."

My stomach clenches. I don't answer. I'd have to admit to Sergey I'm ready to go head-to-head with the Rossis. In the last few weeks, Nora's brothers have spotted their thugs hanging out near the pub. Something is coming, I can feel it, but I don't know what. And I'll be damned if I sit back when Nora's involved.

But I'm not telling my brothers anything about the Rossis. It's staying an O'Malley issue, and there's no reason to alarm them.

Plus, Sergey is still the only one who knows I'm with Nora. The others think I slept with her and no longer am anymore. At least, I assume since Maksim and Dmitri haven't tried to convince me to stay away from her again.

The driver pulls in front of the gym, and we get out. Sergey and I both work out, shower, and I turn to him. "I'm headed to the pub. You want to come?"

"Yeah. I've got nothing else going on."

We head to the bar. When we turn the corner, Nolan lands a punch in a guy's face. But he gets up, runs at him like an animal, and takes Nolan to the ground. Sergey and I jump out of the car and pull them apart.

"Let me go, Boris," Nolan yells.

The stranger attempts to get out of Sergey's hold. "Get off me, you motherfucker."

"You better watch your mouth," Sergey warns.

I glance at him and realize he's the same guy who was in the pub the day Molly got groped. My stomach drops. *He's a Rossi.*

A black car, similar to mine, pulls up to the curb. The window rolls down. A man points a gun and barks, "Let him go, or I shoot."

None of us move. My pulse beats in my throat. Sergey and I exchange a glance.

"Last warning!"

"Sergey, let him go," I demand and continue holding Nolan, not trusting he won't try something.

Sergey releases the man, and he runs to the car. He gets in, and they take off.

"What the hell happened?" I ask.

"He came back. He won't leave Molly alone. Rossi piece of shit." Nolan spits blood out of his mouth and onto the sidewalk.

"Rossi?" Sergey asks, glaring at me.

"Yeah. We had three of them in here. Boris didn't tell you?"

Shit.

Sergey's face hardens. "No, he didn't."

I open the door to the pub. "Let's go inside before someone calls the cops."

Nolan walks in, and Sergey palms the wooden door and slams it shut. He spins and seethes, "What the hell are you doing, Boris?"

I cross my arms. "Mind your own business."

"How many times are you going to deny reality? You faced off with the Rossis, and you kept it from us? Your own brothers? After everything we've been through together?"

Guilt floods me. "Sergey, it's not what you think."

"Not what I think? It's the Rossis," he growls.

"Keep your voice down, little brother," I warn.

Sergey steps closer so we're eye to eye. "I don't know what's happening to you. We're your brothers. *Your* blood. Ivanov is your last name, not O'Malley, or have you forgotten it?"

"Don't insult me."

"This is not our war. We don't need the Rossis causing trouble for us. Our people are in enough jeopardy."

"You don't think I know this?"

Sergey shakes his head. "I think you've forgotten a lot of things lately."

"Don't be dramatic," I accuse.

"Do you even know what day it is?"

A chill runs down my spine. I'm not sure what day it is. I've not been paying attention to anything except trying to figure out how to solve the business issues and give Nora the life she deserves.

Sergey's jaw twitches, and he blinks hard. It suddenly hits me what day it is. Twenty years ago, our mother committed suicide. Sergey found her. I was eighteen. Dmitri was twenty-three. Maksim was twenty-five. Sergey had barely turned thirteen.

He pushes past me. "We made a pact to protect our people from him so no family ever had to go through what we did. Today of all days, you should remember why we still wake up each morning and get out of bed. When you remember where you come from and who your allegiance should be to, let me know."

My gut flips. "Sergey."

He ignores me and keeps walking down the street.

"Sergey," I yell, but he doesn't turn around.

Shit, shit, shit!

I lean against the door with my eyes closed until I hear Nora say, "Boris."

My stomach twists faster.

She's standing in front of me, holding a brown bag of groceries. "Why is Sergey upset with you?"

"Don't worry about it. He'll cool off," I tell her in an attempt to avoid the truth. "Let's go in." I turn to open the door.

"Boris." She grabs my arm.

I freeze.

"It's about me, isn't it?"

"No."

"Don't lie to me," she sternly says.

I spin. "It's not about you. It's about the Rossis. He just needs to cool off, and he'll be fine."

Worry fills her face. "How did the Rossis come up in conversation?"

I sigh. There's no point hiding the truth. She's going to find out from Nolan. "When we got here, Nolan was beating up the guy from the other night. One of Rossi's thugs pulled up with a gun, and they drove off."

"A gun!" Nora gapes.

"Don't worry about it. Everyone is fine."

She stares at me in horror. "How can you say that? One of you could have gotten killed."

"But we didn't. Come inside."

"Boris—"

"Go inside, Nora," I roughly command, take her bag out of her hands, and open the door.

Her face turns red with anger, and she brushes past me. She goes straight to Nolan. "What happened?"

He spins and starts filling her in.

I take the bag back to the kitchen and unload it.

Nolan comes in and starts making a sandwich. "Where's Sergey?"

I sigh. "He's pissed off I didn't tell him what happened with the Rossis."

"Why? It's not his business. It's not your problem, either. You were just here when it happened. Why are his panties in a twist?"

I almost tell him it is my problem. That I love his sister and am over all the Irish/Russian bullshit and am sick of hiding. I'm tempted to tell him no matter who wants to come at him or me, there's no escaping it—I will be part of the solution to take them down.

Instead, I say, "How long have I known you?"

He throws a few slices of ham on bread. "Too long." He takes a bite of the sandwich.

"Yeah. That answer your question?"

Nolan drops the sandwich. He swallows his food and locks eyes with me. "Boris, this isn't your fight. The Rossis aren't people you want to have as enemies. It's an O'Malley war. Don't step into it when you have no reason to."

Nora comes into the kitchen. There's an expression on her face I'm not sure how to take. I'm trying to decipher it when my phone rings.

I groan then answer it. "Maksim, I'm sorry I forgot—"

"We must have a target on our backs or something."

My blood turns cold. "What are you talking about?"

"The mayor sold the land out from under us. That piece of shit."

"I thought we were closing tomorrow?"

"Not anymore. The new owner of the land is already listed on the city website," he seethes.

"Who is it?"

"Lorenzo Rossi."

The hairs on my neck rise. "Lorenzo? Giovanni's son?"

"Yes. And he's already contacted me to buy it from him."

I swallow the lump growing in my throat. "For how much?"

Maksim's voice fills with disdain. "Triple what we were buying it for."

"That motherfucker."

"Yes. Instead of the city, we have a meeting with him tomorrow. Whatever you had planned, cancel it. We all need to be there."

My chest tightens. "With Lorenzo?"

"Yep. Looks like we're dealing with the devil now. Sergey with you?"

"No."

"I'll see you tomorrow. I need to call him." Maksim hangs up and I put my phone in my pocket.

"What's going on?" Nora asks.

"The city lot we were set to buy—the one we need to develop the millions of dollars in land we've already acquired—well, the mayor just sold it from under us to Lorenzo Rossi."

"Shit," Nolan mumbles.

When I look at Nora, the expression I couldn't figure out is on her face again. But this time, it's deeper than before. It disturbs me. Something tells me everything is only beginning to fall apart.

13

Nora

EVERYTHING WE DIDN'T WANT TO HAPPEN IS COMING TO fruition. My family's war with the Rossi family is slowly dragging Boris in. I find it hard to believe Lorenzo buying the city lot isn't somehow linked to the O'Malleys.

If it was this easy for the Rossis to go after the Ivanovs' business, how much easier would it be for Zamir to learn about my relationship with Boris and take it out on my family?

The building dread in my gut only grows more as the night goes on. And I can't get Sergey's face out of my mind. His hurt and disappointment pained me. It was just as deep as his anger. I was several stores away when I saw his expression and heard the anguish in his voice.

I avoid looking at Boris all night. I stay busy with customers and my staff, but I feel his intent gaze on me. He sends me several text messages, but I don't read them. At the end of the night, I drive Killian home since he's had a lot of drinks. Boris gets in his car with his driver, and when I get to my house, he's waiting for me.

"Moya dusha, get in." He stands outside the car and holds the door open.

I hesitate.

He pushes his hands through my hair and tilts my head so I can't avoid him. Little bolts of lightning streak through my veins. The humming in my cells ramps up. "Have I done something to upset you?" he asks.

"No. It's not—"

"Then get in the car. We'll go to my place tonight."

I close my eyes. Everything about Boris and me represents a future train wreck. "What are we doing?"

His lips press against mine, and his tongue slides in my mouth, owning every atom I have. It dissolves my ability to think about why we shouldn't be together.

He murmurs, "We're going to my place. Get in before someone sees us."

I obey.

When he slides next to me and shuts the door, I say, "Tell your driver not to leave yet."

"Why?"

"Tell him," I order.

He rolls the divider down. "Kirill, stay parked until I tell you to go." Boris presses the button, and the glass rolls up. He pulls me over so I'm straddling him. "Are you going to tell me what's wrong?"

I don't answer. My pulse beats hard, and my heart hurts at the thought of not being with him.

"You've avoided me and my text messages all night."

"I was busy working. You were there."

"Nora, I'm not stupid. Don't lie to me."

My stomach flips. "I love you."

Boris's eyes darken. "Why do I feel there's a huge 'but' next to your 'I love you?'"

I swallow the lump in my throat. "We said we would keep the Rossis and Petrovs away from each other's family."

His voice fills with alarm. "Have the Petrovs done something and you haven't told me?"

I shake my head. "No. Not yet. But how long will it be until they do? What if they already know about us and are planning something?"

"Moya dusha, I told you I would take care of this. I will figure out a way to keep them away from you. Don't create an issue when there isn't one."

"I'm not!"

"You are."

I become angry. "How will you keep them away? The Rossis weren't supposed to become your issue, and now they have.

Your brothers are upset. We're coming between you and them."

"My brothers don't know about our relationship. Everything is fine between all of us."

I know it's for the best and what we agreed upon, but his truth hurts. His brothers should know if he's in a relationship. My brothers should, too. It slaps me in the face harder about what we're doing.

"Sergey knows about us. And I saw him. I don't want you losing your relationship with any of your brothers."

"I won't."

"You already are," I cry out.

"I'm not," he barks.

Silence fills the air. My insides quiver, and my lips shake. He pulls me closer to him. "Have faith in me, moya dusha. I'll make sure everyone stays safe."

"I do have faith in you. But this is more than you can control. I don't want you involved with the Rossis, and now they're coming after your family, too."

"No, they aren't," he insists.

"Do you think I'm stupid?"

"Of course not. I've never said anything even remotely close to that statement."

"Lorenzo Rossi went under your nose to buy the city lot. You were at the bar the night his thugs came in and groped Molly. It's too coincidental. Tonight, you were again part of a fight with them. They pulled a gun on you. They—"

"Did you want me to let Nolan fight it out on the street?"

"No, of course not."

"Then what did you want me to do, moya dusha? Hmm?" Boris asks in a pissed tone.

"I don't know," I admit.

He clenches his jaw.

I hold his cheeks. "I'm not saying you've done anything wrong."

"Sounds to me like you think I'm not handling things for us."

"I never said that."

"Then what are you saying?"

"I don't want you and your brothers involved with the Rossis. I don't want my family involved with the Petrovs. We're putting everyone we love in jeopardy. This is selfish for us to do to our families." As the words come out of my mouth, my chest tightens, and my stomach flips. A couple of tears stream down my face. But I can't continue to pretend we aren't putting people who are closest to us in extra danger.

"We aren't. You need to give me time—"

"The Rossis are coming after your family. It's because of my family. Admit it," I shout.

His face hardens.

I lower my voice. "You don't want me to lie to you, but you lie to me."

"I do no such thing," he claims.

"Don't you? You and your brothers have a meeting tomorrow with Lorenzo Rossi. What would the land he bought off the city be worth if he doesn't have the surrounding parcels you and your brothers own?"

Boris turns and looks out the window.

"Answer me," I order.

He continues to stay quiet.

I move his face toward mine. "Nothing. It's a liability due to the millions it will cost to clean it up. So why would he want it other than to screw you and your brothers over?"

"You're reading into things. We don't know his intentions for buying it."

"Don't you dare treat me like a fool. Our relationship is affecting your business. You could lose millions. It's putting your brothers and you in danger."

"I don't need you worrying about us, Nora. My brothers and I are all capable of dealing with Rossi or anyone else."

I release his chin. "That's the exact attitude that got Sean killed."

"I'm not Sean. Neither are my brothers," he replies in a haughty voice.

"What does that mean?"

He shuts his eyes and sighs. "Nothing."

"No, you said it. Tell me what you meant."

"Nora—"

"Tell me," I demand.

He nods. His eyes turn to slits. "Okay. I will. Sean somehow got on the Rossis' radar. He should have told your brothers so they could help him."

Grief and hurt mix. I seethe, "You're blaming Sean for those bastards murdering him?"

In a firm tone, he says, "No. I didn't say that."

"Yes, you just did."

"No, I meant if your brothers knew, Rossi would be dead, not Sean."

"And you just proved my point."

"No, you're reading into my statement."

I glare at him. "You're a hypocrite."

He sarcastically snickers. "I'm a hypocrite?"

"Yes. You just stated my brothers would have protected Sean, so he didn't get murdered. Yet, you hide the battle you just entered—the O'Malleys' battle with Rossi, by the way, not an Ivanov one—from your brothers."

"It's not the same thing. And my brothers are involved with our land deal."

"Are you going to tell them you're getting involved in O'Malley fights? That the reason Lorenzo is coming after your business is because of my family?"

"You don't know that," Boris growls.

"I do. It's too coincidental. Stop denying it."

Boris rubs his hands over his face. "We need to stop discussing this. All it's doing is creating issues between us."

My insides pitch so much, I feel nauseated. I close my eyes and whisper, "These are real issues. They aren't made up and won't go away. We need to stop putting everyone we love at risk."

The car goes silent, and when I finally open my eyes, Boris's are cold. "What are you saying, Nora?"

"I-I love you. But we can't do this anymore."

The color drains from his face. "You're breaking up with me?"

I can't talk. Tears fall so fast, they drip off my chin.

He angrily says, "How can you say you love me, yet in the next breath, tell me we're over?"

"I do love you."

"Then don't do this. Come to my house with me, and let's forget we had this conversation."

"We can't forget about the facts," I cry out.

In a stern voice, he claims, "I'm handling it. I told you to give me time."

"There is no more time. We've already put your family in jeopardy. What's next? Zamir comes after my brothers or yours, harder?"

Boris holds my head next to his. "Moya dusha, I love you. You're jumping to conclusions—"

"I'm not!"

"You are!"

"I'm sorry. I can't do this with you anymore."

His voice turns so angry, a chill runs down my spine. "If you throw me to the curb, I won't come running back."

"I'm not throwing you—"

"What would you call it?" he spouts.

"Doing what's right for our families."

"Jesus, Nora. I'm so sick and tired of worrying about everyone else. Let's just come clean and be done with it. I'll take the punches from your brothers and we can move forward."

"This is way more complicated than a few punches, and you know it. We agreed the Rossis and Petrovs were risks for both our families. It hasn't changed."

He exhales deeply and scowls. "So that's it? Hmm? You're going to allow Zamir and Lorenzo to break us?"

"No."

"So, you aren't breaking up with me?"

I squeeze my eyes shut. "I love you. I want to be with you, more than anything."

"Then let's be together," he barks.

"What's our future look like? A secret relationship? Always looking over our shoulders? One day we wake up and realize we're old and it's too late?"

He tilts his head. His eyes widen. "Ah. So this is what this is really about. This is about babies, isn't it?"

I can't answer him. The stabbing pain the last time it came up with my brothers returns.

"You don't want my babies?" he asks in a low, hurt voice.

"How? It can't happen. You know this."

"Why?"

"You know why."

"Say it, Nora."

I stay quiet.

So much disgust fills his face, I cringe. He grunts. "Goddammit, Nora. You can't even say it to my face, can you?"

"What do you want me to say?" I cry out.

"Tell me I'm not good enough for you since I'm Russian and not Irish. Go on."

More tears well in my eyes. "I never said that. It's just...it's complicated. You're aware of the dynamics."

He slides me off his lap. Repugnance fills his voice. "Sure, Nora. And they all revolve around the fact I'm Russian and not Irish. Well, you know what? It's getting old."

"Boris—"

He takes a deep breath. In a steady voice, he says, "No. If you want to have Irish babies, then I'm not stopping you. I wish you the best."

"Boris, I never—"

"Stop denying it! I'm never going to be good enough in your brothers' eyes. All because I'm not Irish. I didn't think it applied to you, but it does. You feel the same exact way. Well, don't let me stop you. Go have tons of Irish babies with some Irish prick who will check off all the O'Malley boxes."

My voice cracks. "You're not being fair right now."

His eyes light with rage. "I'm not fair? I've never once tried to hide you from anyone because you aren't Russian. Why? Because I don't give a damn. All I care about is you. And I didn't think you were like your brothers, that it mattered to you, but I've been wrong. You're worse than them. At least they'll tell me to my face I'm not good enough for you. You don't want to admit it and, instead, string me along."

I reach for him, but he grabs my wrist. "It's not true. I—"

"I wish you the best."

My insides quiver, and I stare at him. The air in my lungs becomes thick.

After a few moments of silence, he says, "I'm not going to be with someone who is ashamed of where I come from."

"I don't have anything against your Russian heritage."

He opens the door, gets out, then reaches in for me. Stunned, I take his hand. He pulls me out and leads me to my front door. He grabs my keys out of my pocket and unlocks my door.

"Boris—"

"I love you, moya dusha. I do. I wish you felt the same about me." He turns and leaves.

I stare at him as he goes. I've never had an issue with Boris not being Irish. It's always been my family who stressed I had to marry an Irish man. But I suddenly wonder if I am a hypocrite. Does hiding Boris from my brothers, no matter what the added layer of danger is for our families with the Rossis and Petrovs, make me just as bad as the O'Malleys' standards?

I lock the door when his car pulls away. I slump against it and fall to the floor. I spend several hours crying, my heart hurting, and hating how there are no clear answers to anything regarding Boris's and my situation. But I can't even call it our situation anymore. We've broken up. I'll never have him as mine again. And the realization cuts me.

14

MC

Boris

NOTHING I DO ALLOWS ME TO ESCAPE NORA. HER FACE WON'T leave my mind. The smell of her skin wafts in my nose, as if she's next to me. And I hear her whimpers and "Jesus, Mary, and Joseph" cries.

But she's not with me. I've not seen her since we broke up. Killian keeps asking why I'm staying away. Even Declan and Nolan have come to the gym to see me. I keep giving them excuses about work and needing to stay focused on the issues we have with Lorenzo Rossi. Plus, our longtime designer, Lada, bailed on us. She left us in a lurch. We're in the middle of a twenty-million-dollar new build and already behind. Dmitri hired a new woman named Anna. She's not Russian, which means we're taking a lot of money out of our community. With Zamir increasing his recruiting efforts, it's not the best time for this, but I can't blame Dmitri. Lada left us no choice.

I don't think the O'Malley brothers buy my excuses, but there isn't any other conclusion for them to make. Nora and I hid our relationship from them well. It drives me nuts, not talking to her or knowing how she's doing. The only way to get any information about her welfare is to call her or ask her brothers. I refrain from it all until I finally cave.

Killian and I are due to fight for our annual match. He comes into the gym. I'm covered in sweat and getting in an extra round of cardio. When I see him, I stop jumping and drop my rope.

"Good thing you're working extra hard. I don't want to take you out with a jab tomorrow night."

I grunt and grab my water. "Don't get cocky." I chug half the bottle then wipe my face with a towel.

"Are you going to avoid me forever?"

I freeze. "I'm not. I've told you what's going on."

"Boris, what did I do to piss you off?"

"You didn't do anything."

He crosses his arms and raises his eyebrows.

"Stop looking for problems when there aren't any," I lie and drink the rest of my water.

"Okay. If we're good, then you're coming to the pub after our fight, right? Same bet as always?"

Everything tells me to say no. Seeing Nora is only going to make me obsess over her more. But I'm out of excuses. Killian and I have had the same running bet for as long as I can remember. And I miss my friend. As much as I'm pissed he thinks my Russian blood makes me less of a man for Nora, we've always been as tight as brothers. "Yeah. Tell Nora to stock up on vodka though."

He grunts. "Fat chance."

"By the way, how is Nora? Is she taking days off or working herself into the ground?"

Please tell me she isn't dating anyone.

She's not mine anymore.

"She's become obsessed with remodeling the pub. She wants to update it but is struggling to find the right designer."

"Yeah, well, I'd give you Lada's information, but she fucked us. Dmitri says his new hire, Anna, is good, but I haven't seen anything yet to confirm it. If she's as brilliant as Dmitri claims, I'll get her information for you."

He nods. "That would be great. Thanks."

"I'm not sure if she's Irish though," I say, just to take a stab at him.

He scrunches his face. "So?"

I don't say anything.

"She's Russian? I don't have a problem with hiring one of your people. Nora won't, either."

No, we're just not good enough to mix our blood with yours.

I snort. "She's American."

Shock fills his face. "Maksim having a fit?"

"None of us were too happy," I acknowledge. "Dmitri's got a thing for her. He wouldn't admit it, but it was all over his face."

Killian chuckles. "Well, let me know if you can vouch for her."

"Will do."

"Okay, well, I've gotta go." He holds his fist out, I bump it, and while he walks away, he calls out, "I'll tell Nora to stock up on the whiskey."

"Vodka," I yell after him. My phone rings, and I grab it off the counter. "Sergey, what's going on?"

"Lorenzo increased the price another ten percent."

"He's getting cocky." Anger flares through my bones. I'm running out of patience with this deal. I still don't know if he bought it because of my involvement in the incident at Nora's pub or another reason. I haven't said anything to my brothers. Sergey and I never discussed the fight outside with Nolan, and he's kept his mouth shut to Dmitri and Maksim about it.

The only thing I told him was Nora and I were over, and he didn't have to worry about it any longer. It seemed to appease him. But every time Lorenzo is mentioned, his jaw twitches. And that means Sergey is obsessing over how to fix the problem.

Sergey lowers his voice. "At what point do we enforce our rule?"

The Ivanov rule is simple. No one fucks with us. Zamir may own me once a year, but everyone else on earth plays fair, or they feel our wrath. While I am the one Zamir focused on when we were kids and then when I made the deal with him for our freedom, Sergey's ability to torture men only developed over time. My steadiness comes from hours of Zamir and his head thug teaching me to control my every action. Sergey's is an inherent ability to personalize our victim's crimes. And they all relate back to our mother.

Sergey's voice is deadpan. "Maksim and Dmitri are right. There are additional consequences if we enforce right now."

"So we just allow him to screw us, lose millions, and put our guys out of work?" Sergey barks.

"He's not going to win. We're getting the lot. One way or another, it's going to be ours," I assure him, but my voice is more confident than my thoughts.

Lorenzo gets ballsier by the minute. The turmoil I feel inside is boiling, and every ounce of patience and logic I have is required. He's a big reason Nora and I aren't together. No matter our issues, if the incident at the pub hadn't happened, she wouldn't have gotten upset.

It doesn't matter. I'm not Irish and never going to be. She doesn't think any differently than her brothers.

"It better be. I have to go." Sergey hangs up.

I head to the locker room, shower, and change. I go to my penthouse and spend the remainder of the day trying to forget about Nora.

I get to see her tomorrow after the fight.

It doesn't matter. It's over between us.

God, I miss her.

Unable to control my urge to see her, I call my driver and sit outside the pub. I almost go in, but Killian and Nora step outside. I hold my breath. It's the first time I've seen Nora since I left her on her front doorstep. And the ache I've felt and can't get rid of only intensifies.

There's another guy with them. He's got a four-leaf clover tattoo on his neck. I instantly get nervous.

He puts his hand on Nora's back. It's a friendly gesture to the average person, but a guy with any radar can see he's into Nora, and Killian encourages him.

I'm going to kill Killian tomorrow night.

She freezes then steps away.

That's my girl.

She's not my girl anymore.

I stay outside the pub all night, far enough away no one would see me. After the pub closes, Killian and the Irish guy come out together and walk Nora to her car. He hands her a piece of paper, and she takes it.

Rage stirs and grows within me. I tell myself again, *she's not mine anymore.*

But she should be.

I roll the divider glass down. "Kirill, follow Nora."

"Hidden?" he asks.

"Yes."

We set off. As expected, she goes straight home. When she gets inside, the lights turn on, then off.

I stay outside her house until my alarm rings. I go work out with my brothers, spend the day going through the motions, then meet my trainer, Aleksei.

"Boris, you ready to kick Killian's ass tonight?" he asks.

I've never been more ready to destroy Killian. The pain of losing Nora seems to have tripled in the last twenty-four hours, and I focus all of it on him.

How dare he continue to push men on her.

She's mine. We're meant to be together.

He's going to pay for every thought that ever crossed his mind about my Russian blood.

I warm up. Maksim and Sergey come into the gym.

"Please don't let him take you out with a jab this time," Sergey groans.

"Shut up."

He snorts and goes into the office. Maksim pats me on the shoulder. "Let's get your ankle taped up."

I follow Maksim and barely hear a word he says. All I see is Nora's face and hear her voice. I visualize everything I'm going to do to Killian.

Aleksei comes into the locker room and says some things I pretend to pay attention to, then, "Time to go."

I jump up, crack my neck, then go out into the gym. I notice no one, only Killian, who comes out of the other locker room.

Nothing has changed. His green eyes glow, representing his desire to take me down. There's no friendship when we're in the ring. We're two enemies, and both of us will do anything to destroy the other.

I work hard the entire time to stick to the rules. Round after round, Killian and I beat on each other. My rage during a fight has never been higher, but Killian's is, too. During a quick break between the final rounds, Aleksei wipes the blood off my face. I suddenly wonder what's driving Killian. Did he somehow figure out what is between Nora and me?

I don't have time to figure it out. The bell dings, and we start going at it again. I swing and land a hard fist into Killian's cheek. He goes flying backward and lands on the ground.

The referee counts to ten and grabs my arm. He holds it in the air, announcing I'm the winner.

Killian turns and glances up. His bloody face is swelling, and his green eyes are slits.

I take a moment to catch my breath and reach down to pull him up. When he's on his feet, he wipes the blood off his mouth and says, "Vodka it is."

I smile, unable to stay mad at him. It's Killian. He's been my opponent and friend for so long, I can't let what's between Nora and me ruin our friendship.

There is no Nora and me.

I need to fix it. She's meant to be mine.

I continue to go through the motions, and when I get out of the locker room, Killian is stepping out of his. The crowd has died down. Few people remain.

"I'm catching a ride with you," he says.

"You aren't scared of me?" I jab.

He snorts. "You got lucky."

We leave and get to the pub. My insides flip as I walk inside. I quickly look to find Nora but don't see her.

A brunette comes up to Killian and starts making a fuss over his face. He introduces me, and I say, "I'm going to the restroom then getting some ice. You want any?"

"I already have a bucket waiting for you in the game room," the girl says. "Your brothers are all in there."

Killian cockily squeezes her ass. "Lead the way."

I go to the back of the pub and down the hallway. Once I verify no one is looking, I open the door to Nora's office. She's at her desk and looks up in surprise.

I shut and lock the door.

"Boris," she whispers. Her expression quickly turns to worry. "Oh God, your face." She rises.

I take three steps and slide my hands through her hair then take every piece of her I can get.

My mouth presses against hers, and she gasps, then parts her lips. Our tongues urgently flick the other's. "I miss you," I admit then deepen our kiss and unbutton her jeans.

"We can't...oh... B—" She shudders as my hand slides into her panties and my fingers slip into her sex. Her eyelids flutter.

I shove her pants and then mine down. I circle my finger on her clit and murmur between kisses, "Tell me to stop, or I'm not."

She doesn't. She laces her fingers through my hair and kisses me harder while whimpering into my mouth.

I hold her up against the cold windowpane, entering her in one swift move.

"Jesu—"

I cover her mouth with my hand and thrust into her like a wild animal. Her hot breath penetrates my skin, and her face flushes until she's sweating.

I lean into her ear. "You're mine, Nora. We're meant to be together. Tell me you agree."

She whimpers louder and moves her hips quicker into my thrusts.

"Tell me," I growl.

Her body shudders, eyes roll, and she spasms against my cock.

I pound harder into her. She clutches me tighter, pushing her face into my collarbone and biting it.

"Tell me," I order again.

"Jes...oh fu..." She flies into another orgasm, and I go with her, detonating inside her like a piston out of control.

There's a knock on the door. Nolan's voice booms, "Nora!"

Her eyes widen. She yells, "I'm on the phone."

"You seen Boris?"

"No. Check outside."

I reach up and quietly pull the shade over the window. I murmur in her ear, "Tell me you want to be with me."

"I do. So badly," she whispers in my neck.

"Then let me go tell your brothers about us."

"We can't. Nothing has changed."

I squeeze my eyes shut, take a deep breath, then step back, releasing her. We pull our pants up and stare at each other. "I'm not letting you go, Nora. One way or another, we're going to be together."

Her face scrunches, and she looks away.

I pull her into me and hold her while she cries, but she doesn't push me away. I tighten my arms around her.

There are muffled noises outside the office, and she pulls back. "We can't do this here. And we need to accept our reality."

I hold her cheeks and say against her lips, "I'm not accepting anything. You are mine. We *will* be together. You don't want to tell them tonight, fine. But I'm not staying away anymore."

She shakes her head. "Don't do this to me at work ever again. I-I can't handle it. This is killing me." She puts her hand over her face.

"Let's stop hiding. I'll handle whatever happens."

She takes a few breaths and tilts her head. "We can't. Don't come into my office again. I can't do this. We will never be. I won't harm our families. Sean is already dead. I won't have the death of my brothers be from my doing. Please go."

The truth hangs in the air like a razor, slicing my skin in one slow cut after another.

"Please," she whispers and points to the door, avoiding my eyes.

She's never going to let us be together.

Defeat sets in for the first time. It's clear and finally hits home. Once and for all, I need to figure out how to move past her.

15

Boris

DMITRI COMES INTO THE GYM. "BORIS, I NEED YOU TO GO TO New York with me."

"Why?"

His face hardens. "I need to deal with Anna's ex. You're coming to make sure I don't kill him."

"What fun is that?" I mutter.

He sniffs hard. "If I kill him, Anna isn't going to forgive me. She hasn't said it, but she won't."

"What did he do?"

"I'll have all the details when we get to New York. But he hurt her and is holding her personal items over her head. He also stole her money. I have Tolik on it." Tolik Ivanov is our cousin who handles a lot of things for us. He's connected everywhere and could get a priest to admit what was said in the confession box if needed, without ever laying a hand on him.

"I'm going to babysit you, then?"

Dmitri grunts. "Yeah."

I nod. "A trip out of town sounds good right about now. I'm in."

"Why? What's going on?" A line forms between Dmitri's eyebrows.

"Nothing. Just ready for a change in scenery. Clear my head from all this Rossi shit."

"Can't believe he thinks we're going to hand over our other lots to him," Dmitri spouts as Sergey and Maksim walk in.

"It's time to enforce our rule," Sergey claims.

Maksim shakes his head. "You'll do no such thing. We do not need a war on our hands."

I snort. My patience is wearing thin. Every new offer Lorenzo sends our way is lower. "We already have one."

Maksim steps until he's eye to eye with me. "We are not at war with Rossi. Not yet."

"Keep believing that." I turn and pick up a weight to load onto the bar.

"Boris," he snaps.

I spin. "Don't talk to me like I'm your child."

Sergey sets his bottle of water down. "Boris is right. We are at war. Lorenzo's actions are clearly offensive. When are we going to stop playing defense and end this?"

"We need to give this more time and see how it plays out. Hopefully, he will come to his senses," Maksim advises.

"Are you in la-la land? This is a Rossi. He's an arrogant piece of shit who had everything handed to him from his daddy," I claim.

"Yeah, and his father is now in prison. Lorenzo has more power over the family than ever before. We don't need a war if we can avoid it." Maksim scowls.

"We're already in one," I restate.

"We don't strike first on a crime family."

"He's already taken the first few hits. What else does he need to do?"

Maksim's eyes turn to slits. "First few hits? What are you talking about?"

I glance at Sergey, which is enough to tip Maksim and Dmitri off.

"What are you two keeping from us?" Dmitri asks.

Sergey crosses his arms and stares at the ceiling. His jaw twitches.

I confess, "There was an issue in the pub. Rossi's guys came in, and we had to kick them out. Sergey and I pulled up to the bar and Nolan and the same guy who groped their server were going at it on the sidewalk. We broke them up. One of Rossi's guys pulled up in a black car and aimed a gun at us."

"When did this happen?" Maksim asks.

My stomach flips. "The night you called to tell me Rossi got the land."

Maksim's face turns red. "And neither of you bothered to tell us?"

"It's not relevant," Sergey says, coming to my defense.

"Are you two out of your minds? Of course it's relevant," Dmitri growls.

Sergey sternly replies, "No, it happened minutes before Maksim told us about the lot. Rossi had already bought it. It's completely unrelated."

Maksim points to Sergey and me. "We don't hide important information from each other."

"This has to do with Nora, doesn't it?" Dmitri asks.

"Keep Nora out of this," I bark.

"She wasn't there. We got out of the car, and they were fighting. You can't expect us not to jump in," Sergey claims.

"No, but we expect you to inform us a Rossi pulled a gun on you," Maksim seethes.

"Fine. Message received. Who's spotting me?" I ask.

Sergey steps over and picks up a weight. "Let the old men work out together."

"You better watch it," Dmitri says, pointing at him.

I finish my workout and go home. I spend the day trying to keep busy and not think about Nora. It's impossible.

I need to get over her.

I struggle all day and night. I barely sleep, unable to get her out of my head. I stop myself from texting or calling her. The next day, I fly to New York with Dmitri. When we get to Tolik's, he hands us an envelope of pictures he got from the hospital. They are of Anna. Her ex, Mitch, beat her up so badly, you can't recognize her. It happened a year ago, but there is another set of images from several months ago before she moved to Chicago.

It's a good thing Dmitri brought me. There's no way he's going to not kill her ex without me stopping him. Personally, I think he shouldn't be so merciful toward the guy and beg for Anna's forgiveness later, but that's the difference between us. It pains me not to finish the guy myself, after what he did to her.

After we get all the information from Tolik, we get back in the car. Sergey calls Dmitri and informs us Lorenzo just offered us ten percent less than his last offer for all our lots.

I clench my fists then crack my knuckles. The daily pressure I feel to get past this Rossi issue only grows. He's screwing with us and the O'Malleys, and I directly blame him for a major reason Nora won't let us be together. "He's looking for trouble."

Dmitri nods. "But we don't need it."

"His father has severe legal issues going on right now. Even with his connections, it's going to be hard for him to get out of going to prison. Lorenzo's going to take over. This isn't good. Dealing with this sooner rather than later is best," I insist, reiterating our conversation we had the morning before at the gym.

"Maksim and I both agree we need to wait. You and Sergey need to cool it."

I glance out the window. "He's messing with the wrong family."

"Agreed. But we wait."

The car pulls up to a high-rise building Anna's ex-boyfriend works at. He's a financial advisor and stole a significant amount of money from Anna. We're here to get it back and make sure he never works on Wall Street again.

We go into the building and get through security after giving them our licenses and getting visitor's badges. When we get off the elevator and go into the office suite, a red-haired woman greets us when we walk in.

She isn't Nora.

I need to get over Nora.

She shakes our hands, and I hold it longer while checking her out. She says, "I'm Robin. Can I get you something to drink?"

"No, thank you," Dmitri says.

I linger on her different body parts and order a latte, just to see how she reacts. She blushes.

Guilt fills me. I'm not really interested in her. I want Nora. But Nora's made it clear we'll never be together. And I haven't been able to get past her no matter what I do. So maybe I need to spend some time with someone else.

Robin leaves to get my drink.

"Seriously? We aren't here to get you a date," Dmitri reprimands.

I shrug. "She's a sexy woman."

"Can we stay focused?"

"Don't worry. I'm on."

Robin comes back, and I flirt with her all the way to the conference room while checking her out like a pervert until she's as red as her hair.

Dmitri and I deal with the suits. He makes his demands, and on our way out, I grab Robin's business card and wink.

As soon as the elevator door shuts, Dmitri slaps my head.

"What the fuck is that for?" I growl.

"You aren't here to get some ass."

"You're the one in the relationship, not me. And until tomorrow, I'm free. So sit in the hotel if you want, but I'm hitting the town. And that redhead looked like the perfect woman to do it with," I claim, once again feeling guilty for even looking at another woman.

Dmitri jabs me in the chest. "You better be ready at seven tomorrow. Workout, breakfast, then we finish this and get back to Chicago. I don't need you with a hangover or off your game."

"Have you ever known me to not deliver?"

"No. But this is too important to screw up."

"Don't worry. I know my role," I claim.

Dmitri and I get to the hotel and have dinner. I start texting the woman from the financial office but stop.

What am I doing?

I call Tolik instead. "Tell me you're free to hit the town tonight."

"If by hitting the town you mean a sports bar and beer, then I'm your man."

"I'm in. Send me the location."

I hang out with Tolik, get to bed early, then meet Dmitri for breakfast. We go through the plan and spend the day "taking care of Mitch."

We get to the airport and on the private plane. I clean my knife and say, "We should have killed him."

Dmitri sighs. "She wouldn't have forgiven me. I know her. She didn't have to say it."

I shut my knife. "We need to take care of Lorenzo. This isn't going to go away."

"We have time. The last thing we need is a war with the Rossi family," Dmitri insists again.

When are my brothers going to wake up and realize he isn't going to disappear? This can only escalate. I confidently state, "We quietly do it. You know this."

In his "don't argue with me" voice, he demands, "We wait. Now, I'm done talking about this."

Everything in life suddenly feels exhausting. I ignore Dmitri for the rest of the flight. We both pull out our phones. Against my better judgment, I cave. I text Nora.

Me: *We need to talk.*

Nora: *I can't deal with this right now.*

Me: *There's never going to be a convenient time to deal with us.*

The dot, dot, dots appear on the screen but then stop and go away. I assume since we're in the air, something might be interfering with the signals.

When the plane lands, it's barely evening. There still isn't a message from Nora. Instead of texting her back or calling, I head directly to her pub. Traffic is backed up on the street, which never happens. Then I see and hear the sirens behind me.

A chill runs down my spine. I get out of the car and run toward the pub. The closer I get, the clearer the picture becomes.

Flames burst from inside the pub and out of the roof. A crowd is on the sidewalk. Molly and Darcey are outside, holding each other and crying.

"Where's Nora?" I shout at them.

Molly points to the building. "She just went back in to get her grandmother's picture."

"You let her?" I growl while shoving through the crowd, screaming Nora's name. I use my jacket, open the door, then cover my mouth with it. Smoke makes my eyes water. I continue to choke out, "Nora!"

The heat from the game room hits my skin. Black smoke permeates the air. I get halfway across the pub when I see her. She's passed out, lying behind the bar. Her grandmother's picture is on the floor next to her.

I pick her and the photo up, continue moving forward toward the back door and into the alley.

"Moya dusha, wake up," I yell, running around the building where the emergency responders are.

She doesn't open her eyes. She lies lifeless in my arms, and I keep ordering her to wake up.

The paramedics pull up as I come around the corner. My insides shake. I stare in horror, willing her to wake up. Things become a blur, and I hop in the back of the ambulance and hold her hand. A non-rebreather mask is over her face. We only get down the street before she opens her eyes and starts coughing. The paramedic attends to her and adds an IV to hydrate her. She seems confused, and her eyes keep rolling, as if she's dizzy. When we get to the hospital, they make me stay in the waiting room.

I pace the hallway. Nora's brothers come flying in. "Where is she?" Killian roars.

"Back in the exam room. We have to wait."

"What the hell happened?"

"I don't know. I just flew in from New York. She's awake, but it's all I know. Where were the three of you?" I accuse. I have no reason to be pissed at them, but the fact no one was there to protect Nora or stop her from running back into the pub angers me.

They nervously glance at each other.

"What?"

"We had O'Malley issues to deal with," Nolan states.

"Like what?" I growl.

Declan clenches his jaw. "You know we can't answer that."

I lower my voice. "What are you getting involved in?"

"Nothing. Stay out of our business," Declan warns.

The doctor comes out. "Nora O'Malley."

"That's us," Killian replies.

"I'm Dr. Amaro. Ms. O'Malley's lucky. Her diagnosis is smoke inhalation, but it's mild compared to what it could have been. We're continuing to give her oxygen and an IV for hydration. I want to keep her overnight for observation. She's still a bit confused, which is normal in these circumstances."

Relief fills me and all three of the O'Malley brothers' faces.

"Can we go back?" Nolan asks.

"Yes. She's in room three-nineteen. Best if it's two at a time maximum so she isn't overwhelmed."

Molly and Darcey run through the doors.

Darcey cries out, "Is she okay?"

"Yes, she'll be fine," the doctor assures them. "If you'll excuse me, I need to get my next patient."

"What the hell happened?" Killian asks again.

"I'm going back to see Nora," Nolan says, and Declan starts walking with him.

Molly scrunches her face. "We were all in the back, helping Nora in the kitchen. Carey called in sick, so we were under-staffed. There was a crash, and the customers started yelling. Sybil told the firemen a man ran in with a black hoodie on and threw something in the game room. It went up in flames in a matter of minutes."

"Did she get a good look at him?"

Molly nods, and tears come to her eyes. "I'm sorry. This is my fault."

"Why is it your fault?" I sternly ask.

Darcey pulls Molly close to her like a mother hen. "It's the same man you threw out of the pub. He seems obsessed with Molly. I was worried before, but now I'm terrified of what he's going to do."

"Rossi?" Killian seethes.

Molly nods.

Killian scowls, and our eyes meet. I pull him aside so we're out of the women's earshot.

"You know what this is, correct?" I growl.

Killian nods. "War."

Nora

MY BROTHERS SEEM TO STAY FOREVER. FIRST, IT'S NOLAN AND Declan. Then, it's Killian with Nolan. After that, Killian and Declan remain. I faintly remember Boris being in the ambulance with me. I don't dare ask my brothers. I'm not sure if I was hallucinating or not. But he's the only person I want to see, and he's nowhere.

So when Molly and Darcey come in, I remove the oxygen mask from my face and ask, "Is Boris here?"

Darcey sits down and picks up my hand. She glances behind her at the door then says, "He left after I told him it was a Rossi."

My heart beats faster. "Where did he go?"

"I'm not sure. He pulled Killian aside then took off."

I close my eyes, take a few deep breaths of oxygen, then remove the mask again. "But he was here?"

Molly's eyes widen. "Boris saved you. He ran into the pub and carried you out the back door. I have your grandmother's picture in my car. He grabbed that, too."

Tears fill my eyes. "He did?"

"Yes. He was a wreck. It's a good thing he showed up when he did. I'm not sure what you were thinking, running back into a burning building," Darcey reprimands.

I don't answer her. I close my eyes and focus on breathing.

"Are you tired?" Molly asks.

I nod and keep my eyes shut. It's nice of them to come to the hospital, but I want Boris. I need to see him more than I ever have in the past.

They take the hint and leave. I only open my eyes when the doctor comes in with the nurse. "Ms. O'Malley?"

I remove the oxygen mask.

"Go ahead and keep it on. Just shake your head when I ask questions," the doctor instructs.

I put it back on and nod.

He smiles. "Perfect." He opens my chart, reads something, then pulls up a chair.

I panic and remove the mask. "Is something wrong?"

"No, not at all. Ms. O'Malley, your blood tests came back from the lab. Are you aware you're pregnant?"

Goose bumps pop out on my arms. "I'm sorry, what did you just say?"

"You're pregnant."

My mouth is already dry from the oxygen, but any hydration I have evaporates at his words.

"I take it you weren't expecting this?" the doctor asks.

I shake my head, gaping. "I'm-I'm on the pill. I've been on the same one since I was eighteen and take it religiously."

"There are many reasons your pill might not be effective."

My blood beats between my ears. I put the oxygen mask back to my face and breathe.

Jesus, Mary, and Joseph.

What the hell am I going to do?

He gives me a sympathetic look. "Do you know how far along you might be?"

"I-I-" The image of Boris and me having sex in my office pops into my head.

How long ago was that?

"Maybe a month."

He puts his hand on my arm. "Is there someone you would like me to get in the waiting room?"

"No! Please! Don't tell my brothers."

The doctor holds out his hands. "I won't. But is there someone you want to call?"

Boris. What would I say? Hey, guess what? You know that time you screwed me in my office, and I told you to take a hike? Yeah, well, we're having a baby.

Oh, my God.

"Is my baby okay? From the smoke?" I ask and start to cough.

The nurse fills a cup of water and hands it to me once I stop. I drink almost all of it.

"I believe so, but we'd like to do an ultrasound and a few other tests just to make sure."

I blink hard.

Keep it together.

"Okay." I look at the nurse. "I want my brothers sent home. Please have all of them come in at the same time so I don't have to repeat myself. Have them bring the two women who were here, if they are still in the waiting room."

She pats my hand. "I'll go get them."

"Please remember not to say anything."

She pretends to zip her lips. "Secret is safe with us."

"Thank you."

I spend the next fifteen minutes convincing my brothers I'm exhausted, going to spend the night sleeping, and to leave. Molly and Darcey do what I suspect and help get them to agree.

Before they leave, Darcey hands me my phone. "The fireman pulled your purse out of the back office. It's in my car, but I thought you might want your phone."

"Thank you."

After they all leave, the doctor comes in. I spend the next hour in tests, and they announce everything is okay with the baby.

I breathe a sigh of relief. I'm wheeled back to my room. Once I'm back in bed and everyone is gone, only then do I let my tears freely fall.

I stare at my phone, debating about texting or calling Boris, but I don't know what to say. All I hear in my head is his voice, filled with disappointment, saying, "You don't want my babies?"

It was never true. The only man I've ever wanted to be with is him. But everything we were cautious about seems to be happening. The Rossis are out to get my family and him, and now I wonder how I'm supposed to ever protect a baby from it all.

Eventually, I fall asleep. At some point, I wake up. It's dark, and I think I'm dreaming. His scent flares in my nostrils. My body is curled into his chest, humming with energy how it always does around him. His beating heart thumps against my ear.

I slowly look up and remove the oxygen mask. "Boris?"

His arms tighten around me. He kisses my forehead. "You scared me, moya dusha."

Against my will, I become a sobbing mess.

"Hey, shhh," he soothes, but I bury my face in his body. My own shakes, and I wonder why life has to be so cruel. Why do there have to be any dynamics to a person loving another?

And how is it fair to have to worry about your child's safety beyond the normal scope of life?

Boris places his arm over my IV and scoots down in bed. "Careful you don't pull this out." He releases his hold on my arm and puts his lips to my forehead. "We have to figure out a way to be together, Nora. Whatever it takes so you're comfortable telling your brothers is what I'll do. But we can't stay apart anymore."

"No. I never wanted to," I admit.

He strokes the side of my hair. "Don't run from me anymore. There can only be one option, and it's us together."

I lift my head. "I have to tell you something."

He drags his finger down my cheek, and I shudder. Even in a hospital room, his touch electrifies me. "Don't give me an excuse to leave you. Let me worry about your brothers and all the other issues. Please. I just want you, Nora."

New tears soak his chest. I shake my head. "It-it's not that."

"No? Then what is it?"

"I didn't know. I swear, I took it."

He gently kisses my lips. "Your nana's photo is safe. One of the girls from the pub has it."

I kiss him, not sure how he's going to respond or what my news will do to us. "Thank you for saving it, and me. But that isn't what I need to tell you."

He cups my cheeks. "Okay. Whatever it is, tell me."

I stare at him with my insides shaking.

"Moya dusha?"

"I...the doctor came in and..."

His eyes fill with worry. "Is something wrong he didn't tell us about?"

"No...um...nothing like that."

He breathes a sigh of relief. "Okay. What did he say?"

Just spit it out.

"I'm pregnant."

Boris freezes.

"Say something," I whisper in a shaky voice.

He holds my face. "Did you say you're pregnant?"

"Yes."

He stares at me, and my stomach flips.

"I'm sorry. I really did take my pill. I—"

He cuts me off with a kiss. A deep, all-consuming, hungry kiss that makes my toes curl.

"You aren't mad?" I ask when I come up for air.

"No. Are you?"

I get teary-eyed again and shake my head. I admit, "Not mad...scared."

He pulls me closer and cradles my head on his chest. "I need you to trust me, Nora. Whatever comes our way, I will protect you. I will handle your family and all the other issues, we'll figure out together. No one will hurt you or our child."

"Don't tell my brothers yet. Please. Give me some time to figure out how to tell them."

"We've already thought about this enough. We need to tell them," Boris insists.

"Please," I beg. "I don't want them to hate you. Or me."

He snorts. "They could never hate you, moya dusha. Your brothers love you. I'm the one they will be upset with. But you're carrying my baby. We can no longer pretend this isn't between us. And I will not have you or our baby anywhere but with me."

"Promise me you won't say anything until we discuss how to tell my brothers. Please."

Boris takes a deep breath. "All right. But we aren't dragging this out. I want your things moved into my place. You can't stay on your own anymore."

The hairs on my arms rise. "Why? Did something happen?"

His voice turns cold. "Did they not tell you?"

"What?"

"Rossi is behind the fire at the pub."

"Yes. The girls told me."

"So you understand why I don't want you left alone?"

I slowly nod then yawn.

He kisses my forehead and picks up my oxygen mask. "You need to rest."

I stroke his cheek. "Killian is coming back tomorrow morning to get me. This isn't the place to talk to him."

His face hardens under my hand. "Am I supposed to pretend forever?"

"No. I promise. Give me time to recover with my brothers. They will protect me so you aren't worried. I'll figure it out."

"Nora, I want you with me. This is our baby. I'm the father. We need to be together."

"We will be. I only want to be with you. I love you, but I need you to give me a little bit more time so we can tell my brothers the right way. Please."

He sighs. "Okay." He holds my mask near my face then kisses my forehead. "Go to sleep. I'll be gone before Killian gets here. But I'm not going to wait forever. We need to tell them."

I nod. "We will. I promise. Before I sleep, I have one more question."

"What is it?"

"Where did you go? The girls said you left after you found out it was a Rossi."

He clenches his jaw. In a low voice, he replies, "I found the man who torched your pub. He's in the garage, waiting for me."

1 7

$\mathcal{MC}$

Boris

WHEN IT'S STILL DARK, I LEAVE NORA SLEEPING IN HER hospital bed. I text Killian fifteen minutes before he's due to arrive.

Me: *Where are you?*

Killian: *On the way to the hospital to pick up Nora.*

Me: *I'll meet you there. We need to talk.*

I grab a coffee and sit in the waiting room to wait for Killian. When he walks in, he raises his eyebrows. "What's going on?"

"I have him."

His eyes turn to slits. "Where?"

"In a place I can destroy him."

Killian nods. "My brothers are out looking for him. I was up all night searching for him, too. Let me text Declan and Nolan." He pulls his phone out of his pants and types quickly. "Where did you find him?"

"At his house."

Killian licks his lips. "Let me find out when Nora is getting discharged. Where should I tell my brothers to meet us?"

"I'll take care of him."

Killian crosses his arms. "He torched my sister's pub. The one my grandmother built."

"Yeah. And your sister is lying in a hospital bed. Do you really believe Lorenzo doesn't know about Emilio's attempt to burn the place to the ground? He would have gotten approval to do something that public. So you and your brothers create a schedule. Nora doesn't spend a moment without one of you or me, if needed. Who knows what Lorenzo will do when he discovers Emilio missing?"

Killian's face hardens.

In a stern voice, I add, "Nora needs to recover. I will handle this. You take care of your sister."

"My brothers can go with you, then."

"No. Emilio is in a location my brothers and I own. It is not a place we bring anyone. And it's too risky to transport Emilio. I will take care of this and text you when it's over. Any information I find out, I will disclose to you."

Killian shakes his head. "This is an O'Malley war. You shouldn't involve yourself."

I step closer to him. "This is not just an O'Malley war. Lorenzo is trying to fuck my brothers and me. We have a Rossi target on our back as well. And I've been at the pub for both incidents. Don't play your Irish/Russian bullshit with me, Killian."

He moves his head back. "I didn't say anything about Irish/Russian—"

"I'm done discussing this. Emilio is staying put until I dispose of his body. My brothers will not allow me to bring anyone to our property. You will take care of Nora and wait. If you or your brothers attempt to follow me or find out where I'm going, I will have my family take care of Emilio. Are we clear?"

Killian shifts on his feet then scrubs his face. He grumbles, "Fine. But you make the motherfucker pay."

I sniff hard then look over my shoulder. I lower my voice. "You won't hear from me for a few days. But mark my words, from the moment I step foot in front of him, until the last breath he takes, he will be in pain."

Killian's eyes turn cold. He nods.

I leave and text my driver on the way out of the hospital. He pulls up to the curb when I step outside. I get in my car. The last time Nora was involved with my victim at the garage, I lost my cool. I should have extended Cormac's life and gotten more information out of him. I can't afford another mistake. I text Sergey.

Me: *Meet me at the garage.*

Sergey: *When?*

Me: *I'm heading there now.*

Sergey: *Give me five, and I'm on my way.*

I stare out the window at the blur of the passing landscape. My thoughts race faster through my head than the cars on the expressway.

Nora's pregnant.

I'm going to be a father.

I have to protect her and our child.

I don't like the growing tension between the Rossis and Nora's family, nor mine. And my time with Zamir is coming soon. I feel it in my bones. I usually get this sick sense a few months before he calls. It's earlier than usual, but the last time, it had been fifteen months. It's like he wanted me to sit on pins and needles waiting for his orders.

I'll have security on Nora at all times unless she's with her family or me.

We need to figure out how to tell her brothers.

I'm not sure what the best way to break the news to her family she's with me is, but I want to get it over with. I already let this go longer than I ever should have. I could have had security on Nora and dealt with everything else.

My thoughts never stop spinning. By the time I get to the garage, I'm stressed and angry. Like always, I direct my driver to leave, go into the main room, then wait for Sergey.

If I enter the next area, I'm going to tear into Emilio. It's something I feel when I box. The usual calm I have when I torture and kill is nowhere. Without Sergey to keep me in control, I don't trust myself.

I change into the clothes we keep in the garage. There are always several sets so my brothers and I are prepared for anything. Then I pace the small space, taking deep breaths.

I hear the car pull up. The second room is soundproof, but this one isn't. Sergey walks in with Adrian.

"Where're Maksim and Dmitri?" Sergey asks.

"I didn't text them."

"Why? Since when do we come to the garage without them?"

My night with Cormac comes to mind, but I don't tell my brother. I avoid looking at Adrian. What happened is between Nora and me. I focus on Sergey.

"You missed our workout. Maksim and Dmitri were worried you were with Zamir. I was, too."

"Yeah, well, I'm not."

"Who's in there?" Adrian asks.

"Emilio Rossi."

Their eyes darken. Sergey barks, "Why do you have him?"

"He torched Nora's pub, and she almost died."

"Jesus. Is she okay?"

"Motherfucker," Adrian mutters.

"She spent the night in the hospital from smoke inhalation. Killian is taking her home today."

"Rossi would had to have approved a move this public," Adrian says.

"You don't know that. And we can't afford any wrong moves right now," Sergey warns.

"Of course the prick knew. And after I deal with Emilio, I'm going after Rossi," I seethe.

Sergey points at Adrian and me. "Until we know for sure, no one is doing anything to Rossi. You don't just take out the head of the mob without a solid plan. There are consequences. We need to cover our asses at all times. Don't make a stupid move. Maksim is right about this."

Adrian paces. "You're right. We also risk the land falling into someone else's hands if Rossi disappears."

The vision of Nora lying in her smoke-filled pub, passed out on the floor fills my mind. "Rossi is not going to get away with this. I don't buy for one minute he didn't give the order to torch the pub. He almost killed Nora."

Sergey grabs both my cheeks. "Listen to me, Boris. He will not get away with it. But there is a time and place for everything. This is the time for information. We need to secure the city plot so our people can continue to work and not fall into Zamir's grasp. We cannot risk a war with the Rossi family."

"Let the O'Malleys take care of Rossi. They are already at war," Adrian adds.

"He's right. We're already stepping over the line by taking care of Emilio," Sergey insists.

I step away from him and pick up my black gloves. I slide them over my hands. "Since you're both here, you can make sure you stop me from killing this piece of shit too soon."

"Let us get changed," Sergey says.

"Adrian, hold off. I need you to get something for me."

"What?"

"Fill the gas tank."

Adrian nods, gets what I asked him for, and comes back.

We spend three days trying to get as much out of Emilio Rossi as possible. He's third cousins with Lorenzo and mid-level on the totem pole. We hoped to find out why Lorenzo bought the city lot and his real motive, but Emilio proves to be too low in their family organization to know anything.

Every second I spend torturing him, I take great pleasure in. He torched Nora's pub. He almost killed her. My baby could have died as well. So every slice of my knife and cry from his mouth gives me a bit of satisfaction.

I've never been conscious of much while I'm in the middle of harming someone. There's always a mission, and the only thing I focus on is my task at hand. This time is different though. It's personal to a different degree.

Several times, Sergey or Adrian stop me. They make me go into the other room to cool off.

The last time, there was barely any life left in Emilio, but we still haven't gotten any useful information.

"It's time to finish this guy off. He's about to go into shock," Sergey says.

Adrian leans against the desk and glances at his watch. "He doesn't know anything. I've got a date tonight, so if we can move this along, I'd appreciate it."

"With who?" Sergey asks.

"That waitress from Kipichi."

"The stuck-up one from Brazil?"

"Yep. And I know just how I'm going to make her apologize for being so bitchy to me most of the time."

Sergey whistles. "She's smoking."

"Yeah, so let's get this over with," Adrian agrees.

I don't say anything. I get up, go into the other room, and lean into Emilio's ear. He's probably too far gone to understand me, but I say, "Since you almost killed my woman and child with fire, it's only fair you get the same."

I pick up the red gas tank I had Adrian get. I pour it over his head, and he screams in pain as it fills his open wounds. I pour some in his mouth then step back as he chokes.

We've always used plastic to cover the floors, walls, and ceiling. And the room is built as an incinerator. No matter what punishment we give out, we're prepared. Sometimes it's necessary to do something besides burn everything to ashes. In this case, not a bone or fingernail will be left of Emilio.

I nod to Sergey.

He takes the box of matches, steps in front of Emilio, and strikes one. "You should never underestimate the O'Malleys. But your biggest mistake was you fucked with the Ivanovs."

He tosses the match so it hits Emilio's mouth. His body erupts in flames from the inside out, and he screams but only for a few minutes due to his voice box burning.

Adrian, Sergey, and I watch him burn for a minute, then shut the door and go into the other room to avoid the flames and fumes.

I start to strip out of my clothes. "I'm getting in the shower. I have something else I need to take care of. Give him another minute then turn the incinerator on. Can you two clean up?"

"Yeah, we got it," Adrian says.

I throw the clothes in the burnable bin, text my driver, and shower. I put on the clothes I came in and go straight to Killian's.

Nora's on the couch with a blanket around her. It takes all my willpower not to pull her into my arms. After I get past Killian, I sit in the chair across from her. "You okay?"

She smiles, lighting up my dark world. "I'm doing a lot better."

"Good."

"Is it done?" Killian asks.

I turn back to him. "Yeah. I just finished it."

"Did he pay?"

I raise my eyebrows. "I'll tell you what you already know. An Ivanov believes a tooth for a tooth, tenfold."

He nods, pats my back, then walks toward the kitchen. He calls over his shoulder, "I'm making Nora our nana's Irish stew. You hungry? Want to stay for dinner?"

I lock eyes with Nora. "I'm starving. Think I'll hang here tonight if you don't mind."

"Stay. We were going to play cards later if Nora is up for it."

"Count me in, then."

18

Nora

A Few Weeks Later

MY BROTHERS HAVE ME ON LOCKDOWN. I CAN'T GO ANYWHERE without them hovering over me. It means I haven't seen a lot of Boris. The pub hasn't reopened yet. A fire restoration company did the best they could. The good thing is the firemen got to the pub and put the fire out before it spread past the game room. But there was some smoke damage to the main area.

"When can I reopen the pub?" I ask my brothers. It's the first time I've been here since the fire.

"The city has to deem it safe. The inspection is in a few days," Killian replies.

"Should I be worried?" Every time they mention inspection, my chest tightens. My biggest fear is they will shut my pub down, and everything my nana worked for will be gone.

Nolan shakes his head. "No. The fire restoration company said as long as the game room is closed up, you shouldn't have any issues. We can start tearing it apart after the inspection."

"Don't touch it. Until I know what the design will be, let it sit."

Nolan's eyes widen. "Are you crazy? The regulars are going to have a fit without the game room."

"Don't you mean you?" I smirk.

"Yeah, me included."

I tap my fingers on the bar and stare at the plastic covering the entranceway. "I need to find a designer. I can't hold off on remodeling much longer, but until I do, nothing is to be touched."

Declan snorts. "Just pick one. Stop being so picky."

"It's important I find the right person. I don't want to lose the authentic feel. Not every designer gets it. Actually, no one seems to, based on the ones I've spoken to."

"Boris said he might have someone for you to interview. His old designer bailed, and they were trying someone new out. I'll ask him," Killian says.

"No, I'll ask him. This is my business. You've all done enough. I can handle it."

Declan's phone rings. His face darkens. He exchanges a glance with my brothers and answers it. "Tell me you have good news." He continues to glance between Killian and Nolan.

Chills run through me.

"Tonight?" he says.

Killian cracks his knuckles.

I murmur to him, "What is going on?"

"Nothing. Stay out of it."

"We'll be there." Declan hangs up. He tells my brothers, "Be ready to leave at seven. Call Boris. See if he can watch Nora and if she can stay at his place tonight."

I huff. "Watch me? I'm not a child who needs a babysitter. And where are you going?"

"If we're not with you, Boris needs to be. We've already explained this," Killian states.

A night with Boris is all I'm craving. I haven't touched him in weeks since the hospital. But my bad feeling grows. "Where are you going to be all night?"

"It's not your business," Declan states.

"Don't—"

"Nora, don't ask questions we won't answer. Let's not waste our breath."

"Boris, are you able to watch Nora tonight? My brothers and I need to take care of something," Killian says into his phone.

"I don't need a babysitter," I claim again, which is stupid on my part since it gives me a perfect reason to be with Boris.

Killian shoots me an annoyed look. "I'll tell her to dress up. Can she stay at your place?"

Why do I need to dress up?

My insides turn to Jell-O, thinking about a night with Boris. But I'm not happy my brothers aren't informing me where they are going.

"Great. I'll tell her to be ready by six. Thanks." Killian hangs up. "Pack your overnight bag and put on your best dress. The new restaurant Boris and his brothers invested in has the grand opening tonight. He'll pick you up from my house at six."

"Tell me where you're going tonight."

"No. Stay out of it. Let's go. I'll take you to your place so you can grab clothes. It's already four."

"Do I need to worry about you three all night?"

Nolan snorts. "No. We can handle ourselves."

"Don't be cocky," I hurl.

"I'm not. There's nothing you need to stress over. Go have a nice night out. The new restaurant is supposed to be amazing. It'll be good for you to do something fancy and not pub related anyway."

I cross my arms and glare at him, but my body is already throbbing at the thought of Boris's hands on me.

Killian begins walking toward the door. "Come on, Nora. Time's ticking."

We go to my house, and I stare into my closet. I call Boris.

His deep, rough voice sends a delicious chill down my spine. He answers, "I can't wait to get my lips on every part of your body tonight."

I shudder and smile. "How fancy is this place? Nice or cocktail?"

"Cocktail. Don't wear any panties."

"What?" I softly laugh.

His voice lowers. "You heard me. If you put them on, I'm going to make you remove them in the car."

I twirl my hair around my finger and debate about whether to wear a green or black dress. My fancy clothes are limited. "How would you make me do that?"

He growls. It's low, but I don't miss it. My loins pulse some more. "No panties. Wear that sparkly green dress you wore to your cousin's wedding."

"That was years ago," I say, holding the phone to my ear, and pulling the dress out of the closet.

"Yeah, and my dick hurts every time I think about you in it."

I bite my lip and put the dress on my bed. I rummage into the back of my closet and pull out a pair of black stilettos.

"It's been killing me not seeing you," Boris admits.

I freeze. "Me, too."

"You're feeling okay?"

"Yes." *Just hornier than a whore in church.*

"You've been taking the vitamins the doctor gave you?"

"Mmhmm. Everything is good."

"Did you figure out how to tell your brothers?"

My heart races faster. "Not yet. But—"

"I'm not going to allow this to go on much longer. We need to tell them. I want to move your things in and be together. This has gone on way too long."

"I know. I want to."

"Then let's get it over with and tell them."

"We'll talk about it tonight. Okay?"

He releases a long breath. "Fine."

I stick my head out the door to make sure Killian isn't in the hallway and step back into my room. "Is this considered our first date?"

"No. If it were a first date, I wouldn't be able to do the things I'm going to do to you tonight."

I swallow hard. "I guess I'll have to adhere to your no panties rule then."

Sergey's muffled voice comes across the line. Boris says, "I have to go. I'll pick you up at six."

"Bye." I put my phone in my pocket and finish packing. Killian takes me to his house, and I get ready. When I walk out, Boris is already here.

He's wearing a black button-down shirt. The top three buttons hang open, and his chest tattoos are on display. The shirt, tucked in to perfectly tailored slacks, is formfitting and stretches across his torso and arms just right. The scent of his skin hits my nostrils and goes straight to my loins.

I'm suddenly fearful I made the wrong decision not wearing panties. The hum in my body I always have around him feels more intense. Heat blazes through my cells, and I try to breathe normally.

"Nora, you look nice." Boris quickly tears his eyes from me and says to Killian, "I'll drop her off tomorrow."

Killian nods. "Thanks."

My lust turns to worry. "Killian, whatever you're doing tonight, please be careful."

He scoffs. "Stop fretting. You look great. It's good to see you out of your pub attire. Go have a good time."

Oh, I plan on it.

If you only knew.

I don't linger. I don't trust the throbbing in my veins to not give my attraction to Boris away. I step away, and Boris puts his hand on the small of my back to guide me outside. It sends all my flutters into overdrive, and I once again think about how I'm not wearing panties.

The moment we get into the car, he straddles me on his lap. My dress bunches to my hips. His palms slide under my dress and onto my bare ass cheeks. My lips and tongue press against his, and I moan into his mouth.

He grunts, slides his palm forward, and teases the hole of my sex. "Fuck, you're wet."

I move closer to him. The friction of my nipples against his chest makes me gasp. Everything seems so much more sensitive than ever before. I try to sink onto his finger, but he doesn't let me. He slides it forward to my clit, and I shudder.

"Oh, Jesus, Mary ...oh..." I slide my tongue back in his mouth and shimmy my breasts against him.

His arm tightens on my back. He moves his hand between us. He pumps three of his fingers in my sex and circles the heel of his palm against my clit. He bites my neck over my beating pulse.

Adrenaline explodes in my toes and quickly climbs through my body. "Jesus, Mary, and Joseph," I cry out, shaking hard.

He growls, "I'm tired of staying away, moya dusha. We're telling your brothers tomorrow. I scheduled the moving company." He pushes harder and moves faster against my clit.

I can't respond. I'm panting and moving my chest faster against his, trying to maintain the pleasure consuming every part of my body.

His lips move to my ear, and he sucks on my lobe. He slows down his hand.

I beg, "Please, don't stop." I grind my lower body faster on his palm.

"You're mine, moya dusha. We tell them tomorrow."

The adrenaline slows, bringing my buzz to the edge of the cliff. My voice is raspy and desperate, and I've never felt so needy. "Oh God. I need more. Please."

"Tell me you agree. Say yes," he demands then slows further.

Any reason I have to say no flies out the window. I crave what he can give me. Not just now but in our life together. I want it as badly as he does. But at this moment, I can't think about the consequences or how we're going to tell my brothers. I feel a desperation I've never felt before.

"Yes. Now, please."

He groans. "Good girl." He slides his fingers out of me and creates a pattern of pinching and rubbing my clit.

"Jesus, Mar...wh...oh God!" I cry out as all hell breaks loose in my body.

I don't feel the car stop or hear Boris lock the doors. I fall into the curve of his neck, panting. The earthquake in me digs so deep, I feel it in my bones.

When it finally slows, I stay curled up to Boris, inhaling his sexy scent.

His lips brush against my ear. "I love you. You're the mother of my child. I won't have you anywhere, except in my bed every night from now on. Do you understand?"

Reality hits me and what I agreed to. I slowly pull away and look at him. "What are we going to tell them? I still don't know how to do this."

"I will tell them."

"They will attempt to kill you."

Boris snorts. "No one's killing me, Nora. Do not worry about this anymore. Now, we're going into the restaurant, and we're going to have a good night with my brothers, like normal couples do. And the entire time, my cock's going to be hard, looking at you in your little dress."

Not worrying is easier said than done. "But—"

He puts his fingers that were in me in my mouth. He commands, "Suck."

I close my eyes and obey. The taste of my orgasm only makes me crave more.

"Mmm." He licks behind my ear and murmurs, "I've been dying to taste you. For weeks, I've dreamed about your sweet pussy. So get every drop of your juice off me, moya dusha. If I taste you right now, we're not going into the restaurant. And I promised myself I would take you out for a nice night like you deserve."

I shudder, suck harder, then pull away. "Let's go to your place."

He sniffs hard and licks his lips. "No. I'm feeding you first. You're going to need the energy when I keep you up all night." He kisses me quickly, moves me off his lap, and yanks my dress down. He brushes his finger over my nipple.

I inhale sharply.

"My mouth has missed these, too."

"We don't have to go inside," I try again.

His heat-filled eyes sear into mine. "But we are. I'm tired of hiding and not showing the world you're mine. Let's go." He pulls back, gets out of the car, and reaches in for me.

At first, I almost step away from him. I'm so used to hiding my affection for him. But I lean into his chest, enjoying being his. I wonder how we're going to tell my brothers.

He kisses the top of my head and says, "Let's not worry about your brothers tonight."

"I'm not," I lie.

He snorts. "I can see it on your face, Nora."

I wince. "Sorry."

"No more anxiety. Let's have fun tonight."

"You're right."

He guides me into the restaurant, and the hostess seats us. Sergey is already at the table with Eloise. I've met her once before. He brought her to the pub, but she turned her nose up, like it wasn't good enough for her. But since Sergey's into her, I smile and say hi.

He raises his eyebrow at Boris when he sees me but quickly recovers. He stands and kisses my cheek. "How are you feeling?"

I smile. "All better."

"Good."

Boris pulls out my chair, and I sit. Maksim joins us with a woman named Jade. I've known her for years. I don't understand why he's with her, either. She's a cold fish. But at least she never looked down at my nana's pub. There's small talk, but all I can concentrate on is Boris's scent and the humming in my veins. All I can think about is getting through dinner and going back to his place.

Dmitri is the last to arrive. He brings his new girlfriend, Anna. She sits next to me. I immediately like her. She asks, "Are you from here?"

"Yes. I've lived here my entire life. You?"

"I just moved from New York City."

"I love it there. What made you move?"

Anna pauses then replies, "My brother and his wife live here. They're having a baby, and I thought it would be nice to be near them."

I smile. "That's nice. My sisters and brothers all have kids. It's fun being an aunt."

Well, not all my brothers. Only Sean.

My pregnancy brain is making me misspeak.

Don't get into how your brother was murdered, with a stranger.

Anna asks, "They are here in Chicago?"

I blurt out, "Oh, yeah. The O'Malleys would never leave Chicago. That would be a sin, according to my grandfather."

And another mistruth. Sean's wife, Bridget, left and took my nieces and nephews, too. She said she needed to get away from the O'Malleys' issues and keep her kids safe. Bridget is from New York and part of the O'Connor family, which is another crime family we have close ties with. She believes her family can keep her kids safer than ours. Not seeing her and her children breaks my heart. We were close, and since Sean's death, she doesn't want anything to do with me or any of us.

Anna beams. "Ahh, you're Irish. That explains your beautiful red hair."

I touch it. "Yes. It's hard to escape in my family."

Boris slides his arm around me and drags his finger down my bare arm. He twists a lock of my hair around his finger.

Heat singes my face. The humming in my veins turns to buzzing. I inhale sharply.

I turn to him. *Please take me home now. God, I want every part of you in and on me.*

Boris leans near my face, looking at me like he could eat me up in the restaurant. He says, "Anna is Chicago's newest, up-and-coming interior designer."

My cheeks burn. I tear my eyes away from Boris. "You're an interior designer?"

"Yes," she says.

"Do you design restaurants?"

"I worked on several over the years before I started my business, but I've not designed one on my own before."

"Could you?"

"Yes, I suppose."

Boris adds, "You two should meet up and discuss this. Nora's been struggling to find someone good, haven't you?"

"Yes. There have been some issues," I admit.

Boris leans closer to my ear. His hot breath hits my skin. A new surge of tingles race down my spine. He strokes my neck from my ear to my collarbone. Against my will, I squirm in my seat. *Why didn't I wear panties? Am I going to stain the seat?*

He confidently says, "But all of them are going to go away. Sometimes a clean slate is best, don't you think?"

I nod, hoping he's right and there aren't any issues when we tell my brothers, but I know it's asking for the impossible.

He strokes my cheek, and my insides throb so hard I shudder.

Why does everything feel so intense tonight? Is it because I haven't seen him in weeks?

I struggle between wanting Boris to touch me and telling him not to lay a finger on me until we are in the car alone.

Anna clears her throat, pulling me out of my lewd thoughts. "Well, I'd love to meet up and talk with you if you want."

"I would. Very much. Please."

"Okay." Anna pulls out her phone, and we exchange information.

A waitress comes over and puts bread on the table. Maksim orders wine and champagne for everyone.

Boris slowly strokes my neck, and I close my eyes. My heart rate increases. I swallow hard and make the mistake of looking at him.

He glances at my lower body and licks his lips. His eyes are a blow torch straight to my pussy. I squirm again.

"Imagine finding all the Ivanovs here tonight," a man sneers behind me.

Boris's face hardens, and his brothers and he all exchange glances.

"Lorenzo. Didn't expect to see you here, either," Maksim replies in a deadpan voice.

Lorenzo Rossi. Oh God.

I glance at Boris, but he scowls at Rossi.

"Time's ticking. I'm getting impatient," Lorenzo says.

Dmitri leaps off his seat and gets in Lorenzo's face. He bites out, "Don't threaten us."

Boris and his other brothers jump up and crowd around him.

"Or what?" Lorenzo replies, and three men behind him step forward.

Maksim steps between Dmitri and Lorenzo. In a firm voice, he states, "We're having a night out. If you have something to discuss, we'll do it at a different time. Not now."

Lorenzo scoffs. "Tomorrow. And I expect to move forward."

"You don't make demands from us," Dmitri growls.

Lorenzo lowers his voice. "I own this town. You know it. I know it. Everyone knows it. The price just went down another ten percent."

Dmitri clenches his fists, and Maksim pushes Dmitri back. He points at Lorenzo. "We're done with this conversation."

Lorenzo laughs, and he and his posse begin to walk away. When he gets to the front of the table, he freezes and stares at me. "Aren't you an O'Malley?"

My skin crawls. I swallow hard, and my face heats with anger. I know he gave the order to burn my pub. My brothers confirmed it. I didn't know he knew what I looked like. My insides shake with rage and fear.

Anna grabs my hand.

"What's it to you?" Boris growls.

Lorenzo's grin widens. "Oh, how the Irish have fallen."

Boris and Sergey almost leap over the table, and Maksim and Dmitri grab both of them, holding back their brothers.

Lorenzo strolls across the restaurant and sits at a table with his men several rows over. Women are already seated, and the waitress begins filling their wine glasses.

"Dinner's over," Maksim orders.

Boris puts his arm around me, and we all leave.

When we get in the car, I'm shaking. "How does he know what I look like? How are we going to keep our baby safe?"

Boris pulls me into him. "Because I'm going to kill him."

19

Boris

NORA WAS AWAKE ON AND OFF ALL NIGHT. WE'D HAVE SEX, she'd fall asleep, then she'd wake up, and we'd start all over again. I'm not sure if her desire for me is greater or if mine is for her, but now that she's back in my arms, there's no way I'm letting her spend one more night away from me.

My plan is simple. I'm going to tell Killian, and once he calms down, I'll talk to Nolan and Declan. I'm sure Killian will tell them before I do, but if anyone deserves to know about Nora and me first, it's Killian.

I scheduled the movers to pack up Nora's house. She wasn't too happy when I told her it was happening today, but she only stayed mad a few minutes. I made her beg me and admit she wanted to be in my bed every night.

She's curled into me, asleep. I stare into the morning light, focusing on the crashing waves of Lake Michigan, stroking the curve of her stomach.

I need to kill Lorenzo as soon as possible.

He gave the order to torch her bar.

He knows what she looks like.

That bastard came after my woman and child.

My phone vibrates, and I grab it off the nightstand. I quietly say, "Killian."

"Can Nora stay with you longer? We aren't going to be back. It might be a few days or a few weeks."

The hairs on my arms rise. "Why? What's going on?"

"I can't discuss it. We're fine though. Can you take care of Nora?"

"Yeah."

"The inspection for the pub is tomorrow at ten."

"I'll handle it."

"Thanks. I gotta go," he says.

"Let me know when you're coming back."

"Will do."

I hang up, and Nora stirs. Her eyes flutter open. "What's wrong?"

I scoot lower and pull the covers around us. "Nothing. Killian and your brothers won't be back for a few days or possibly weeks. He wanted to make sure I'll take care of you."

"A few weeks?" she nervously cries out.

"They're fine." I tease her nipple with my fingers and kiss her jawline. "Do you want me to take care of you, or do you want to sleep?"

She softly inhales and shivers.

"Should I let you rest?" I slide my hand to her slit and drag my finger through her wetness.

She closes her eyes. "Why do you feel so good?"

I dip down to her breasts and cockily mumble, "I always feel good." I suck on her nipple, and she arches off the bed. "Jesus, Mary...oh..."

I grunt. Every time she yells her Irish blasphemy, it's like a shot of Viagra to my cock. Not that I need the little blue pill. I spend half my day with an aching dick, since I can't keep my mind off her.

I don't like that we can't tell her brothers today and get past our lie, but I am glad we don't have to rush over to Killian's. "I'm not allowing you to leave my bed today."

She grips my head and breathes, "No?"

I glance up at her. In Russian, I say, "No. I'm going to eat your sweet pussy so many times you can't move tomorrow."

Nora doesn't know Russian, but her face turns crimson, as if she knows every word I'm saying. My dick hardens further. I flick my tongue on her nipple, tease her sex with my digit, and continue to speak in Russian. "Your family may think you need an Irishman, but you need my big, Russian cock, don't you, my sexy little vixen?"

Her chest rises faster, and her green eyes blaze with lust. She can't seem to get enough of me, and I'm digging every moment of her insatiable need.

I slide my arms under her and move on top of her frame. I hold my body weight up with my knees and forearms to not risk hurting our baby. The second my cock slides over her clit, she whimpers.

"Fuck, you're always so wet, moya dusha."

She latches her arms around my shoulders and tries to widen her legs, but my legs stop her.

"Greedy girl," I tease her and rock my hips faster over her swollen nub.

She trembles. Her moans get louder, and when she's full of sweat and shaking harder, I roll off her and sit up, pull her on me, and slide her over my erection.

"Oh God!" she whispers.

I fist her hair and hold her head in front of me. "I want you to marry me, moya dusha."

Her green orbs widen, and she freezes.

I reach for the table and open the drawer. I pull out the ring I bought earlier in the week. I hold it up. "Forget about anything you're worried about with your family. Tell me you'll marry me."

She bites her lip, and tears fill her eyes.

"Say yes," I urge her, my heart beating faster.

She quietly asks, "Is this..." She swallows hard and lifts herself off my erection. "Is this because of the baby?"

My head moves back, surprised she would doubt my love for her. I wrap my arm tighter around her. "The only woman I've ever wanted is you. Years ago, I should have made you mine."

"But if I weren't pregnant, you wouldn't be asking me?"

I put my hand on her stomach. "Our baby is making us do what we should have years ago, which is form our life together and tell your family about us. It doesn't make my obsession with you more or less. I've always wanted you as mine. I've always loved you. Do not use our child as a reason to tell me no."

"I didn't say no."

My mouth turns dry. "You didn't say yes. Do you not want to be my wife?"

She puts her hands on my cheeks. "Of course I do."

"Then say yes. I want you as my wife, not just because you're my baby's mother."

Her lips twitch. "So, I'll be an Ivanov."

"Yes."

"We haven't told my brothers about us yet."

"What do they have to do with you marrying me? Is their reaction going to change how you feel about me?"

"No."

"Is their opinion going to make you want to keep our baby away from me?"

Her eyes widen. "God, no. Why would you say such a horrible thing? You are the father of my child. Of course I want you involved in his or her life in all ways."

I hold the ring up again. "Then your brothers have nothing to do with this decision. Tell me you'll marry me, moya dusha."

She slides her hand through my hair. "My brothers will insist on a Catholic wedding. Assuming they don't kick me out of the family."

I groan. *The O'Malleys and their Catholicism.* "I won't allow them to disown you, Nora. But all of you barely go to church, minus funerals and weddings."

She shrugs. "We're Irish. You know the O'Malleys."

"Fine. I'll pay the priest."

She bites a laugh. "It's a little more complicated than that."

"Doubt it." I glance at the ring. "You still haven't said yes."

She blinks a few times and leans closer. Her hot mouth ruins me. Every second I spent wanting her but never taking her was wasted, and I'm not able to stand her not being part of me in every way. I wrap my arms around her. I slip my finger into the ring and palm her head. I firmly repeat, "Say yes."

"Yes," she murmurs against my lips.

I groan. "Tell me again, louder. Tell me you're mine."

Her green eyes sparkle. She pulls back and stares at me. "Yes. I'm yours. I've always been."

I kiss her again, feeling as if my world is suddenly whole. As if all the darkness and evil surrounding me won't be able to suck me in and annihilate me someday.

It can't if I have her. She's my beautiful perfection of happiness.

But I also know we still have issues to deal with. And I'm not sure what her brothers are going to tell her to do regarding me.

I hold her cheeks and admit everything I'm worried could happen to tear us apart. "I love you. No matter what your family says, promise me you won't go back on your word. That even if they tell you to leave me and raise the baby as an O'Malley, you won't."

Pain flashes in her eyes. It scares me at first, but then she says, "We're having a baby. No matter what my brothers say, I will not leave you, nor would I ever attempt to keep our child from you. If they do not accept us together, then they do not accept our child. I will not be ashamed because our baby is not full-blooded Irish."

I release a breath of relief.

"And I love you. You're right. We are past the point of this secret. If they make me choose, I choose you."

I take her hand and slide the ring on her finger. "I promise you, no one, even my brothers, will come first over you. There is only us and our child from now on. And anyone, Lorenzo, or even Zamir, who tries to do anything to harm us, I will destroy."

Fear crosses her expression, but my fiancée is not naive. She understands more than I ever anticipated in the past. She slowly nods then slides her hands into my hair. When her lips meet mine in a fury of fire, it's an unspoken vow of the future.

I push every disturbing thought out of my head about the realities of the Rossis and Petrovs. I sink into her and the world that is only ours.

20

Nora

TRUE TO HIS WORD, BORIS HAS MOVERS SCHEDULED. I DON'T even go to my house. Boris keeps me in bed all day. The company packs everything up, and by early nighttime, Boris's penthouse is full of my stuff.

Four guys with the moving company stand in front of me, waiting for instructions. I twist my hair around my finger, staring at the furniture and boxes. "What are we doing with all these extra things?"

Boris says something in Russian to the movers, and the men nod and step out of the room.

"What did you say?"

"I told them to grab a coffee and come back." He sits in my armchair and says, "So, what are we keeping, and what are you making me give up?"

"Huh?"

He points around the room. "What are you attached to?"

I glance at my old furniture compared to Boris's expensive, designer leather furniture. For some reason, I laugh.

Boris arches an eyebrow. "What's so funny?"

"My furniture looks like a homeless person trying to compete with a runway model compared to yours."

He studies his couch then mine. A grin forms, and he sits farther back in the chair and pats the arm. "But it's comfy. You want to keep yours or mine?"

I sit on his couch then swing my legs on it. "You're being nice, but this is high-end and way better than mine. My furniture makes your luxury penthouse look dumpy."

"So, you want to keep mine?"

I snort. "Is this even a question?"

He rises, puts a blanket over me and a pillow behind my back. "Tell you what, you relax and tell me what to keep or donate. Once we know what you want, then we can go through my stuff and get rid of it so we don't have two of everything."

"So we're really doing this, huh?"

His face falls. "Are you having doubts?"

"No. I just didn't expect to have all my stuff in your house when you picked me up for dinner yesterday. And what happens to my house?"

"Sell it. Rent it. Whatever you want."

"That easy, huh?"

"Yeah. I think we have enough complications without letting what's easy be difficult, don't you think?"

I think for a moment. "Yes. You're right. But I want to take some time to decide what to do with the house."

He bends down and quickly kisses me. "Fair enough. There's no rush. Take all the time you want. Now, what furniture pieces do you want?"

I scan the room. The only thing is a wooden rocking chair my grandfather made for me when I was a little girl. I point to it. "The chair. Everything else can be donated."

Surprise fills his face. "You sure?"

"Yep." I pat the back of his couch. "I'm going to embrace living in luxury."

An amused expression appears. "That was easy. Should we go through all your kitchen stuff?"

"Nope. I'm not attached to anything, except the four green coffee cups and teacup set that was my nana's. Oh, and my omelet pan. Everything else, I'm sure you have."

"You're making this too easy," Boris teases.

I shrug. "Everything else will be my clothes and personal items. Guess we're done here. Do your guys unpack, too?"

"Yep. Let me call them back."

"I was joking."

"I'm not." He picks up his phone and rattles off some Russian. He sets his phone on the table then picks up my feet and sits under them. Within minutes, the movers are back in the penthouse, removing the furniture and kitchen boxes, and Boris is giving me a foot massage.

"I think it would have made more sense to let me go to the house," I say.

Boris snorts. He leans toward me and slides his hand under the blanket and up my inner thigh. "But then we would have missed all our fun today."

Heat rises in my cheeks. Tingles trail his fingers. I take a deep breath. We've been in bed all day, yet, I can't seem to get enough of him.

One of the movers says something in Russian, and Boris looks up, replies, then turns to me. "Want them to put your clothes in your closet, or do you want to point as they unpack?"

I've never had an extensive wardrobe. I spend so much time at the pub there hasn't been a point. Most of my wardrobe is jeans and O'Malley pub T-shirts. "I'm feeling quite lazy. Let them have at it."

Boris gives orders in Russian, and they take the four boxes into the bedroom. When they're done, they unpack the remaining box with my personal care products and organize them in the bathroom. Within fifteen minutes, everything is complete.

Boris rises and hands them a wad of cash. They leave, and he spins with a huge grin.

"What are you so happy about?"

He sits back down and picks up my feet. He teases, "There's no going back now, Nora O'Malley. You're mine."

I push the thoughts about my brothers out of my mind and try to enjoy our happy moment. He's all I've ever wanted. I've always wanted to be a mom, and now I get to be one with his child. The light catches my diamond, and I trace it with my finger. "I think this is the fanciest thing I've ever worn or owned."

Boris snorts. "Now I can spoil you the way you should be."

I crawl over to him and straddle him. I push his hair off his face. "I have a doctor's appointment tomorrow. Do you want to go with me?"

His smile grows. "Yes. Killian said your pub inspection is at ten. When is the doctor's appointment?"

"Two thirty."

"Perfect." He puts his arms around me, and his phone vibrates. He pecks my lips, pulls it out, and his face falls.

My gut drops. "What's wrong?"

He turns away from me, and his face hardens. His heart beats faster.

"Boris?"

"It's Zamir."

"What does he want?" I ask in a panicky voice.

Boris says nothing and locks eyes with me.

The chill down my spine grows colder, and I shudder. "But it hasn't been a year yet."

"It's not on a calendar. I knew this was coming."

"How?"

"I felt it."

My pulse increases. "So...what does it mean?"

His jaw clenches. "We shouldn't discuss this. Don't worry about it."

I gape at him. "You just proposed to me. I'm carrying your child. Don't ever again tell me not to worry about it."

"It's not good for you or the baby if you're stressed."

"Then tell me what the text means."

He loudly exhales. "It means I wait. He'll call, and I'll go. When it happens, you will stay with your brothers or mine until I am back."

I already know the answer, so I'm unsure why I ask. "And how many days will you be gone this time?"

His eyes darken. "You're asking questions I cannot answer. If I could, I would."

Fear lances me. I cup his cheeks. "Don't go."

He slowly inhales. "I don't have a choice."

"But—"

He fists the back of my hair and glides his tongue in my mouth. His hand slides in the back of my pants, and he tugs me as close as possible. When we come up for air, he says, "We will not live our days worrying about this. He will no longer steal parts of my life. Do you understand?"

His eyes morph into the boy I used to know—the one who didn't know how to kill or torture or live with secrets. He had hope and innocence, and I see it for the first time since I was a girl. But there is also vulnerability and pain. It scares me. I'm not used to seeing anything but confidence with Boris.

His lips brush against mine. "Tell me you understand, moya dusha."

I hold his head firmly. I never realized how much Boris feels like a prisoner of Zamir's until now. And a soul-crushing pain stabs at my heart. "I understand."

I do the only thing I can think of to try and show him my love. And I spend every moment we have over the next week wrapped around him.

We go to the inspection the next day, and the city allows me to reopen the pub. I work with Darcey to handle more duties so I can be at home more. We go to the doctor's, as excited couples do when they are having a baby.

The entire time, I sit on pins and needles, wondering when Zamir will call upon him and what it will continue to do to him, year after year.

My brothers don't contact Boris or me for a week.

"Why aren't they back or calling us?" I fret.

"I don't know. But Killian said they were fine. Worrying isn't good for the baby. Go to your appointment with Anna. Adrian will take you since I have my meeting."

"Can he stay out of sight? It's embarrassing to have him standing over me," I ask.

Boris snorts. "It's Anna. She's with my brother."

"So?"

"I bet she comes with a bodyguard."

"So, he can stay out of the way then?"

Amusement crosses Boris's face. "I'll tell him to give you space."

"Good." Something else occurs to me. "Did you tell your brothers about the baby?"

Boris shakes his head. "We will tell your brothers first. Unless I have a reason to tell mine sooner."

I go to the pub, which is the first time I've been away from Boris all week. I point to a corner booth. "Why don't you sit there?"

Adrian arrogantly smirks. "Is this your way of telling me to stay out of your way?"

I wince. "Want something to drink? Or eat?"

"I'm good. I'll just sit back and pretend I'm here for..." He glances around.

I snap my fingers. "Hold on."

I go behind the bar and pull out the newspaper Darcey always leaves for me to read when we're slow. I grab a bottle of water and put both on Adrian's table. "You can read."

He glances at the paper. "Sure."

"Do you want—"

He puts his hand in the air. "I'm good, Nora. Pretend I'm not here. Do what you gotta do."

"Okay. Thank you."

"Yep."

The phone rings, and I rush behind the bar to get it. "O'Malley's."

"Why aren't you answering your phone?" Boris says.

I put my hand in my pocket. "Oh, sorry. It's off. Is everything okay?" I ask, worried Zamir texted.

"Yes. Killian called."

My chest tightens. "And?"

"Your brothers are coming back late tonight."

My nervous flutters take off.

"Moya dusha, please don't tell me you've changed your mind."

No. He's right. I take a deep breath. "We can't keep doing this." I twist the old-fashioned cord around my finger. "My brother—"

"Will need to get over it. Let's do it tonight," he firmly states.

I sigh. "I'm working tonight."

"I thought Darcey was taking the shift? Do you not want to get this over with?"

"You know I do."

A woman clears her throat behind me.

I turn. "Oh, sorry, Anna." I hold up my finger. "I need to go. Anna is here."

He lowers his voice. "Text me when you're on your way home. Leave Adrian in the lobby. Take your panties off when you get in the elevator."

Heat rises in my face, and my lower body throbs. I turn and mumble, "I have to go." I hang up, take a deep breath, and turn back toward Anna. "Anna, how are you?"

"I'm doing well. I love the authenticity of this place." Her face brightens as she looks around.

"I'd like to keep it but not be lost in the past if that makes sense?"

Anna beams. "Sure."

"Why don't we—" I glance toward the door. Two large men are standing at the entrance.

"Sorry. Dmitri has me on bodyguard lockdown right now," Anna tries to joke.

"It's okay. I understand." I point to a booth. "Do you want to sit? Can I get you a drink or food?"

She declines. We spend the rest of the time discussing my vision of the remodel. Before she leaves, I sign a contract with her. I love her ideas and concepts. She seems to understand my vision and promises me she can start right away.

It's three when Darcey comes in for her shift.

"Shoo!" she tells me.

I get in the car and text Boris.

Me: *I'm on my way home.*

Boris: *Don't forget to leave Adrian in the lobby. And you better not have any panties on.*

Me: *Am I supposed to put my jeans back on?*

Boris: *That depends.*

Me: *On?*

Boris: *How fast do you want me to eat your pussy?*

My face flushes, I squirm in my seat, and don't reply back. I grab the bottle of water and drink half of it. When I get to the building, I tell Adrian to stay in the lobby.

As soon as I punch in the penthouse key and the elevator moves, I hit stop, remove all my clothes, then hit the button for the elevator to continue.

When the elevator opens, Boris is waiting. His eyes are flames dancing on my skin. But it's not the Boris I'm used to. His eyes have the vulnerability, pain, and fear I saw the other day. And there's a little bit of the crazed look I witnessed the night he came to my home after he was with Zamir.

He says nothing, coming at me in the same manner he did the first night we were ever together. He punches the stop button, and I retreat against the wall as he moves toward me.

His kisses are rough and hands possessive. But I don't have time to think about it or ask him what's wrong. Within seconds, he's on his knees and my thighs are squeezing his neck. I'm gripping his hair while I scream, "Jesus, Mary, and Joseph!"

21

Boris

Earlier the Same Day

THINGS GET HEATED BETWEEN MY BROTHERS AND ME. THEIR warnings to stay away from Nora anger me. They don't know she's pregnant, or I moved her into my house, or we're engaged. And I promised Nora I wouldn't tell anyone anything until her brothers know.

I don't expect my brothers to say anything to anyone. But it doesn't seem fair for me to tell my family and not Nora's. So once the O'Malleys are back, we can inform all of them.

Mix my brothers' comments with the time clock on the Rossi issues and the looming nights I'll soon be spending with Zamir, and I'm suddenly a bomb ready to explode, waiting for someone to pull the pin.

Sergey comments I should find a different piece of ass besides Nora. It pushes me over the edge, and I lunge at him. After an aggressive verbal exchange, Maksim forces me to the wall, and Dmitri pushes Sergey away.

Maksim growls, "Cool it! All of you! And Sergey is right about Killian. You're playing with fire with Nora. We don't need a war with her family next."

"You can all mind your own business. I know what I'm doing. And you better get your head straight, Maksim," I seethe through clenched teeth.

"About what?"

I shake out of Maksim's grasp. "Lorenzo is not going to wait. He's going to attack us. It'll be dirty, just like his father. Everyone will be in danger. Us. Our workers. Our women. Stop being stupid and give me the go-ahead to take care of this."

"This isn't just anyone. It's the mob boss. We have to strike at the right time. It can never be linked back to us," Maksim reminds me.

I point in Maksim's face. "Figure out a time—this week. If you don't, I will. I'm not letting that little weasel shove us around anymore. We're losing millions because of him. And I'll be damned if I let him continue to threaten us."

"You need to take a breather," Dmitri states.

"You want him coming after Anna?" I fire out.

Dmitri's face hardens. "No. You're right. He needs to be taken down. But Maksim is correct, too. And you're dealing with Zamir right now. What night are you meeting him?"

My gut flips. The sick feeling I always get whenever Zamir is mentioned, or I even think about him, grows. "You know how it works. He reminds me. Then he calls, and I have to drop everything and go."

"So, you see why you cannot move on Lorenzo until we are past the other situation?" Dmitri says.

I sniff hard and stare at the ceiling, clenching my teeth. I'm sick and tired of letting Zamir control my actions. Lorenzo needs to be taken down, but Dmitri is right. If Zamir calls and I'm in the middle of dealing with Lorenzo, I'm screwed.

Maksim puts both hands on my cheeks and makes me look at him. "We all want the same thing. One thing at a time, little brother."

"I want him tracked. At the very least, it's time to follow his every move," I growl.

Maksim nods. "Okay. I will implement it immediately. He won't shit without us knowing."

I step back. "I've gotta go. I'll be late for my session with Aleksei." I get to the door, and Dmitri stops me. "You tell us when Zamir calls."

I close my eyes briefly and nod.

Dmitri pats my back, and I leave. Sergey is close on my heels.

"What are you doing?" I grumble.

"Going to the gym with you."

"You babysitting me again?"

He grunts, and we get in the car. "When did Zamir contact you?"

I sigh. "Last week."

"Why didn't you tell me?"

"So you could watch my every move?"

Sergey cracks his knuckles. "Until we take control of the Zamir situation, it's never going to end. At what point do I ignore the rest of you?"

A bad feeling bursts in my veins. I lower my voice. "Ignore us? What's going through your head?"

His jaw twitches. "The thing about ghosts is they reappear. And the only way to get rid of them is to send them to hell."

Since I found out Nora is pregnant, one of my ongoing thoughts is how to kill Zamir. But I don't want my little brother anywhere near him. What I need to do to Zamir could backfire, and I don't want my brother caught in the crossfire. "We've been over this. Whatever you're thinking is impossible. Get it out of your head."

"Let's have Obrecht track him."

The air thickens. "We'd be setting Obrecht up for a suicide mission."

"You're underestimating Obrecht."

"No, I know Zamir better than any of you." The truth hangs in the air. Sergey can't deny it.

"Then start using it to your advantage."

I shift in my seat. Irritation festers. "You got something you want to get off your chest?"

The twitching in Sergey's jaw intensifies. "Do you ever wonder why this happened to us? What made Zamir look at our family and say, 'Those boys. They're the ones to turn into monsters.'"

I groan. "Oh shit. You're not getting all philosophical on me now, are you?"

Sergey's voice turns angry. "He didn't only see the devil in us. He saw he could control him and our every move."

"He doesn't control any of you. He gets me once a year. That's it," I claim, trying to deny Sergey's statement, not wanting to give Zamir any more power over me.

Sergey scrubs his face. "Sometimes, I'm not sure how the four of us are related."

"What the fuck does that mean?" I angrily spout.

He points at me. "The one thing he stressed to us was to bleed out your victim slowly." Sergey puts his fingers in quotes. "When you control your knife, you control life."

"What's your point?"

Sergey's eyes turn to slits. "Zamir places all his faith in assuming we'll never go after him. He takes for granted our fear not to destroy him. He believes he holds the knife. Right now, he does. But we're letting him. We need to take the knife and control his life."

I lean closer. "Did you smoke weed today? I feel like you're talking in tongues right now."

His face turns red, and he belts out, "Goddammit, Boris! This isn't a joke. You of all people know this. We need to bleed that motherfucker out. Slowly kill him and find out about every part of his operation we can."

A lump grows in my throat. "Are you listening to yourself? You're talking about the impossible. There is no slow bleed with Zamir. He'll find out and destroy all of us. And why do you have to know every part of his operation?"

Sergey's eyes darken.

The bad feeling I had at the beginning of this conversation worsens. I try to calm my voice but keep it firm. "Sergey, answer my question."

"To take it over."

My blood chills. I sit in stunned silence for several moments, gathering my thoughts. I finally ask, "Why would we want to do that?"

"To burn it and everyone who's a part of it to the ground. Leave no stone unturned in the Petrov operation."

Fear percolates inside me. "Little brother, you do not understand what you are saying."

"Think about it."

"I am," I insist.

He turns in the seat more. "If we run his operation, we can slowly destroy it all. If we only kill Zamir, it won't ever fully die."

I take a few breaths, trying to control the uneasiness growing at exponential rates in my chest. What Sergey is suggesting is dangerous beyond anything we've ever done. The fact he's thinking about this worries me. To try and shove all this nonsense out of his head, I say, "We aren't killing Zamir."

"It's getting old, Boris. I'm not living my remaining years under his control."

"You aren't. You're free," I angrily insist.

"Stop saying that. None of us are. You definitely aren't, but neither are we. Everything we do is centered around stopping him from hurting our people. But it's not enough, and it will never be. Until we take the reins and bleed him dry, he'll always win, always own us, always leave a path of poison wherever he goes."

The car stops outside the gym. I lean closer to Sergey. "We are not getting involved with anything Zamir is operating, whether he is alive or dead. You are speaking with your heart and not your head right now. There is nothing rational about Zamir or his operation; therefore, your thoughts, which make sense when said out loud, don't when implemented. I made a deal with Zamir. It is my place to decide what actions we do or do not take. Get all this out of your head. It is not the way forward."

Sergey's eyes grow colder. Pain mixes in his expression. In a quiet voice, he replies, "He killed her. He knew exactly how to have us hurt her even when she wasn't his prisoner."

All my brothers and I feel different types of guilt surrounding my mother and what we did to her. In some ways, the guilt eats Sergey more. I'm unsure if it's the age he was when everything happened, or finding her lifeless body, or the fact she couldn't look at him when she returned home. Maybe it's a combination of it all. And I wish there were a way to take away all the guilt and pain from him. If I could hold it inside of me instead of him having to carry the burden, I would. But there isn't.

"This still isn't the way," I say in a gentle but stern tone.

He stares out the window with his jaw twitching faster.

I pat him on the back. "Come on. Change quickly so I can knock a few more punches at you."

"Keep dreaming," he mutters as his phone rings. He pulls it out of his pocket and answers it on speaker. "Maksim."

"Boris with you?"

"Yeah, he's next to me. You're on speaker."

Maksim snarls, "Things just escalated."

My pulse increases, and Sergey raises his eyebrows.

"Come back to my place. We can't talk over the phone."

We obey and are soon inside Maksim's.

"That motherfucker sent this." He opens a white, expensive-looking box. A red bow is on the table next to it. Sergey and I peer over it.

"What the fuck!" Sergey says.

"Cover it up," I growl. A man's hand and arm, up to his elbow, is in the box. It's already rotting and stinks.

"The note says, 'Sign while you still are capable,'" Maksim seethes.

I point at Maksim. "He's crossed the line. I told you—"

"I already called Tolik. He's digging up anything we don't know and moving Obrecht to Lorenzo. We'll transfer Kappo to Atlanta."

Sergey shakes his head, scowling. "Lorenzo and Zamir need to be eliminated."

"I'll tell you what I told Dmitri. We wait for Obrecht to do his job. The time has come for us to move on Zamir and finish him. After we deal with Lorenzo, we put Obrecht on Zamir. No one will continue to threaten our family. And when that bastard breathes his last breath, he will stare into all of our eyes and understand what he has created."

I voice my concern. "You're giving Obrecht a death sentence with Zamir."

"No one is more capable than Obrecht," Maksim asserts. "Dmitri is in agreement"

"Me, too," Sergey says.

"I don't like it. I should be the one to figure out how to end the Zamir issue."

"Don't be arrogant," Maksim says.

I stare at my brothers for several moments, rehashing the conversation I had with Sergey. If I agree, then maybe he'll get his crazy idea about taking over Zamir's organization out of his head. I focus on Sergey. "Okay. I'll give my blessing for Obrecht to track him. But no one makes any moves on Zamir without all of us in agreement."

Sergey's eyes harden.

"Since when don't we operate that way?" Maksim asks.

I turn to him. "We do. I'm just reiterating it."

He turns to Sergey.

"I'm good," Sergey replies.

All our phones buzz at the same time. We pull them out.

Dmitri: *I'm throwing a party for Anna tonight to celebrate all her success. It's at eight at our place. Can you all come?*

Sergey: *Yep*

Maksim: *Yes*

Me: *Y*

Dmitri: *FYI: I'm putting Anna on lockdown.*

My chest tightens. The stress I usually don't feel reappears but stronger.

I need to increase Nora's security with this going on.

"I need to go," I say.

"I'm snagging a ride," Sergey declares, and we leave.

When we get in the car, he says, "Way to almost rat me out with Maksim."

"I'm making sure you get those crazy ideas out of your head."

We stay silent for the three blocks it takes to get to my place. "See you tonight," I tell Sergey. I get in the penthouse and text Adrian.

Me: *Is Nora on her way back yet?*

Adrian: *Darcey just got in. She's trying to make Nora leave.*

Me: *We have increased threats. Be extra cautious. If she fights Darcey about leaving, tell her to call me.*

Adrian: *On it.*

I spend the next few minutes fighting the urge to go to the pub and pick up Nora. I don't want to alarm her. Stress isn't good for the baby or her. I add another bodyguard as Nora's driver so she's always with him and Adrian if I'm not there.

I get another text message.

Killian: *We're going to be a few more days. Something else came up.*

Me: *No problem.*

My agitation grows. I pace the penthouse. I'm ready to get the secret about Nora and me out in the open. All it's doing is adding more stress to both of us.

I feel like I'm about to jump out of my skin. It's something I usually feel after I'm with Zamir for days, and I'm not sure what to do about it. Then she texts me, and the need to own every part of her body consumes me.

When the elevator opens, she's standing naked. Her pink nipples against her porcelain skin, red hair, and green eyes take all the anxiety racing in my blood and turn it into a potent concoction of lust. And I put all my energy into her, trying to shake the increasingly bad feeling I can't seem to escape.

22

MC

Nora

"You didn't tell your brothers I was coming?" We're in the car going to Anna and Dmitri's for an impromptu party.

Boris shakes his head. "No."

"Aren't they going—"

My phone blares out a song, and I jump. I reach into my purse and pull it out. "Darcey, everything okay?"

"The city inspector just came in. He said the electrical is outdated and we're shut down until further notice."

Cold crawls down my spine. I shiver and cry out, "They can't do that!"

"What's wrong?" Boris asks.

I hit the speaker button on my cell. "Darcey, tell me exactly what happened."

"A man came in. He had identification. He left his card for you, but he posted on our doors papers we aren't allowed to be open until further notice."

"They can't do that," I repeat, in shock.

"He made me shut everything down. I wanted to call you, but he wouldn't let me. He said it was unsafe for customers to be in the pub and yelled for everyone to leave. He left a sealed envelope for you."

Nausea streaks through me, and I put my hand on my stomach.

Boris pulls me closer. "Darcey, it's Boris. We'll be there in five minutes."

"Okay."

I hang up. "Can they do this?"

He scowls. "Yes."

"My brothers told me they would update the electrical when they started the remodel. But I'm not anywhere close to starting construction. Anna and I only met today," I fret.

"Let's see what the paperwork says. But you can't get worked up about this. It's not good for the baby. The doctor gave strict instructions to avoid stress if possible."

I snort. "Easier said than done."

"Take some deep breaths. I'll handle this for you."

"How?"

"Let's just stay calm." He tries to reassure me, but his expression darkens.

We pull up to the pub; Darcey is outside in her car. The rest of the lot is empty. She gets out and into our vehicle. Worry laces her eyes. She hands me the envelope. It's full of legal documents.

I briefly scan them. "How does this happen? My nana never had one day where this pub was not open."

"Do you think the fire caused the city to look at the electrical?" Darcey asks.

Boris's voice is angry. "No. They issued the permit to stay open. This has Rossi written all over it."

My heart pounds harder. I barely get out, "It's never going to end, is it?"

Boris nods to Darcey. "Thanks for waiting for us to get here. Go home. Nora will call you in the next few days when she has more information."

"Of course." Darcey squeezes my hand then gets out. Once she starts her car and veers out of the lot, Boris tells his driver to go to Dmitri's. He pulls me into his arms. His heart is beating faster, and anger radiates off him. He quietly says, "He'll pay for this."

I glance up. "Why would Lorenzo do this? What is the purpose of harming my pub?"

Boris's face hardens.

"What aren't you telling me?"

"The man who torched your pub is missing. And he'll never find him."

My skin crawls. "And?"

Guilt fills Boris's eyes. "Lorenzo thinks your family is responsible."

There isn't any other reason to say anything else. Boris killed the man. We've never discussed it, but I saw and heard the finality in his voice when he came to see me at Killian's. I knew when he left the hospital he was going to the garage. And I can't be upset he took care of it and my family is being blamed. My brothers would have killed him if Boris hadn't gotten to him first.

We don't say anything else. I wrap my hands around Boris's fist. It's something he suddenly started doing the last few days. He's always been a fighter, but unless he's in the ring, I've rarely seen him clench his hands. Since Zamir texted him last week, they're in a ball most of the time.

I kiss the Russian letters tattooed on his knuckles. "I've added a lot of extra pressure to your life."

He tightens his arm around me and kisses my head. He murmurs, "You're the good in my life."

"I'm worried about you."

He grunts. "You don't have anything to think twice about."

I catch his gaze. "Boris." It's a lie. We both know it.

His fist flattens on my stomach. He dips his head so it's level with mine. "Stop stressing, moya dusha. I'll get to the bottom of all these issues. And you can't do anything about the pub right now. Tomorrow, I'll have Maksim call his contact at the city, and we'll figure this out."

"What about my brothers? When they get back tonight, they're going to be pissed about this. Plus, when we tell them about us..."

He pulls me closer, kisses the side of my head, and says, "I forgot to tell you Killian sent me a message. He said it's going to be a few more days."

"What? Please tell me where they are."

"I'm not lying to you. I don't know anything about what they are doing."

I bite on my lip, worried.

He sighs. "When are you going to trust me when I tell you I'll handle things?"

"I do trust you—more than anyone. But you can't have the weight of the world on your shoulders all the time. It's affecting you. I see it."

"You're imagining things."

"No, I'm not. And don't insult me with your denials."

"Let's stop this discussion now, or we'll be arguing all night over this." The car parks in front of Dmitri and Anna's building. Before I can reply, Boris gets out. He reaches in, pulls me out and into him. "Let's have fun at the party like a normal couple."

"You seem to have a thing for us to act like a normal couple," I tease.

He strokes my hair. His face turns serious. "It's what I want, Nora. You, me, and our baby. A normal, drama-free, happy life."

I smile. "That sounds really nice."

He glances at my hand. "I'm ready for us to tell our families so you can start wearing your ring."

My stomach flutters. There's nothing I want more than to show the world I'm going to be his forever. And I adore my ring. "Me, too. And I'll be Mrs. Boris Ivanov."

He grins. "Are you going to hyphenate your name so everyone still knows you're an O'Malley?"

I shake my head. "No. I love my family. I'll always be an O'Malley. But I don't want anyone questioning who I belong to."

His smile widens, and he says against my lips, "Now that you have some free time, figure out which priest I need to pay off."

I softly laugh. "It doesn't work like that. I think we have to go to classes."

Boris furrows his eyebrows. "Classes?"

"Mmhmm. So the church can make sure we're compatible or something like that."

He arches an eyebrow. "Just pick the priest. I'll handle the negotiations."

"I don't think it's something negotiable."

Amusement appears on his face. "Everything is negotiable."

I don't think it is with the church, but I'm not going to argue. "What if the priest says we have to go to class?"

He smirks. "Then I'll make an excuse why we need to use the restroom since you're pregnant, find a dark room, and spend the majority of the hour making you yell out, 'Jesus, Mary, and Joseph.'"

Heat rises to my face. I playfully slap him on the arm. "Boris!"

He pecks me on the lips and laughs. "Let's go inside before you freeze." He puts his arm around my back, and we go into the building and up to Dmitri's penthouse.

I push the pub issues out of my mind and decide to enjoy the night. We've never done anything with others, except for the restaurant opening, which ended in a disaster. I've always liked the Ivanov brothers, and Anna and I connected right away.

Dmitri's penthouse is similar in design as Boris's. There is an expansive view of Lake Michigan in every room. Similar black leather furniture, grays, and darker wood elements beautifully mix.

Anna takes me into her studio Dmitri created for her. It's a different design than the rest of the penthouse. "These are initial concepts based on what we discussed earlier today. If you don't like it, I won't be offended. I want to make sure you fall in love with whatever we do." She opens a wallpaper book, sets a few floor samples and several paint swatches next to it.

"Wow! That's beautiful!" I run my hand over the textured, creamy white wallpaper. It has small slivers of kelly green running through it, but it's not overpowerful.

She beams. "I'm so happy you love it. It's my favorite, and I think it brings in the Irish charm with an updated feel."

"Yes. And adds a bit of class."

"Agreed!" She picks up several pieces of stone tiles in different sizes and rearranges them into a pattern. "This would be beautiful around the bar and in the game room. We can resurface your wood floor."

I get goose bumps. It's better than anything I could imagine. "I love it. I think it's perfect!"

She nods. "Okay. This will help me create the rest of the design."

Her friends, Steven and Harper, come into the room. She introduces us. I excuse myself and go out to the living room. Boris and his brothers are all huddled together, speaking Russian. Their tone is aggressive, as if they are upset. I go to the window. It's dark, minus the lights of the Chicago skyline.

Boris sneaks up behind me and wraps his arms around me. He rests his palms on my belly, and I tilt my head up. "Hey."

"Everything okay?" he asks.

"Yes. Anna has beautiful ideas. I'm excited."

"She's super talented."

"Yes. How long do you think it'll take for my brothers to remodel the pub?"

"I'll have our guys come over and help if needed. Don't worry about the pub. I will take care of it."

My stomach growls.

He chuckles and rubs his thumbs on my stomach. "Let's get you fed."

Anna, the Ivanovs, and others are at the food table. Anna introduces us to her brother, Chase. I pick up a plate and start to fill it when Boris's phone rings.

My blood goes cold. The air in my chest tightens. It's the ring Boris has for Zamir.

His brothers exchange a glance.

Boris's face hardens. "Excuse me." He walks off and answers the phone. He stops in the entranceway near the elevator.

I follow him. But I don't know what he's saying, since it's in Russian. The call isn't long, but his shoulders tense. When he hangs up, he spins. His eyes have the same urgency, fear, and stress I saw the last time Zamir called him.

"What's—"

"I need to go, moya dusha. I don't have time to talk." He quickly steers me into the living room.

"Where do you have to go?" I ask.

"Maksim, take Nora home later."

Maksim's expression fills with worry. "Sure. Call me later."

Boris nods.

I try again. "Boris—"

He cups my cheeks. "Maksim will take you home. I will talk to you tomorrow."

"Tomorrow? What—"

"Nora, do what I say. Please," he snaps.

"Okay."

He leaves, and I watch him go. Everything feels worse than the last time Zamir called him. Is it because I know the truth now? Or is something worse than usual going to happen?

Dmitri holds out a plate. "Have some food, Nora."

I put my hand over my stomach. "He's back, isn't he?" I'm unsure why I ask. I already know it's Zamir.

Dmitri's eyes widen in surprise.

"Yes. I know. Everything. When does it stop?"

Dmitri firmly replies, "Soon. We're working on it."

"He can't take much more."

"Boris knows what he's doing."

His statement angers me. And so much fear is consuming me, I blurt out, "He may be your brother, but I know him. This needs to end."

"We're fully aware."

I briefly close my eyes then turn to Maksim. "I'm sorry, but please take me home."

He nods. "Sure."

I turn to Anna. "Thank you for having me. Can we talk tomorrow about the design?"

Sympathy fills her face. I wonder if she knows about the Ivanovs and their history. Did Dmitri tell her about Boris's deal he made with Zamir? "Yes. I'll call you in the afternoon?"

"Please."

"Nora," Dmitri says.

I try not to cry, but a tear falls down my cheek.

"We're going to end this," he repeats.

I've heard that phrase too many times to count. It only served as a lie in my experience. I wipe my face. "Killian promised that as well. We all know what happened to Sean." My family knew Sean was into something. He wouldn't tell us what. The final time he left and didn't come back for days then showed up in the pub at three in the morning with blood on his hands. I heard that phrase from Killian even though Sean wouldn't tell him what he was involved in or with whom.

Dmitri takes a deep breath. "We will end this."

I want to ask him how. I want to tell him he and his brothers need to stick their neck out for Boris. He's taken all the wrath of Zamir for them. But I don't. I understand the bond of brothers. Any of mine would try to protect the other in a heartbeat. It's not Maksim, Dmitri, or Sergey's fault Boris is the one sacrificing for them. And deep down, I know they would die for Boris.

I say nothing and allow Maksim to lead me out of the building and into his car. When we get in, Maksim says, "Nora, what's your address? I don't remember the number."

"I don't live there anymore," I say without thinking.

"Oh. When did you move?"

I stare into his icy blue eyes. My stomach flips. "A week ago."

He smiles. "What is your address?"

"It's Boris's penthouse."

The silence in the air is deafening. Maksim's eyes widen.

"My brothers are going to kill him. We're telling them when they return, but please don't tell anyone until they know. Not even Dmitri or Sergey."

Maksim nods. "Okay."

I grab Maksim's hand. I'm not sure if it's my hormones raging all over the place or if the feeling in my gut is a real warning, but nothing has ever scared me more than right now. Tears run off my chin and drip onto my thighs. "Please. You have to make sure my brothers don't kill Boris, and end this thing with Zamir. Boris can't keep doing this for the rest of his life."

"We will end this, Nora," Maksim firmly states.

"He can't..." I look away, my insides shaking, unable to finish my thoughts.

He can't die. Our baby needs a father. I need him.

Maksim rolls the divider down. "Boris's place." He puts it back up. "He will be okay, Nora. And we will destroy Zamir."

I don't look at Maksim the entire ride. When we get to Boris's, he escorts me into the building and up to the penthouse.

"Adrian, what are you doing here?" Maksim asks when we get to the living room.

"Boris called. I'm her security detail."

"Ah. I see." Maksim helps me remove my coat and hangs it in the closet.

Adrian says, "I'll be in the entranceway. If you need anything, let me know."

I sniffle and nod. "Thanks."

He shuts the door.

"Boris said he'd see me tomorrow. Does Zamir tell him how long he'll have him?"

"No. And I don't believe Boris was thinking clearly. He's never been back the next day. You should not expect him home tomorrow."

I put my hands over my face and turn away.

"Do you want me to stay, Nora?" Maksim asks.

I spin back and hurl, "No. I want you to do something so your brother never has to see that evil man again."

Guilt rushes to Maksim's face. He says nothing.

"Thank you for taking me home. I'm going to rest now."

Maksim opens his mouth to say something but stops.

I wait.

He finally says, "If you need anything, call me."

I nod, go into the bedroom, and crawl into bed. The next morning, I force myself to eat for the baby and take my vitamins. Boris walks in.

Relief flies through me. I rush over to him, but he closes his eyes. "I can't be near you right now."

I cling tighter to him. "Boris, whatever—"

"No, Nora. This isn't debatable. I don't trust myself around you right now. I need you to go," he barks.

I try to kiss him, but he turns his cheek.

"Killian is on his way to get you. Adrian will escort you downstairs."

"What? Boris, no! I'm not going to leave you—"

"Get out. What part of 'I don't trust myself' do you not understand?" His eyes bore into mine, and for the first time, I see the devil in them.

Boris has never yelled at me before. I'm not sure what he thinks would happen if I stay. I debate about what to do.

He lowers his voice and closes his eyes. "You can't see me like this. I need you to go with Killian. Tell him you want to stay at his house."

My vision is blurred with tears as I nod. I quickly pack a bag, change, and go out to the living room. Boris is standing in front of the window with his hands over his face.

"Boris," I whisper.

He doesn't look at me. "Nora, I can't talk right now. Please. I will call you later."

Every emotion I felt while waiting for him the last time, then the memory of how he treated me when he finally saw me again, floods my soul. "Promise me you won't stay away from me when this is over."

He continues to avoid me. "I promise. Now, please leave. Adrian will take you down."

I obey him, turn the conversation on Killian about what he's been doing and where he's been at, and try not to cry. I want to help Boris, but I don't know how. He promised he wouldn't do what he did the last time, but all I can feel is how I did then. And I'm scared Zamir made him do something worse than ever before.

23

M̃C

Boris

With Zamir

THE ABANDONED WAREHOUSE IS FORTY MINUTES AWAY. I HAVE
two minutes to spare and run inside. A man is naked. His
limbs are spread out as far as possible so he's on his toes. His
wrists and ankles are restrained by a rough metal, sharp
enough it will slice him to pieces if he moves.

I freeze. I recognize him. His name is Jake, short for Jakub.
He's a Polish immigrant I went to school and hung out with.
Every now and again, we run into each other. The last time I
saw him was about a month ago. He was with his wife and
three children. Their baby was only a few months old.

Zamir walks up to me, leans into my ear, and his signature
musky scent flares in my nostrils.

My gut churns as usual. I struggle more than normal not to show any reaction to him.

Zamir puts his hand on my cheek. In his sinister voice, he says, "Cut out his kidney, heart, and liver so I can feed it to his wife and children."

I swallow the bile rising in my throat, looking the devil in the eye. "You don't want me to torture him?" I ask, trying to push the thought of his family dining on his organs out of my mind. Plus, Zamir has never had me kill a man without tormenting him for days.

"No. And make it quick. Feeding time is soon."

I struggle to remain composed. And I call upon Satan, but he doesn't seem to be anywhere inside me. All I can see is Nora and our unborn child, and I can't seem to get my feet to move.

"Now," Zamir growls.

I put on the gloves Zamir's thug holds out. I step in front of Jake and do it as quickly as possible, avoiding his eyes and trying to drown out his screaming. I place each organ in the bucket provided.

"Brand him," Zamir orders.

I slice off his thigh skin and put the five-pointed star with a circle around it on his femur.

When I finish, Zamir says, "Shower."

I'm confused again, but I don't question anything. I strip, throw my clothes in the bag his thug holds out, and I stand in the corner, over the drain. He sprays me down with cold water and throws me a towel. I dry off and put the T-shirt and shorts Zamir always supplies on.

I leave in a daze. Zamir didn't even keep me one day. I drive several miles, detour down some backroads, then pull over when I'm somewhere in the country. Knowing what Zamir has in store for Jake's family never leaves my mind, along with the vision of Nora holding our unborn baby. I can't escape it. I barely make it out of the car before I throw up.

I stay in my car all night, wrestling with my demons, trying to get the devil to leave me alone. I've always hated myself for doing Zamir's work, but something about tonight is hitting me harder than ever before.

When the sun comes up, I return home. I park in the garage, and Killian calls.

"We're almost back. I'll be at your place in fifteen minutes to get Nora."

"Sounds good."

"Thanks for watching her. I know this was longer than expected."

"No problem. I have to go." I hang up quickly, not wanting to deal with Killian or the lies I still have to create. And as much as I want to wrap myself up in Nora, I don't trust what might come out of my mouth if I am around her right now. I might break and tell her what Zamir made me do. And I don't ever want her to know how far I've fallen.

I shoot a quick text to my brothers I'm back and turn off my phone.

I need to get upstairs and get Nora out the door.

If I see Killian right now, I'm going to tell him about us. I won't take any of his Irish/Russian bullshit, either. He may end up dead. So I need to get Nora away from me.

When I step into the penthouse and see her pained face and the love she has for me swirling in it, I almost crack. I don't deserve her or a sliver of her affection.

When she leaves, I spend the next twenty hours pacing the penthouse, not sleeping, thinking about every problem my brothers, Nora, and I have.

When the darkness of night begins to morph into the morning light, I turn my phone on. There are several messages.

Sergey: *Want me to pick you up for our workout?*

Me: *I'll meet you there.*

Sergey: *You okay?*

I don't respond and go to the gym. My brothers are already there. They all stop talking, and their typical concerned expressions fill their faces.

Maksim is closest to me and embraces me first. "You alright, dear brother?"

I step back, crack my neck, and lick my lips. My mouth feels dry suddenly. The visions haunting me return. I firmly state, "It's over. Where are we at on Lorenzo?"

"Obrecht is on it. We will know more later today," Maksim states.

"I'm tired of waiting. Nora's bar is shut down because of him. He's gone too far. Tell Obrecht to give us the entry point, or

I'll figure it out myself." I angrily shove past Maksim and go into the locker room. I throw my bag down and put on my shoes. I go back out and rack weights on the bar to bench press.

Dmitri stands on the opposite side and helps. "You filling this?"

"Yep."

Maksim starts, "Boris—"

"We aren't talking about it. Every year, you want to talk about it. I always tell you the same thing. I've not changed. There's nothing to say. It's over. Can we please focus on our current problem?" I shout.

Maksim's eyes turn to slits. "I'm worried about you. Out of all of us, you're the man who demonstrates patience the best. But I haven't seen it this week."

I slam a weight on the floor. I step toward Maksim. "What do you not get? The Rossis torched Nora's bar. She could have died. They put her out of business. And you know they were behind Sean's death."

"I know Nora means a lot to you, but—"

"I love her. She's carrying my baby," I growl.

My brothers' eyes all widen. They gape at me. Silence fills the room.

It wasn't my plan to blurt it out. I meant to keep my promise to Nora to tell my brothers after I told Killian. But the pressure of the last few days and all the ways I'm failing Nora and my child are building.

I soften my voice. "I've always loved her. You all know that. No matter what Killian thinks, she has my baby in her belly. And this is no longer only an O'Malley war with the Rossi family. This is our war now, too."

Maksim is the first to recover. "How far along is she?"

"Maybe six weeks."

Dmitri smiles so big, I can feel his happiness. He steps forward and embraces me. "Congratulations. But I hope the baby gets Nora's stunning good looks and not your ugly mug."

"I'll second that," Sergey says and hugs me, too.

Maksim shakes his head. "An O'Malley-Ivanov. Good God." He chuckles and puts his arms around my shoulders.

All I want to feel around my relationship with Nora and the baby is happiness. But I won't rest until they are safe. "I want him dead, Maksim. And he needs to see my wrath."

"He will. For everyone's safety—Nora, Anna, us, and the O'Malleys—I need your head back in the game. No past, no future. We cannot make old mistakes. Patience is what I need from you."

I scowl. I'm not going to sit back and be patient anymore. Where has my patience gotten me?

"We're in this together. Do not jump the gun. We wait for Obrecht. He will not let us down. Then you can execute with perfection, which is what you do," Dmitri agrees.

Sergey pats my shoulders. "Listen to the old, wise ones."

Dmitri slaps Sergey's head.

"Ouch."

"You better watch those old comments."

I lie down on the bench. "Fine. I will give it a few more days. But I will not wait forever."

Dmitri steps behind me to spot. "Have you thought about the beating Killian is going to give you?"

I grunt and lift the bar off the rack. "It's a good thing I fought him before he found out. I barely took him out that last fight."

We work out, shower, and I agree to wait until Obrecht gives us information on Lorenzo. We're walking out of the gym when Viktor calls Dmitri. It's clear something is wrong.

He finishes his conversation and hangs up. "That mother—"

"What is it?" I ask. Chills run down my spine.

"Lorenzo just tried to deliver a package to Anna, insisting she sign for it. It was wrapped how the other package was. They wouldn't accept it, but the guy said he'd be back."

I bark, "Do you still want me to be patient? He already came after Nora. Now he's coming after Anna."

Maksim growls, "We do this the right way. The dynamics have not changed since our conversation earlier. We wait for Obrecht. He will give us an update today."

Dmitri scowls. "So help me God, if he or anyone comes near my Anna, I will slice him to pieces in the middle of the street."

"Have security pull the video footage. I want to see who this delivery person is," Sergey says. "I'll go with you."

"I need to talk to Killian. Nora can't be left alone," I claim.

"Boris, let me go with you," Maksim says.

I sarcastically reply, "Are you going to step between us when he tries to beat me to a pulp?"

Maksim sighs. "No. I'm going to try and talk some sense into him before he tries to kill you."

"Good luck with that." Sergey snorts.

"Looks like you got the easy job today." Dmitri pats Sergey on the back. "Let's go. Good luck, Boris. I hope we see you again," he teases.

I grunt, and we part ways. I text Killian.

Me: *Where are you?*

Killian: *The gym.*

Me: *We need to talk. I'm on my way over.*

Maksim says, "How is Nora?"

I stare out the window. "I made her leave when I got back." I send her a message.

Me: *I'm on my way to tell Killian about us. I'll call you after.*

I stick my phone in my pocket.

Maksim says, "Zamir's never let you go so quickly before."

"Unless we're going to discuss how to kill him, drop it."

Maksim sighs. "We have to figure this out. We can't keep having you do this every year."

"I said to drop it. Tell me how we eliminate him from earth or shut up about him."

We drive several minutes and pull up to Killian's gym. As we're walking in, my stomach flips. I grumble, "Can't believe I'm bringing you to do this."

"Don't worry. I'll let him take a punch first."

"Gee, thanks. Guess I underestimated the brotherly love."

Maksim arches an eyebrow. "Don't get me started on all the ways you could have handled this."

I ignore him, scan the gym for Killian, and make my way to the back corner. There is only one other man in the gym. Killian's trainer holds the bag he's punching.

"Killian," I call out.

He takes a final punch and turns. Sweat drips down his shirtless torso. His face is red, and his chest heaves for oxygen. He glances at Maksim in surprise and says to his trainer, "Patrick, give me a minute."

Patrick nods and leaves.

Killian snatches his bottle of water off the ground, drinks half of it, then wipes his towel on his face. Slightly out of breath, he asks, "What's going on?"

I've had years to think about how to break it to Killian I love his sister. I've had over a week to think of how I will tell him she's pregnant with my baby. Nothing seems to come to mind to soften the blow. I blurt out, "Nora's pregnant. We're getting married."

Killian blinks. Then his eyes widen, and the beast I've only seen in the ring, the one who will do anything to kill me, enters his eyes. He lunges at me so fast, I don't have time to react. His first punch knocks me to the ground. He gets three additional punches to my head before Maksim and Patrick pull him off me.

"What the fuck, Boris!" he yells.

"I love her. I always have."

"Calm down," Patrick yells.

"I'll kill you for ever touching her," Killian growls.

"Because you'd rather have assholes like Cormac with Irish blood with her, right?"

Killian attempts to lunge at me again, but Maksim and Patrick hold on to him.

"Don't ever come near my sister again."

"I'm marrying her. She has my child in her belly. Get over it," I yell.

He slips out of Maksim and Patrick's hold and flies at me. We both hit each other. Maksim and Patrick try to break us up, and Nora's voice rings through the air.

"Killian! Boris! Stop!"

It's enough to make Killian and me freeze long enough so Maksim and Patrick can pull us away from each other.

We turn our heads toward Nora. Her green eyes are red, as if she hasn't slept, and tears fall down her cheeks. She holds her stomach and winces as if in pain. "You both need to stop."

I shake out of Maksim's grasp and go to her. "Moya dusha, are you okay? Is something wrong with the baby?"

She reaches for my face. "No. The baby is fine. But I'm coming home. I need you."

I pull her into me, and she sobs. I murmur in her ear, "I'm sorry. I couldn't... Shhh."

"What did you do to hurt my sister?" Killian growls.

I hold Nora tight to me and spin. "I—"

"He's done nothing except respect my wishes to not tell you about us."

Hurt flies onto Killian's face. "How could you lie to me, Nora?"

Her eyes pierce into his. In a low, cold voice, she says, "You know why."

Killian clenches his jaw and looks away.

Nora steps in front of Killian. She grabs his chin and makes him look at her. "If you are going to disown me for being with a man I love, a man who's been a brother to you, a man who has done nothing but take care of our family, then do it now and tell me to my face. But whatever you tell me, I will walk out of here with him. Sean was not your decision to lose. I am. So make up your mind right now."

Killian swallows hard. "You should have told me."

"You didn't make it very easy."

The pain on Killian's face morphs into guilt.

I state, "We have a problem. Rossi needs to be taken care of. We can be enemies or work together and be stronger. It's up to you. But I will be marrying Nora and in our child's life. We want you in it, too, but I will not beg or ask you again."

Killian glares at me. "She needs to get married in the Catholic Church."

What is with these O'Malleys and their Catholic Church?

They don't even go to church on Sundays.

I need to find out what priest I need to pay off.

"Yes. I've already agreed."

"And the baby needs to be baptized in the church as well. All O'Malleys are."

Might as well get it all over with.

"Our baby will carry O'Malley blood, but he or she will have the Ivanov name," I state.

"O'Malley will be their middle name then, as well as any future children you bear. They will not lose their Irish heritage."

"That is up to Nora."

He glances at her. "This is important. You know it is."

She nods. "Okay. They will have O'Malley in their name. But their last name will be Ivanov. And I'm not hyphenating mine."

Shock fills his face again. "Why would you not want to keep O'Malley? The world should know where you come from."

"I don't want two last names. You aren't winning this one, Killian."

I try to hide my satisfaction about Nora only taking my last name.

He shakes his head. "O'Malley is—"

"I am a woman. Not a man. The tradition is to take your husband's last name. You want the Catholic wedding and baptism and middle names. I gave them to you. The conversation is over."

Killian growls as he sighs.

Nora's voice shakes as she quietly says, "I need you to get over this. And quickly. I do not want to lose you, Nolan, or Declan. I need you to help me with them. Please."

His face hardens, and he pulls her into an embrace. "Okay. I'll handle them."

She cries again, and he hugs her tighter.

"Can you name the baby Killian?"

She laughs through her sobs. "I'll think about it."

"Nora, have you slept?" I ask.

She shakes her head. "Not a lot."

"Can you go into the office and lie down? Maksim and I need to talk to Killian before we go."

She hesitates.

Killian glances at me then puts his arm around Nora. "I'll be right back." He leads her to the office. He's in there for several moments. I nervously glance at Maksim and Patrick.

Patrick puts his finger in the air. "I've always respected you. But you've played with fire, Boris. The rest of our family isn't going to like this."

"Tough shit. Make them," I reply.

"I'll have my wife say some rosaries for you." He pats me on the back and calls over his shoulder, "I'll start working on the rest of the family today."

Maksim raises his eyebrows, steps close to me, and mumbles, "Do Nora and her brothers go to church?"

I snort. "Nope. I need to find a priest I can pay off."

24

Nora

"NORA—"

"You told me you'd help me with Declan and Nolan. Don't get me in private and try to go back on your word," I tell Killian.

He holds his hands in the air. "I'm not."

"It's not right, Killian. Boris has always been like a brother to you. When you need him, it doesn't matter he's Russian and not Irish."

"You know how our family is, Nora."

"It doesn't make it right."

"The Ivanovs aren't a crime family. There are going to be complications."

I point at him. "Then uncomplicate it for me. And the Ivanovs might not be a crime family, but they are on the right side of the Rossi battle. Boris is going to kill Lorenzo. So make it known to our uncle."

Killian's eyes widen. "How do you know this?"

"He loves me. And you know Boris. He isn't going to let Lorenzo get away with torching the pub. Plus, he told me."

Killian gazes out the glass overlooking the gym. He locks eyes with Boris. "You love him?"

"Yes."

He crosses his arms and turns back to me.

I close my eyes and lower my voice. "You've always been as close to me as Sean. I need you to make sure everyone accepts Boris. And my baby."

"Your baby has O'Malley blood. Our uncle will require an alliance." Our uncle is the head of our crime family. Everyone in the family does what he says.

"Then, please, do whatever you need to so I am not cast out of the family. But the Ivanovs are not the enemy here. And make it clear it is only for the Rossi issues."

Killian's voice is firm. "It's not cut and dry. You know Uncle Darragh. An alliance is either with the O'Malleys on all things, or there is no alliance."

I put my hand over my belly. "Then I will voluntarily leave the family."

His eyes widen. "Why would you say such a thing?"

"I do not want my husband, the father of my child, involved in our decades of issues. It is the Rossi issues and nothing else. Make it clear, Killian."

He shakes his head. "Uncle Darragh—"

"Try! For me! My baby! Your blood!"

He scrubs his face in frustration. "I can't guarantee anything, but I will do my best."

I sigh and look at the ceiling. "Erin and Nessa—"

"Can stick their snotty noses up their ass. If anyone wants to talk trash about you in our family, they'll have to deal with me."

I smile. "Thank you."

"I will speak with Uncle Darragh, but from now on, no more secrets, Nora."

"Okay."

He grabs a few towels off the shelf. "We don't keep blankets here. But lie down and rest. You look like you haven't slept in days."

"I haven't," I admit.

"That can't be good for the baby."

I don't argue. I slide onto the sofa, and he puts two towels over my body, then several under my head. He crouches down so his face is next to mine and smirks. "Killian is a great baby name."

I push him away. "Get out of here! Plus, you stink and need a shower."

He smells his armpit. "Nah. The chicks dig it."

I roll my eyes.

He winks and leaves, and I sigh in relief.

One brother down. Two to go.

I close my eyes. I'm not sure how long Boris, Maksim, and Killian talk, but I fall asleep. When Boris wakes me up, I have a fuzzy blanket over me, a pillow beneath my head, and it's the afternoon.

"Nora," Boris's Russian accent cuts into my sleep.

"Hmm?"

He softly chuckles, and his lips brush against mine. "We have to go."

I open my eyes. "Hey."

He strokes my cheek. "You were so passed out, I had Adrian bring blankets and a pillow while I went to my meeting."

I glance around and realize I'm still in Killian's office. I sit up and reach for his face. "Are you okay?"

His expression falls. "Yes. I'm sorry. I couldn't... Zamir...after..." He sighs.

"It's okay. But I need to come home and be with you."

He slides onto the couch and pulls me onto his lap. I curl up to his chest. "Nora, I'm taking you to stay with Anna tonight."

I look up. "Why? I want to be with you."

"All I want is to have you home with me. But this isn't about that."

A bad feeling fills me. "No?"

"No. We need to deal with Rossi."

I swallow the lump in my throat. Earlier, I told Killian Boris was going to kill Lorenzo, but now panic seizes me.

Lorenzo killed Sean.

I grab Boris's shirt. "Don't go. Please. You just got back. Something bad is going to happen. I can feel it."

"Nothing is going to happen to me, moya dusha. I need you to stay with Anna. I don't want you alone. Lorenzo is a risk to you and our baby. He needs to be eliminated."

No matter what I say to Boris over the next few hours, he doesn't change his mind. My hormones are all over the place, but it's the same feeling I had the night Sean was murdered.

I call Killian and beg him not to let Boris go, but he tells me it's happening and necessary.

I spend most of my time with Anna, crying. She's worried, too, but tries to distract me by showing me designs for the pub, but it doesn't work very well. After twenty-four hours pass and they still aren't home, I'm pacing, pulling on my hair, and holding my stomach.

My baby needs a father.

Lorenzo pulled Sean's beating heart out of his body.

Boris pulled Cormac's out.

Who is deadlier?

"You should try to rest, Nora. I'll stay awake and let you know when they call," Anna says.

"Something is wrong. It has to be. This is too long."

"Nora, you need to lie down. This isn't good for the baby. Come on." She takes my hand, leads me to the guest bedroom, and tucks me under the covers.

My distress makes me blurt out all kinds of things. "I told Killian not to let Boris go. No matter what was going on, I begged him to stop Boris. He can't take much more. I know he can't."

She strokes my hair. "They're going to come back."

"What if they don't? This is so long. My baby... I want it to know it's father...to know Boris and be loved by him." I begin to sob hard. I keep seeing Sean's dead body in the morgue. The lack of sleep and stress of the last few days isn't helping my anxiety.

Anna embraces me. "Shh. They will be back. Your baby will have a father."

I cry myself to sleep. At some point, I wake up. Boris is holding me. His hair is wet. The scent of his skin and security of his arms bring me instant comfort.

My nerves hum. I turn more into him. "Are you really here?"

He holds me tighter. "Yes."

"I've been so worried."

He kisses me. "Stop worrying. He's dead. He'll never mess with you or your family again."

Sean's killer is dead.

I start to cry all over again.

"Shh. I'm here. Everything is okay," he murmurs.

"Did Lorenzo admit he killed Sean?"

"Yes."

I nod, tears falling. "Thank you."

He pulls me tighter to him. "You need sleep, Nora. I'm worried about all this stress on you. It's not good for the baby."

I reach up and kiss him. It's deep, hungry, and I slide over him more.

He groans and cups my ass cheeks. "I've missed you. But you're going back to sleep."

I glide my tongue into his mouth again and frantically circle it, wanting and needing every part of him I've been craving for too many days.

He pulls away. "Sleep now, moya dusha. Tomorrow when you wake up fully rested, I'll take care of you."

But I don't listen. "I'm awake," I mumble against his lips and run my hands through his wet hair. My clit shimmies along the smooth skin of his growing erection, and I moan into his mouth.

"Jesus, you're wet," he mumbles. His tongue slides back in my mouth, but then he pulls away. "You need to rest."

"No. I need—" I part my legs more and rock my hips, sinking over his cock and whimpering, almost as in relief. "Yes. I need this. Us," I breathe.

"You need to rest," he repeats, but it's half-hearted. His erection grows harder inside me. He shocks me with tingles, stroking my spine with his thumb and knuckles.

Our mouths urgently connect. We're water and flour mixing until every part of us is so combined, we morph into something deliciously divine. And it can't exist on its own.

"Jesus, Mar...oh God!" I whimper. My body is a vibrator on high-speed frequency, held captive by Boris's warm, muscular arms.

"Moya dusha," he growls, along with other Russian I don't recognize or understand, then licks my jaw to my ear in one hot stroke.

I shudder harder, pushing my knees into the mattress so his cock can go deeper, and panting for air. Heat bursts in my veins. Sweat coats my skin. Arousal and his scent swirl in my nostrils.

One palm grips my ass. The other covers my breast while his thumb circles my nipple. He moves me faster, thrusts harder, and a double dose of adrenaline combusts so quickly, I see white light.

"Jesus, Mary, and Joseph," I scream.

His teeth scrape on the top of my shoulder, creating a trail of zings. He grunts and groans as my pussy spasms, desperately trying to clutch him as his thick girth slides against my walls.

"Boris...oh..."

He barks out Russian as his cock swells, spiraling me into another pandemonium of euphoric bliss.

In the aftermath, I slowly lift my head off his chest. "So it's over then? War with the Rossis?"

Something crosses his expression. The room may be dark, but I see it.

I slide my hands to his face and sit up more. "Boris?"

"I won't lie to you, moya dusha. But I also won't give you more details than necessary. This is for your safety."

Anxiety tightens in my chest. "What do you mean? Lorenzo is dead. What else is there?"

His dark, cold eyes pierce through the blackness of the night. "Nothing will be over until we destroy every one of the Rossis and Petrovs."

My skin turns clammy. New fear ignites. "I-I don't understand. How would you ever do something of that nature? It would be impossible."

His voice gives me chills. "By creating a war between the two families."

25

Boris

"IT'S BECAUSE OF THE IVANOVS THAT LORENZO AND HIS TOP guys are dead," Killian states to his uncle Darragh. I've met him several times over the years. For Nora not to be kicked out of the O'Malley family, he needs to accept our union with an Irish blessing. And it requires me to create an alliance with him.

Darragh's stone-cold gaze fixates on me. He removes his tweed cap, scratches his bald head, then takes a drag off his pipe. In his Irish accent, laced with a smoker's rasp, he says, "The Ivanovs are not a crime family. What benefit do you bring to the O'Malleys?"

Before we killed Lorenzo, I told Killian I had a debt with Zamir. We were about to go inside the strip club Lorenzo was in when it came up, so there wasn't time to disclose my truth to him.

Family is everything to me. It is to Nora as well. I cannot leave this room until I have formed an alliance with the O'Malleys. I will not have my future wife or child disowned by those she loves. So I dig down and pull out the bullet to destroy any doubt the Ivanovs are not a family to be dismissed.

"I planted evidence the Petrovs killed Lorenzo. Killian can confirm this. War will break out among the families. It is up to us to keep the casualties in balance so neither side becomes stronger than they currently are. Without our alliance, you will have a hard time maintaining equilibrium. It puts your family at risk. However, with the help of my family, we will destroy them both."

He scowls at Killian. "You helped create a war with the Petrovs?"

"To destroy them."

Darragh slams his hand on the table. "You did not have my permission to do this."

"It was not his choice," I cut in. "This was an Ivanov decision. He came to avenge Sean's death. We did not inform him what we were doing until it was done," I lie. "And now we are in this position."

Darragh leans across the table so his butt is off the seat. "You don't know what you have done. Zamir Petrov is not a mob boss to go after. And this is why you are unfit for an O'Malley. You do not have experience with men like him to know better."

I snort. "I learned to torture and kill directly from Zamir. All of my brothers have, too. I was seventeen. My little brother,

Sergey, he was only twelve at the time. No one knows how Zamir works better than my brothers and me. And I've been in the pit of hell with him too many times to count, so while I understand your initial reaction, you're misinformed."

Killian's eyes widen.

Darragh's turn to slits. "So, he owns you then." It's a statement, not a question.

"No. I bought my brothers' and my freedom. He owns me only one time a year."

"Then, he owns you all year."

The truth slices through me. I don't waste my breath denying it. "And you should see why there is no other option for the Ivanovs but to destroy his reign until there is nothing left but ashes blowing in the wind."

Silence fills the air.

I continue, "Elimination of the Rossis and Petrovs increases your power. But you need us. And we need you."

"They kill each other off. We will take out more of those bastards when the body count gets too low on whatever side," Killian adds.

Darragh sits back. He takes another hit of his pipe. "Killian, you and your brothers keep playing both sides of our family. You cannot be in a war between crime families, going in and out when you see fit. This notion you have about who you are and what you can be at different times is exactly what landed my Liam in prison. It's what led to Sean's death. You are an O'Malley. A threat against any O'Malley is a threat against us all. As the head of this family, I'm telling you to listen to me closely. If you plan on taking part in any of this war, you must pledge your allegiance to me and this side of our family. Your brothers as well." Darragh has always been blind to his son, Liam's, ways. He's in prison because he was stupid. He assumed having the O'Malley last name and being his father's son, he was untouchable. But Liam has never morphed between worlds. Since he's close with Killian, who tried to stay out of the O'Malley business, Darragh has always given Killian a guilt trip, since he refused to take part in the incident that got Liam locked up. Darragh thinks if Killian had been there, Liam wouldn't have gotten caught.

Killian's face hardens. "My brothers and I have seen the error of our ways. The three of us are ready to pledge."

"You understand there is no going back?"

Killian nods. "Yes."

He has a coughing fit, then takes another long hit off his pipe, holds it in his lungs, then slowly releases it. He points to me. "If you want my blessing to marry my niece, you agree no Ivanov makes a move during this war without my prior consent."

My stomach flips. "No."

He raises his eyebrows. No one ever tells him no. In shock and anger, he spits out, "No?"

"Ivanovs do not take orders from anyone. We do not wait to act if there is an issue. I will commit to a discussion if there is time, filling you in on any action taken, and working side by side. My child's blood has both of ours coursing through its veins. There is no reason for me to do anything but work with you."

The scowl doesn't leave his face.

"Your brothers must come to me and agree to this as well."

"They will," I assure him.

"And you will marry my niece in a Catholic church."

Here we go again.

"Tell me what priest I need to pay."

He doesn't hesitate. "Father Antonio at St. Patrick's. I will inform him you will contact him."

Killian's eyes widen in surprise.

Did he really think the priests aren't corrupt, too?

"How much do I offer?"

"Irish get it for $1,000. He will charge you $30,000 for the wedding and $20,000 to convert."

Irish prick.

"I have to become Catholic?"

"Of course. My niece will not be married to a non-Catholic. What are you, by the way? Are you a Russian Jew or Protestant?" he says both as if they were so disgusting, he needs to go take a bath.

"Neither." I only believe in Hell. If God existed, my brothers and I wouldn't know anything about torture or how to murder men. How the O'Malleys can hide behind their shield of faith, go to church, then turn around and commit sin the next minute baffles me. But if it's what I need to do for Nora, I will.

"You will give Nora money to make ongoing donations to the church each year."

"How much?" I ask, getting irritated.

"$25,000 a year."

"Anything else?"

"There will also be the $5,000 confession fee."

"Confession fee?"

He points in my face. "You will go into your marriage free of sin. The morning of your marriage, you will take the sacrament of confession and make it right with God before saying 'I do' to my niece."

I glance at Killian.

He's nodding, as if this is perfectly normal.

What the fuck? I want to reach over and slap him on the head and tell him to wake up.

I almost tell Darragh to fuck off, but I remind myself his alliance for the war and Nora staying in good graces with her family is essential. It's a battle I don't need to take on. "Done. What else?"

"Baptisms will cost you $10,000 per child."

"Done."

"Your children must carry the O'Malley name."

"Their middle name will be."

His expression gives me the impression I've appeased him, but then he says, "Nora will hyphenate her name."

Here's my battle.

"No. She doesn't want to. She will go by Ivanov. There will not be a hyphen."

"She's an O'Malley," he barks.

I slam my hand on the table and growl, "She's marrying me. I am an Ivanov."

Tension fills the air. The smoke of his pipe thickens in my lungs. My heart beats harder. I will not have my wife forced into doing anything she doesn't want, especially when it concerns taking my name.

Killian clears his throat. "Uncle Darragh, Nora has spoken to me about this. It is true. She does not want to hyphenate."

His eyes widen. He jerks his head toward Killian. "Why would she not want to keep the O'Malley name?"

Killian quietly says, "No other woman in the family has hyphenated."

"They married Irishmen. He's Russian."

I clench my fists under the table. The references to my Russian blood not being as good as Irish blood is getting old. "Do we have an alliance or not? There is work required to monitor the Rossis and Petrovs. I need an answer. Do the Ivanovs have the O'Malleys' support, or does my family take full control of this war?"

"You have O'Malley support after I speak with your brothers."

"Fine." I get up, tired of this entire conversation. Darragh is a necessary pain in my ass I need to accept.

My brothers and I meet with Darragh and solidify the alliance. He makes it clear to the O'Malleys he approves of our marriage. Nora is relieved and doesn't seem as stressed.

I visit with the priest, slap down cash for the total cost of everything. I add an extra $10,000 and tell him the mass I have to convert at will be condensed to fifteen minutes.

Nora wants to get married in the spring, so she spends time designing the pub, wedding, and baby nursery with Anna.

Things stay calm over the next few months. Dmitri and Anna are getting married this weekend. She and Nora have become close between working together on projects and hanging out. The pub remodel started, and the grand reopening is soon.

We sit on pins and needles, waiting for the war between the Rossis and Petrovs to start. But our evidence, pinning Lorenzo's murder on the Petrov family, hasn't shown up yet. And my brothers and I believe Lorenzo might have been working with Zamir. It's the only reason we can come up with why Lorenzo chose to buy the city lot.

As much as I enjoy an everyday life with Nora, uneasiness grows in my belly. Then I get the call.

There's a blizzard, and it's barely five in the morning when Killian's deep voice says, "They found it."

It's all he has to say. A chill runs down my spine. I call an emergency meeting at Maksim's. My brothers and I arrive in the lobby at the same time and take the elevator up. We're in a heated conversation in Russian when Maksim says in English, "Take a breather for a moment."

A woman is with him. She's not Jade, his *on and off again* girlfriend he's had for years. Maksim tugs her closer to him. "This is Aspen."

After introductions, she leaves with Adrian. We shifted Nora's security to Bogden, another one of our bodyguards. We needed Adrian to work with Obrecht on a few issues, but now those are settled. Maksim tells us he's added Adrian to watch over Aspen.

"When did you meet Aspen?" Sergey asks.

"In Vegas," Maksim replies. We went there for Dmitri's bachelor party a few weeks ago.

"She's why you disappeared both nights?"

"Yes."

Dmitri's lips twitch. "How did you find her?"

"By luck. She works for the zoning office."

The city lot reverted out of Lorenzo's name. We cut a deal with the mayor to buy it. But there are zoning issues based on what Lorenzo changed before we killed him.

Maksim turns to me. "I don't think you came here to talk about zoning issues."

"I wish."

"What's going on?"

My chest tightens. "Giovanni Rossi's men found the evidence we planted. He's declared war."

"It took them long enough to find it," Sergey points out.

I look at each of my brothers. "The war has started. We must be prepared."

We divide up who will do what, have a few more heated conversations about whether we should be utilizing force to get the city lot rezoned, and add additional security to Dmitri's wedding.

They need to know about Zielinski.

"Killian has Liam watching Giovanni's visitors." Liam is serving time with Giovanni. He only has a year left on his sentence.

Maksim's eyes turn to slits. "And?"

"Bruno Zielinski showed up." He's the head of the Polish mafia.

Dmitri's color drains from his face. "Visiting with Giovanni?"

"Yes."

Maksim finally says, "If the Zielinski family is making any alliances with the Rossis, we need to know."

"Killian is already on it," I reply.

We go our separate ways, and the next night, celebrate Dmitri and Anna at their rehearsal dinner. Aspen isn't with Maksim, and my brothers and I all wonder why but don't ask him.

On the morning of their wedding, I wake up to a text. And it makes my blood go cold. I pull Nora as close to me as possible.

Maksim: *A second war has started. We must prepare.*

M

Nora

"JESUS, MARY, AND..." I YELL. ADRENALINE EXPLODES IN MY cells, and I pull Boris's face into my sex.

His phone rings, and he sucks me harder until I'm screaming.

He wipes his mouth on his arm and reaches for his cell. He shoves his fingers, wet from my arousal in my mouth, and answers, "Maksim."

I suck, trying to catch my breath.

Boris snorts. "Nope."

Boris removes his fingers, sits up on the side of the bed, and takes a deep, controlled inhale. "You going to let me have some fun?"

The hairs on my arms stand up.

"Good. I won't hold it against you for pulling me out of my warm bed."

I groan. He may have just gotten me off, but I'm hornier than a teenage boy looking at porn. And I don't want him to leave.

Boris covers the phone. "Moya dusha, I need to go to the garage."

My pulse pounds harder.

He returns to the phone. "Sure. You call the others yet?" He drags his finger over my nipple, and I gasp. "Call Dmitri. I'll phone Sergey." He hangs up and taps his screen.

"What's going on?"

He holds his finger up. "Sergey. Meet at Maksim's. We need to go to the garage." He grunts, tosses the phone on the bed, and lunges over me. His tongue flicks my ear, and he murmurs, "Wes Petrov is in the garage."

I freeze. Wes is Zamir's son. Maksim overreacted to something and broke up with Aspen the night of Anna and Dmitri's rehearsal dinner. Her friends took her out to the Cat's Meow. Somehow, she ended up in Wes's VIP suite and on his lap. Maksim, Adrian, and Sergey had guns and knives out, threatening Wes and his thugs to get Aspen and her friends out of the room. Wes sent Aspen a gift box with a snake in it, which bit her. She ended up in the hospital, almost dead. I knew Wes's time on earth was limited after harming Aspen, but it still makes me anxious.

"Oh no, you don't." Boris widens my legs and says something in Russian then thrusts in me.

"Oh God," I moan.

"We have all the control at the garage. You know this," he murmurs, nibbling on my neck.

"Yes," I agree in a shaky breath.

"Good." He shoves one arm under my shoulders and the other hand between our bodies and onto my clit. "Then there's nothing for you to worry about, except resting up. I'm going to be hungry when I get back."

He quickens his thrusts and fingers. The room becomes an echo chamber of my Irish blasphemy and his Russian. And we both come quickly.

I barely have time to breathe when he lifts his lips to mine and deeply kisses me. He pulls back. "We need to go. I'm taking you to Maksim's so Aspen isn't by herself. I'm sure Dmitri will bring Anna, too."

I spend the next few days with Aspen and Anna in Maksim's penthouse. The three of us get along really well. I'm glad none of us are by ourselves.

"Maksim said your pub remodel is almost finished?" Aspen asks.

Excitement swirls in my bones. "Yes. Next month is the grand reopening. You'll be there with Maksim, right?"

"Yes. Do you mind if I invite Skylar, Hailee, and Kora? They are always looking for new places to try out, and they've never been in your pub before."

"Of course. Killian drilled me about Hailee. He'll be more than happy to see her."

And I'll tell him to keep that slut, Becky, away.

Becky is a woman I can't stand. I've known her for a while and never liked her. Something about her rubs me the wrong way, and she's all up in Killian's business lately.

"I'll put their names on the list." Boris and Killian are insisting we keep the opening private for security reasons. They said there are too many Ivanovs and O'Malleys under one roof. Boris is closing the gym for the night and having Leo on the door. And they are putting guys around the neighborhood to watch out for any riffraff.

"How's the wedding planning coming? Did you decide on which dress?" Anna asks.

"Yes, I ordered the long sleeve one to appease my auntie. But I talked with the seamstress the next day. She's going to redesign it, rip the shoulders out, and give me some cleavage." I glance at my breasts, which are a lot bigger than before I was pregnant. "If I'm going to have these puppies, I might as well show them off. Plus, my auntie will have a heart attack. She only said long sleeves for the church, so I'll claim ignorance before she faints."

Anna and Aspen laugh, and my phone rings.

I pick it up and answer it. "Hey, Killian."

"Nora. I'm with Liam. He wants to go to lunch."

My chest tightens. I love Liam. We're blood. But he's always pulled Killian and Sean into trouble. I walk down the hall into the guest bedroom. "I can't. I'm on lockdown."

Alarm fills Killian's voice. "Why? What's going on?"

"Nothing to worry about. And I won't discuss anything over the phone."

"I'm coming over," he says.

"I'm not home. I'm at Maksim's with Anna and Aspen."

"Liam and I will bring lunch to you then. He wants to see you. And—"

"Nora!" Liam's voice booms over the line.

My heart rate increases. "Hey. How are you? Are you okay?"

"Please tell me I can come see you. My mom is hovering over me. She's making me regret I got parole. You know how she is."

His mom is my auntie, who made me get long sleeves for my wedding gown. I quietly admit, "Yep. I do know."

"And I know you missed me, too, right?"

I smile. "Yeah, I did."

"Killian said you're pregnant? And it's Boris's?"

"Yes." I shut my eyes, preparing to hear him tell me all reasons I should be with an Irish man. But he surprises me.

"Boris is a straight shooter. I'm happy for you."

I open my eyes and stare at the crashing waves of Lake Michigan. "Thank you."

"So, are you going to have lunch with me?"

"I'm on lockdown right now. I can't go anywhere."

"It's okay. As Killian said, we'll come to you."

I take a deep breath and don't respond. I don't know why I'm cautious about an innocent lunch.

"Do you not want to see me?" Liam asks, his voice dropping several octaves and laced with hurt.

And my heart hurts from it. He's always been my favorite cousin, more of a brother to me. We were close growing up. "Of course I do. Killian knows where I am. Come over."

"Great. I'll see you soon."

I hang up and continue to stare out the window. It's been several years since I last saw Liam. I visited him once, but Killian and Sean didn't like how the other prisoners eyed me over. Liam saw it, too, and insisted I not return, and my brothers were in agreement.

I've spoken with Liam a few times over the phone, but something made me keep my distance after Sean passed. I'm unsure why. Liam was in prison when Sean died. He didn't have anything to do with whatever Sean was involved in, but something inside me told me to stay away.

When I go into the living room, Anna is working on her computer. "Where's Aspen?"

"Her pain meds kicked in, so she went to take a nap."

"Oh. I guess it's just us then. Killian is coming over with my cousin, Liam. They're bringing us lunch."

Anna smiles. "That's nice. I've not met Liam before, have I?"

"Ummm...no."

"Why are you looking at me funny?"

I open my mouth to speak but then shut it.

Anna tilts her head. "Nora, what is it?"

I try to find the words. I've never had to explain to anyone my cousin was in prison for murder. Everyone I know already knows my family's history. But Anna's from New York. She's new to the O'Malley world. I finally blurt out, "He just got out of prison."

Anna's eyes widen. "Oh. Okay." She smiles.

"He's a good person," I quickly add.

"I didn't say he isn't."

"Sorry. I'm not used to explaining this to people. And he isn't the first O'Malley to spend time locked up. I shouldn't be weird about this, should I?"

Anna shakes her head. "No. I have some friends in New York whose family members went to prison."

"You do?"

"Sure. It's New York."

I twist my hair around my finger. My anxiety only grows. I wish it wasn't and I could turn it off, but I can't.

"How long was he in prison?" Anna asks.

"Fifteen years. He killed a man."

"Wow. That's a long time. You must be excited to see him."

"Yes."

She rises and walks toward the kitchen. "Well, I hope they bring something good. I'm ready to eat. I'll grab stuff to set the table for lunch."

I follow her. "Why doesn't this phase you?"

She takes a set of plates out of the cabinet. She spins. "I think prior to Dmitri, I would have been anxious. But I married a killer. You're marrying a killer. What I used to think of as black and white no longer is. I do not know the circumstances of what he did. So unless you tell me Liam is a horrible, dangerous person who will hurt me, I will not judge him. And I do not believe you would allow anyone to come near me who is out to harm me."

"No, I wouldn't."

"Okay, then. Here." She hands me the plates. "I'll get the silverware and some bottles of water. I would wake Aspen, but Maksim said it was better for her to rest."

My phone rings, and I answer it.

Killian says, "Nora, the security guard won't let us in."

"Hold on." I go to the entrance hallway. Anna's bodyguard, Viktor, is sitting on a chair near the elevator.

"Viktor, my brother, Killian, and cousin, Liam, are downstairs. Can you tell security to let them up?"

His eyes turn to slits. "Liam O'Malley?"

I get nervous again. "Yes."

"Didn't know he was out," he mumbles, picks up his phone, and calls security.

When Killian and Liam get out of the elevator, the men all nod to each other.

Liam picks me up off the ground in a hug. "Look at you."

I get emotional, and tears fall. "Are you okay?"

He chuckles and puts me on the ground. "Of course I am. I told you to stop worrying about me."

I wipe my face. "Let me look at you."

He gives me a cocky grin.

I laugh. "You look good."

His reddish-blond hair is the same as when he went inside. He has more tattoos on his arm and hand, mostly Irish clovers and Celtic crosses, and his bluish-green eyes are as friendly yet piercing as before. His body is more muscular than fifteen years ago. The wrinkles around his eyes weren't there, either.

"You've been lifting a lot."

He puts his hand on my small baby bump. "You're naming him after me, right?"

"Nope. It's going to be Killian," my brother claims.

I laugh. "Come in. Anna's setting the table."

"Who's Anna?" Liam wiggles his eyebrows.

I swat him with the back of my hand. "Don't get any ideas. She's Dmitri's wife."

"Okay, but if you have any single friends, send them my way."

I introduce Liam to Anna. We have lunch, and everything feels how it used to before Liam went away. And it scares me. It's like Liam was never gone. He's just as charismatic as ever. I see my brother and him falling right back into the same relationship they've always had.

The voice in my head keeps reminding me Sean isn't here. I don't know why I can't get past it. But the longer everything is perfect with our lunch, the more I worry about my brother.

Then Killian pulls me aside. "Nora, where's Boris?"

"With his brothers."

"Doing what?"

"You'll have to talk with him."

Killian tilts his head. "You know, and aren't going to tell me?"

I don't answer.

His jaw clenches. "When is he coming back?"

"I don't know."

Killian pulls me farther down the hall. "Tell me what you know, Nora."

"No," I firmly say.

"I'm your brother. Your own blood. Do you not trust me anymore?"

"I never said anything of the sort. But you need to discuss this with Boris, not me. I don't know the details. And please tell me you aren't going to let Liam get you involved in anything."

Killian angrily shakes his head. "That's not fair. He served his time for killing that prick."

"Yes, and he's always gotten you involved in things you shouldn't be. If you had been there the night he—"

"Jesus, Nora. Not you, too." Guilt fills Killian's face. He's always allowed Uncle Darragh to make him believe Liam wouldn't have gotten caught had Killian gone with him.

"It's true. You made the right choice. I don't want you getting swayed by him."

"I'm a thirty-eight-year-old man. I'm not a child anymore. I do have a brain."

I put my hands on his cheeks. "Yes. And you're loyal and fearless. Those traits scare me at times, Killian."

He steps back. "You don't have anything to worry about. When Boris gets back, tell him to call me."

"I will."

When they leave, Anna says, "Liam is charming."

I nod. "Yes." And that's what scares me.

Another day passes before Boris returns. I don't need to ask him about Wes Petrov. The Ivanov brothers' eyes all tell me he's dead.

When we get to our house, I tell Boris about Liam's visit and my conversation with Killian. "I'm not fair, am I? Killian is correct. He served his time."

Boris's eyes pierce mine. "Yes, he did."

"So, I'm unfair?"

"I didn't say that."

I tug on my hair. "I love Liam as a brother. But I don't want anything to happen to Killian, Nolan, or Declan."

Boris pulls me into his arms and sniffs hard. "I will watch over your brothers."

"How?"

He kisses my head. "Don't worry about this, moya dusha. We are slowly eliminating problems everywhere. Let's try to be grateful for the dangers that no longer surround us. We are slowly winning this war."

I'm unsure why a new fear nags me. It's unsettling, and I tighten my arms around Boris. It's different from what I felt when I was around Liam.

Boris of all people should know better than to claim any sort of victory. He's a betting man. He understands cards can turn at any time. And a silent war means every side can hide and strike in ways you least expect.

27

Boris

One Month Later

NORA'S GREEN EYES GLANCE UP. I FIST HER HAIR TIGHTER.

She digs her nails into my ass and squeezes my balls with her other hand.

"Fuuuuck, you're naughty," I growl, put my arm on the bathroom wall to steady myself, and try not to choke her with my cock.

She opens the back of her throat, shimmies her hard nipples on my thighs while moaning, and sucks harder before grazing her teeth against my shaft.

I stare down past her red hair at her round ass cheeks, which are slightly shuddering as she pushes her breasts against me quicker.

Nora's body is a neon sign, lighting up with the slightest touch. She's always reacted to me, but the further along in her pregnancy she gets, the more intense her sensations are. The number of orgasms I've given her just by touching her nipples is too many to count.

She can't seem to keep her hands off me lately. This morning is no exception. I tried to shower so I didn't wake her. The minute I stepped out, she pushed me over to where the rug is, dropped to her knees, and started sucking me off.

Now, I can't decide where I want to look. Her flushed cheeks glow. She possessively works her lush mouth on my cock. Her creamy white ass sticks slightly in the air every time she rubs her breasts over my thighs. So my eyes dart over all of her. And something about the fact she's six months pregnant with our child turns me on more.

My balls tingle and tighten. Sweat pops out on my freshly washed skin, but hers glistens as well. I'm on edge, trying to hold out a little longer, but tremors course through her body, and her savage moans echo in the air. She sucks me so hard, I explode into the back of her throat.

"Moya dusha!" I growl.

She swallows every drop of me while continuing to slide her gorgeous tits on my thighs and shaking.

Jesus Christ, she's perfect.

I pick her up and set her on the counter, slide my digits into her sex, and finger fuck her in every way possible. The entire time, I ravish her precious mouth, muffling her cries.

She orgasms almost the moment I touch her. And I don't stop playing with her until she's coated in sweat and limp as a rag doll in my arms.

My alarm on my phone rings, and I groan. "I have to get ready, moya dusha."

Satisfaction and lust swirl in her green eyes. She tries to catch her breath.

I kiss her again while murmuring, "Don't wear panties at the opening tonight."

Her lips twitch. "Are you going to get dirty with me in front of our guests?"

I grunt. "Don't wear them, and you'll find out." I kiss her some more then pull back. I tuck a lock of her hair behind her ear and put my other hand on her belly. "I have to go, or I'll be late."

She smiles. "Go."

"By the way, you suck my cock like a champion." I wink at her.

She laughs and pushes me in the chest. "Go."

I chuckle and get dressed in my closet. When I come out, she's in a green silk robe. It matches her eyes and barely covers her ass.

My pants become tighter. "Are you trying to torture me?"

She bats her long lashes and innocently says, "What?"

I groan, bend down, and kiss her on the lips. "I'm going to be late for my meeting with Sam."

"Go! It's a big day for both of us. I'll see you tonight."

I don't go though. I spin her back into my chest and untie her robe. My hand slides to her breast, my other to her clit, and within seconds, she's crying out, "Jesus, Mary, and Joseph!"

When she calms, I kiss her neck and murmur, "No panties. Have a nice day, moya dusha." I peck her on her flushed cheek and leave.

The ground is soft enough for the cleanup to continue on the city lot. Maksim and Aspen figured out how to get the zoning issue taken care of. After several years of buying adjoining lots and dealing with the problems Lorenzo created for us, we're finally able to move forward with our development. Our workers will continue to stay busy and feed their families through honest work instead of falling prey to Zamir.

I'm a few minutes late when I arrive. I locate Sam and shake his hand. "Are we all set?"

"The weather is cooperating, so let's hope we don't have any surprise snowstorms or freeze warnings over the next few weeks. Grab a coffee. I've got everything handled." He nods toward a food truck.

"Great." I cross the street as Sergey's driver pulls in. He steps out of the car.

I order two coffees. I hand him one. "You're late. And what's that?" I point to teeth marks outlining a purple bruise on his neck.

He smirks.

"Since when does Eloise mark you?"

He grunts. "It wasn't Eloise."

"Who was it?"

"Someone new."

"And she bites?"

More cockiness fills his face. "What you should be asking is, why did she have to bite me?"

I raise my eyebrows.

He takes a sip of his coffee. "Sam good to start?"

"Yep. We need this weather to stay stable."

"Forecast looks good. I think we're past the issues on this project."

My gut flips. I'm unsure why, but it's so fast, nausea hits me. I inhale a sharp breath.

Sergey furrows his brows. "You all right?"

I put my hand on my stomach. "Yeah."

The machines turn on, and Sergey and I watch for several moments as they break ground.

"So, are you and Eloise officially done?"

Sergey shifts on his feet. "We were never officially anything to be officially done, were we?"

"Good point."

His phone rings, and he answers. "Tim, what's going on?"

He shakes his head, and his face hardens. "I'll be right over." He puts his phone in his pocket.

"What's wrong?"

"Tim said dozens of pallets of steel were stolen."

"You'd need to bring in machinery to do that."

Sergey's eyes turn to slits. "Or keys to ours."

My chest tightens. "Don't tell me one of our guys is a thief."

Sergey's jaw twitches. "I'm going to find out."

"I can't leave right now. Darragh texted me this morning. He'll be here in ten minutes."

"What about?"

"I don't know."

Sergey pats me on the back. "Good luck with that. I'll call you when I know the full situation."

He leaves, and I call Dmitri.

"Boris. Did they break ground yet?"

"Yes. But we've got another problem. Maksim with you?"

"No. He and Aspen were visiting her dad then meeting Anna to look at a location for their wedding. What's going on?"

"Sergey's going to the north lot. Tim called. Pallets of steel were stolen."

The line goes quiet. Dmitri finally says, "That isn't easy to do."

"Exactly."

"Shit."

"Yep. I can't go over there right now," I say.

"I'm not far from the north lot. I'll meet Sergey and help him talk to the crew."

"Call me when you know something," I say as Darragh's car pulls up next to me.

"Will do," Dmitri replies. The line goes dead.

The window rolls down. "Get in," Darragh orders.

This old man needs to learn I'm not his little peon to order around.

I bite my tongue, reminding myself this isn't the fight to pick with him right now. I open the door and slide in. I wait for him to speak.

"How much is this cleanup costing you?"

"Four million for all the parcels, two-point-five is for this lot alone."

He whistles. "That's a lot of money for clean dirt."

I don't respond. It may be a lot of money, but no one deserves to live on contaminated land. My brothers and I pride ourselves on constructing high-quality, safe buildings. We don't skip steps when it comes to our business.

"How much will you make on this project?"

We have an alliance with the O'Malleys, and I may be marrying his niece, but it doesn't involve Darragh knowing all the details about us personally or professionally. "Enough."

His lips twitch. "Seems like a lot of work with a lot of red tape."

I don't like where this conversation is going. "What did you come here to talk to me about, Darragh?"

He scratches his chin, grabs his pipe, then cracks his window open. He flicks his metal lighter and inhales. Smoke fills the car. "You know what's funny about war?"

I'm not in the mood to play games, but I decide to see where this goes.

"What's that?"

"Casualties happen at all times. You don't always see it, but they're there. Some are slow deaths. Others are quick. But power shifts. Secret civil wars erupt within organizations. You must prepare for it."

The hairs on the back of my neck rise. "Has something happened?"

"Besides you taking out the two mob bosses' sons?"

"We've already gone over this. I explained why we killed Lorenzo. I also told you why there wasn't time to discuss Wes's demise. I'm not rehashing this again."

He snaps, "That's not the point."

"Then spit out whatever it is you're trying to say. I've got business to handle. It doesn't involve playing guessing games all day."

He takes another drag of his pipe. "The order has changed. Ill-prepared men are stepping into both Lorenzo and Wes's shoes. There is chaos. But neither the O'Malleys nor the Ivanovs can afford mistakes."

My stomach drops as it did earlier when I was with Sergey. "Why would their chaos create mistakes for us?"

He clenches his jaw and turns so he's facing me. "This will not leave this car."

"Go on."

His face turns solemn. Chills run down my spine. In a grave voice, he declares, "I only have one child left. Liam will rule the O'Malley clan."

God help them.

He points at me. "Ah. I see it in your face. You already know how ill-prepared he is. And it's not his fault, you know? Prison for fifteen years doesn't allow you to grow into the man you're meant to be. It's stifled his development. He can't make the best decisions because of it."

No, he's always made stupid decisions.

"What is your point? Why are we having this conversation?"

"He needs to get prepared." Darragh takes another puff, looks out the window, then says, "And sooner rather than later." He begins to cough.

I freeze. Goose bumps pop out on my skin. He continues to hack until his face is a tomato color. I reach for the bottle of water and hand it to him.

He takes a sip, wipes his mouth, then takes another puff of his pipe. He slowly inhales it, as if it's oxygen and not a toxic poison. After he exhales, he turns back to me. His eyes are bloodshot and watery. "Do you know why Killian, Nolan, and Declan needed to pledge their allegiance to me?"

So you could trap them.

"Loyalty," is all I respond with.

Darragh leans closer, as if he's about to tell me a secret. "They will be Liam's advisors. He will naturally choose them. And because they've always been loyal to him, they will agree. But if they are already in this life, there will not be any hesitation."

I don't want Nora's brothers involved in any of the O'Malley business. Besides the war to eliminate the Rossis and Petrovs, they shouldn't be anywhere near all the shit Darragh is involved in. But everything Darragh says is true. They would step up and help Liam. He would come to them, put on his charm, and any guilt they have about his problems being O'Malley issues would sway them to go against everything they've fought hard to stay out of.

Darragh starts coughing again, pulls out a handkerchief, and covers his mouth. When his fit is over, he glances at the blood-speckled cloth, then clenches it in his fists.

I acknowledge the elephant in the room. I quietly state, "You're dying, aren't you?"

He closes his eyes briefly then swallows hard. He avoids looking at me.

"How long do you have?"

His voice is cold. "Less than a year."

"Fuck," I mutter.

He huffs. "That's what I said."

Silence fills the air. I'm not very good with words, nor am I a stranger to death. But I feel for Darragh and Liam. My father got ill and wasted away in front of us. So I take deep breaths and try to calm my racing pulse.

Darragh's green eyes, usually piercing, fill with fear. "They aren't prepared—none of them. I blame myself. I should have pushed the three of them to take their roles when Liam was in prison. I thought if they made the choice themselves, it would be better. But it's put our entire family at risk. If others see their weakness, they will step up. That goes for their sisters' bastard husbands as well. There will be an internal war within our clan. And external families will use it to destroy us."

Blood pounds between my ears.

He points to me. "This is your problem now, too. You will be part of our family."

I misunderstand what he says. I hold my hands in the air. "I'm not looking to take over. I have Ivanov issues to deal with. No offense, but I have no desire to get involved in your business. And I would never try to hurt Liam or Nora's brothers."

"Yes. I understand your position. And I am not asking you to take over. It is Liam's birthright. But you have more skills than all of them. They will need you to help run things."

Oh, fuck no.

"Darragh, I appreciate your confidence in me, but—"

"It is in your child's best interest to step in and guide them. A threat against any O'Malley is a threat against your blood. There is no choice here."

I grind my molars. I stare out the window at the machinery working on the lot. This is what I want my child to inherit, not the O'Malley crime issues. But Darragh isn't stupid. Everything he says is right. I knew going into things with Nora she was an O'Malley and what it meant.

I turn to him. "I will always watch out for Nora's brothers. But your son, he has never made smart decisions. You've made excuses for him. Maybe he's changed over the last fifteen years, but my gut says he hasn't. I hope I'm wrong."

"He has changed. I've seen it," Darragh insists.

I snort. "How?"

"You ever been locked up? Had all your freedom taken away?"

While I've never been to jail, I have been Zamir's prisoner. So I'm not sure how to answer the question.

Darragh removes his tweed cap and puts it on his lap. "I have. And the only thing you have a lot of inside is time. It makes you think. Some men don't take advantage of it. But you underestimate my Liam. He is wiser. He understands the errors of his past. And I was once like him. I see myself in his eyes. If I could morph, so can he."

I clench my jaw. I hope Darragh is right, but until Liam proves to me he's changed, I'm not going to trust him blindly.

"I need you to help advise him so he can lead and keep our family safe."

I glance out the window, and the machinery has stopped. All the workers huddle together, pointing at the ground. My heartbeat picks up.

I tap the window. "Something is wrong. I need to go."

"Give me your promise," Darragh orders.

I turn. "I vow to love Nora and our child. I promise to watch out for Nora's brothers the best I can. I give you my word. If Liam has changed, I have his back. But if he hasn't, and anyone I care about gets hurt, you won't need to worry about the wrath of the O'Malleys. I'll strike him down so fast, he won't see it coming." I open the door and step out. I turn back. "I'm sorry about your diagnosis." I slam the door and trot over to the part of the site where the workers are.

"Sam, what's going on?" I holler.

He comes toward me and shouts back, "There're bones."

A chill runs down my spine. "Like animals?"

He stops in front of me. His face is white. "Human. And they all have a five-pointed star with a circle around them."

28

Nora

I SPEND AN HOUR FIXING MYSELF UP FOR THE GRAND reopening party. I haven't seen Boris all day, and he's not answering my calls. I finish my hair and makeup and go into my closet. I start to put on underwear but then remember he doesn't want me to wear any, so I skip it. I'm trying to zip my dress when Boris's aggressive Russian startles me. I jump and step out of the closet.

He turns the shower on, undresses, and continues speaking hostilely, then barks something out and tosses his phone on the counter.

I step behind him and put my arms around his waist.

He inhales sharply then takes his hands and slides them around his body and onto my ass. "How was your day, moya dusha?"

"Good. I get the feeling yours might not have been?"

He stays silent, and worry fills me.

"Boris, what's wrong?"

He sighs and spins. He takes the backs of his fingers and strokes my cheek. "You look beautiful, moya dusha."

I reach up and lace my hands behind his neck. I sternly say, "Tell me what is wrong."

He glances at the ceiling, and his jaw clenches.

"Boris?"

"I don't want to worry you, Nora."

"That's exactly what I'm going to do if you don't tell me whatever is bothering you."

He nods. "I'm sure you're going to hear about it tonight. They had to stop the cleanup."

"Why?"

The color drains from his face. "They found bones."

A horrible feeling crawls across my skin and sinks into my soul. "What kind of bones?"

He swallows hard. "The kind Zamir had me brand a five-pointed star with a circle around it into."

The pagan symbol for devil worship.

It hits me how much I don't know about what happens when Boris has to go to Zamir. All the sadistic things Zamir must make him do flashes in my mind, but nothing probably comes close to reality. I'm sure whatever I imagine is a thousand times less harsh than the truth. I step closer to him. "How did the bones get there?"

The vulnerable look I've only seen in Boris's eyes a few times appears. Genuine fear swirls in the darkness, pooling within the boy I used to know. It almost breaks me. But now is the time for me to be strong for him. When he doesn't answer, I firmly order, "Tell me."

"Zamir had to have planted them."

My chest tightens. "Why would he do such a thing? Doesn't that put him at risk?"

Boris shakes his head. "No. He's a ghost. His tracks are always covered. He did it to send me a message."

"What kind?"

He wraps his arms tight around me. "I'm not sure. But my brothers and I are increasing security on you, Anna, and Aspen."

"Okay. I'm not going to argue."

"The authorities have opened an investigation."

My stomach flips. "Do you think anything is linking you to this?"

"The branding on the bones is all. Only Zamir and his thugs know about it. Unless he planted something else on them."

I shudder, and my voice cracks. "Like what?"

He licks his lips. His forehead creases. "A hair? I don't know. It's the only thing I can think he could have planted to link them to me. I always wear gloves. And my entire body is covered."

"We need to talk to Uncle Darragh tonight."

"Why?" he asks in surprise.

My stomach twists. I don't want Boris to owe Darragh anything, but I won't have him go to prison. "Did you notice after Liam got convicted, no O'Malley has since?"

Boris squints. "What are you getting at?"

I take a deep breath. "About a year after Liam went away, I heard my nana and Darragh speaking. He assured her no O'Malley would ever go to prison again. And they haven't. I don't know the details, but anytime an O'Malley has been in trouble, evidence disappears. If you want to crush this now, we need to speak to Darragh."

Boris's face hardens. He shifts on his feet.

"What's wrong? My uncle can help."

"Nothing." He puts his forehead on mine and closes his eyes. "I'm sorry, Nora."

I cup his cheeks. "For what?"

"Putting you and our baby in danger. Adding stress in your life and especially on a day you've worked so hard for."

I slide my hands into his hair. In a stern voice, I say, "*You* are my life. And you do not apologize for Zamir, ever. Do you understand me?"

He stays quiet.

"Kiss me, zip up my dress, and get showered. We can't be late."

He obeys, and I deepen our kiss until I'm breathless, buzzing, and my insides are quivering like Jell-O.

"That's more like it," I mumble. I spin and shake my booty. "Zip."

He drags his finger down my spine, and I shiver. His lips hit my ear, and his digits stroke the top of my ass crack. "No panties. Good girl."

My body hums, and I reach for his thighs and squeeze. "Zip. Or we're staying home."

He does then gets in the shower. After he gets dressed, we leave the penthouse and get into the car. I sink into his chest and lace my hand through his.

"Are you excited?"

I nod. "Yes. I know I can't be at the pub as much, with the baby coming and all, but I'm excited to have it open again. And I think my nana would love what Anna designed."

"You both did a great job."

I glance up and wince. "We have to meet with the priest Sunday after mass."

Boris groans. "What for?"

"The O'Malley private blessing."

"What's that? Darragh didn't tell me about that, nor did Father Antonio."

"After mass, he sprinkles holy water on us and says a prayer for our safety, fertility, and happiness."

Boris snorts and places his hand on my stomach. "I think we're good on the fertility piece." He kisses my neck. "I'm happy. And I'll keep you safe." His hand slides to my inner thigh.

I softly laugh. "It's a big deal. If we don't do it, I'll hear about it from my auntie for the rest of my life."

"This is a family thing?"

"Yeah."

He grins. "Okay. I should make my brothers go, too, then?"

"Is this their kind of thing?"

Boris chuckles. "Nope. But I'm making them go. What time is this shindig?"

"You should already know this, since you're converting during it," I remind him.

"Oh, yeah. I forgot. Such an exciting event," he sarcastically says.

"Mass is at ten. Everyone normally comes to the pub after."

He puts his face next to mine. "Is there anything else I'm not aware of?"

"No." I pick his hand up and kiss it. "Thanks."

He sniffs hard. "Guess it would be hard to pay the priest off for this one, huh?"

I bite my smile and pat his cheek. "You did good on everything else."

The car stops in front of the pub, and he steps out, then reaches in for me. We go inside, and to my surprise, it's full. Everyone yells, "Congratulations," blows noisemakers, and Irish pub music starts playing.

"What are you all doing here already?" I ask.

My uncle Darragh hugs me. He blinks hard, cups my cheeks, and says, "Your nana would be proud."

It makes me tear up, and I hug him again. "Thank you."

The next few minutes are chaotic as everyone in the pub approaches to embrace me.

I finally get a chance to escape my family and pull a chair up to one of the new round booths. Aspen, Skylar, Kora, and Hailee are sitting in it.

"There's the superstar!" Aspen beams.

"Anna's the one who designed it. She gets the credit, not me. She even came over and made my brothers redo things she didn't think were perfect," I reply just as Anna slides into the booth.

"You all did great," Skylar claims.

"Did you see Killian?" I ask Hailee.

Aspen shakes her head, and her eyes widen at something behind me.

"What?" I turn to where she's staring. Becky has her arms draped around Killian, and she's kissing him.

I turn back. "What's that slag doing here? I didn't have her on the list," I address Hailee. "He's not that into her... God, he can't be..." I glance behind me, shoot them a dirty look, then focus on Hailee again. "He probably didn't know you would be here—"

"It's fine, Nora. We've only spoken a few times."

"Well, don't look now, but Mr. Melt Your Wet Panties is checking you out, Hailee," Kora claims.

She blushes and sits up straighter. "Who?"

"Do not all look right now. But my guess is Hailee will deem him as, cocky bad boy, maybe you've been in jail but I don't care, take no prisoners unless it's me because your body is a sanctuary, and I'm ready to have you dip into me wherever you want, so please come to mama," Kora says. She holds up her drink, and Aspen and Skylar clink it before taking a drink.

Hailee looks around. "Where is he?"

"I said not to look, but you should get on your knees and thank Jesus because I think he's dying to get on his. With you in front of him, of course." Kora takes a long drink.

Hailee leans into her. "Where?"

I lean in as well. "Yes, where, Kora? I know everyone here. Tell me where to look so I can give Hailee the details on whoever this stud is."

"Oh! I see him. Yep. Hailee, he's got fuck-me eyes, and I'm positive he's directing them at you. He's not even bothering to look away even though Kora and I are staring at him." Skylar holds up her hand and waves.

"Skylar! What are you doing?" Hailee asks.

"Oh! He's coming over!" Kora claps.

"Holy...yeah. Hailee won't do him. She'll chicken out," Aspen says.

Hailee nudges her. "Why do you say that?"

"You always do when it comes to the bad boys."

"Well, I sat in the wrong seat. Where is he?" Hailee asks but can't get far around Aspen.

"Yeah, who..." My pulse beats hard in my throat. Liam's fixated on our table. He saunters across the bar and toward us.

Anna says in a bubbly voice, "It's Nora's cousin, Liam."

"How do you know him?" Kora asks.

"Nora and I had lunch with him. He's super charismatic and nice. He's funny, too."

"You've been holding out on us, Nora," Skylar teases.

Liam's cocky, charming smile melts my heart and makes me worry, all at the same time. I've missed his grin. I want him to be happy. But I'm not sure if I should warn Hailee about him or not. She's a nice, innocent girl. Killian would have been pushing it for her on the dangerous side, now that I think about it. But Liam's past makes Killian look like an angel.

"Nora, are you going to introduce me to your friends? All stunning lasses, by the way," Liam asks, staring at Hailee.

"Umm..." I pick up a glass of water and take a long sip. Hailee's cheeks burn to the color of my hair.

She's going to freak out when she finds out he's been in jail.

I should tell her.

How?

While my heart goes into a panic, Anna steps in and makes introductions.

Darcey comes over. "Nora, I don't mean to interrupt, but Darragh said to come get you. He's talking to Boris near the back."

"Oh. Okay. Thanks."

She nods and leaves.

I rise, and Liam pulls my chair back. "I'll keep your seat warm while you're gone." He winks.

I force a smile. "Sure." I glance at Hailee, whose face is getting redder from Liam's intense gaze. "I'll be right back."

"Take your time," Liam says.

I go to the table where my uncle sits. Boris is next to him.

"Is everything okay?" I nervously ask.

Boris puts his arm around me and pulls me onto his lap. "Your uncle said he has something for you."

I look at Darragh. "What is it?"

He reaches under his suit jacket and pulls a small box out. "This was your nana's. She gave it to me for when Liam gets married someday. I want you to hold on to it."

My chest tightens. "What is it?"

He nods for me to open it.

I slide the top off. My nana's gold trinity knot with emeralds and diamonds is in it. I take a shaky breath and get teary-eyed, remembering all the years Nana wore it for special occasions.

"Before your nana died, she gave me this. She prayed every day Liam would get out of prison and find a good lass to make him happy. She said she wanted Liam's wife to know she was welcoming her into the family. Even though she wouldn't be here in body, she was here in spirit."

I tear my eyes away from the necklace. "Why are you having me hold on to it?"

"You are the only granddaughter your nana trusted. I am getting old. It is important to me you fulfill her wish."

I grab his hand. "You aren't that old."

Something passes in his expression. It's almost a calm acceptance. "There is only one thing guaranteed in life. Death. Please take this and do as your nana wished."

I wipe my face. "Okay. I will."

He pats my hand. "You've always been a good girl." He removes another box from his pocket. It's longer than the other box. "This is for you."

I hesitate but open it. Three Irish pewter baby spoons with platinum twisted into a Celtic design on one side and O'Malley engraved on the other are in it. I get emotional again. "These are beautiful."

"My gift for your baby. Do not ever let him or her forget they are half O'Malley."

"I won't. But you should give these to the baby when you see him or her," I insist.

He rises and holds his arms out.

I embrace him.

He says, "Your mother, father, nana, and daideó would all be proud of you. Is there anything you need from me before the wedding?"

I freeze.

He pulls back. His eyes turn to slits. "Nora, what is it?"

"Can we talk in my office?"

He nods. "Yes. Of course."

I motion for Boris to stay. When we get to the office, I say, "I need you to make something disappear for Boris."

He arches an eyebrow. "Oh?"

I've never spoken to my uncle before about any of his criminal activities. My stomach flips, but I take a deep breath. "They found bones during the cleanup."

He nods. "Yes. I heard."

I twist my fingers. I didn't know what I planned on saying to my uncle. But now I realize I'm going to have to disclose Boris's secret, which I don't want to do.

I open and close my mouth several times, not sure what to do or say.

Darragh puts his hands over mine. "Nora."

"Yes."

"I've already taken care of it."

"You have? How?"

"I learned about it almost as soon as it was discovered. I have eyes everywhere in this city."

"But why would you take care of it? I'm confused."

He smiles. "Because you love him. He will be an O'Malley as much as he is an Ivanov. And anything that could possibly bring him down, our family will destroy."

I gape at him.

He leans closer and, in a stronger voice, claims, "*We* are O'Malleys. We get ahead of things. We slaughter anyone who attempts to take us down. But we never leave any of us to fend for ourselves. Don't ever forget that." He takes my hand and puts it over his heart. "And make sure you teach your baby, and your husband, what being an O'Malley means, in here."

29

Boris

Nora is still with her uncle Darragh when Adrian arrives. I don't want to ask Darragh for help. But I also don't want anything linking me to those bones. I don't know what Zamir's intentions are, and avoiding life in prison is the only option.

But I'm going to owe Darragh. I already know what he wants. In some ways, it's already a given. I'm not going to let Liam take Nora's brothers down. I'm not convinced he has changed. He's more mature than fifteen years ago, but I'm not putting my full faith and trust he will not lead Nora's brothers down a destructive path. So I'm naturally going to interfere if I see anything going astray. But I can't commit to having Liam's back if he makes bad choices.

I'm going to have to if Darragh saves my ass.

Adrian motions for me to meet him at the front of the pub. When I get up there, he nods to the door with an amused expression. "Want to take care of that?"

Obrecht is outside, scowling at Leo.

I open the door and step out.

"Sorry, man, strict instructions," Leo says in Russian.

Obrecht wasn't on the list. He's been tracking different movements in the war, and I didn't expect him to be here, especially when Maksim told him he's strictly on the bones issue.

"Leo, let him in," I instruct in Russian.

Obrecht throws him some more daggers with his eyes. "Tell this meathead I don't need to be on a list with the Ivanovs. Oh, wait, on second thought, remind him I am a goddamn Ivanov," Obrecht growls and walks into the pub.

I glance at Leo, who looks unfazed at Obrecht's outburst.

I pat Leo on the shoulder. "Probably best if you add him to your mental always-let-past list. But good to reiterate I can always count on you."

He grunts, and I go inside.

Obrecht is already making a beeline toward the back door with Adrian and motioning for my brothers to join him.

We go straight into the back alley.

"Where's Sergey?" Maksim asks.

"I assumed he was already out. I didn't see him, and I was at the front of the bar," Dmitri replies.

"I'll check the bathroom." I return inside, and the back of Nora's red-haired head and Darragh's bald one are in the sea of people in the main room.

I search for Sergey in the bar area with a quick glance. Since he's as tall as I am, it's hard to miss him. When I don't see him anywhere, I check the men's room, but it's empty.

Where did he go?

I check Nora's office and the kitchen. The only other place in the pub is the basement or the break room Nora had built for the staff. It was previously an oversized storage closet.

The door's shut. I turn the knob, open the door, and freeze.

Sergey has one of Aspen's friends—I think her name is Kora, but I've only met her once in passing and didn't pay too much attention—bent over the table.

"Your sweet, tight pussy needs my Russian cock, doesn't it?" my brother growls in Russian, thrusting into her and holding her wrists out to the side. They are tied up in the grand reopening ribbon. His other hand is strumming her clit.

"Oh God... I'm coming...oh God," she shrieks and arches off the wood.

He takes his hands, splays them on her back with her hands underneath his.

Get it, little brother.

I shut the door, step outside, and stand against the wall. Several minutes pass. I patiently wait, glad to see him doing anyone besides Eloise and hoping this woman isn't a nasty bitch.

He finally opens the door, steps out, and closes it. He doesn't see me and starts walking toward the bathroom.

I clear my throat, and he turns.

"Having fun?" I ask.

He smirks.

I nod toward the alley. "We have business to discuss."

"I'll be out in a minute." He steps into the bathroom.

Kora comes out and turns red when she sees me. Well, redder, since her skin glistens and face is already flushed.

"Sorry. Thought this was the bathroom."

I point to the women's room.

She holds her head high and hurries past me, disappearing through the door.

Sergey comes out, and we go to the alley.

"Where were you?" Dmitri asks in Russian.

"In one of those round booths with the O'Malleys. Easy to miss," I continue in Russian, covering for him.

"Okay, well, now that we're all here, tell us what's going on, Obrecht," Maksim orders.

Obrecht crosses his arms and leans against the brick wall. "Kacper and Franciszek Zielinski just got arrested. The examiner found their DNA all over the bones. Since it's already in the system for their prior convictions, it popped right up."

Confusion fills me. "Zamir planted this on Bruno's sons?"

Obrecht's voice is deadpan. "No. The O'Malleys did."

The blood drains down my body, leaving chills in its path. "How..."

Obrecht pushes off the wall and steps closer. "It seems your new family likes you more than you think. Darragh and Liam had a meeting with a few influential people today. In secret, of course."

Darragh and Liam. Shit.

Don't be an ungrateful idiot. This is keeping you out of prison.

I owe Liam now.

Darragh is about to die. He made sure Liam was part of this to tie me to him. It was a smart move on his part. Can't say I blame the man.

Adrian cracks his neck then asks, "Why pin this on the Zielinskis?"

I glance around to make sure we're still alone. "Liam told Killian Bruno visited Giovanni Rossi in prison. We should ask him."

"Zamir isn't going to be happy his plan for the bones didn't go according to his wishes. We need to strike before he does again," Sergey insists.

"He's not popped up yet," Obrecht claims.

Sergey's jaw twitches. "The next time he messages Boris, we need to be ready. It's the perfect opportunity for us to destroy him."

I shake my head. "I've told you—"

"Sergey's right. It's our only opportunity. If we're all prepared with a plan, we can take him out," Maksim states with a confidence I've never heard before during our discussions about Zamir.

"What's changed? You know he has eyes everywhere. We could have a siege of his thugs upon us in seconds."

"It's a risk we have to take," Sergey insists.

My skin crawls. "I don't like it."

Dmitri sniffs hard. His eyes turn cold. "There are no more options. We need to eliminate him. We have families to protect. I'm tired of worrying about Anna every time she steps away from me. And she wants to try for a baby. Zamir needs to not be on this earth when my child is born."

Adrian snorts. "Guess we don't need to worry about the Ivanov lineage with you two. I'll tell our mother to get off Obrecht's and my backs."

Obrecht groans. "She is getting worse. I can't deal with her phone calls anymore. I could knock up anyone at this point and she'd be happy. All it does is make me want to double bag it."

"Can you two concentrate on your dicks later?" Sergey asks.

"That's rich, coming from you," I add.

He ignores me. "Zamir's time on earth has reached its limit. I won't let him harm any of us anymore. The debt we owe him, we've paid for a thousand times over. Our family will no longer be his pawns."

"You're getting lots of practice going deep today, little brother, aren't you?" I dig again. I've never caught my brother having sex before. Didn't know he was into bondage, either. I make a mental note to ask him about it later.

Questioning expressions fill the others' faces.

"This isn't a joke," Sergey snaps.

I hold my hands up. "Chill. You're right."

Maksim's voice lowers. "It's settled. We form a plan. The next time Zamir calls, we execute. Adrian, get Liam and Darragh. I want to know why they pinned this on the Zielinskis."

Adrian doesn't take long to bring Liam and Darragh outside.

Darragh gives me a knowing look then lights his pipe. He inhales and starts to cough but gets control of it quickly.

"This better be important. You pulled me away from a smoking-hot lass. If she leaves while I'm out here, I'm chopping all of your balls off," Liam says.

"Shut up," Adrian demands. "And she'll still be here."

"How do you know? You have ESP?"

A cocky expression fills Adrian's face. "She's friends with Skylar and came with her."

"So?"

"So, I haven't shown Skylar a good time yet."

"Which one is she, Liam?" Obrecht asks.

"Exchange your dick stories later," Darragh snaps. "What is this about?" He inhales again and pulls his handkerchief out when he erupts in coughs.

When he stops, I ask, "Why did you plant evidence regarding the bones against the Zielinskis?"

"How did you know?" Liam blurts out.

Darragh doesn't seem fazed. It's as if he knew we would find out.

He wanted me to know he saved my ass.

Darragh steps closer in our circle. "The head of the Polish mob visits the head of the Italian mob in prison. Why do you think that is?"

"We aren't sure yet," I admit.

Darragh points to my brothers and me. "You've recruited his people, given them enough to feed their families and not turn to him. Instead of staying in your community, you've crossed the line into his. You've put another target on your backs."

Maksim addresses Liam. "What do you know about this?"

"I was in the laundry room on my shift. Two of Rossi's top guys were talking. They didn't say Ivanov, but there was enough to put two and two together. Giovanni agreed to come after you to help put you out of business if Bruno aligned with him against Zamir."

"And you only are telling us this information now?" Sergey seethes, stepping toward him.

Liam gets in Sergey's face. "I had to verify I was correct. It's the same thing my father would do. I'm not the same hothead who acts without thinking anymore."

"You should have told me," I state.

Liam spins and barks, "So you could start a war with the Zielinskis without absolute certainty? And what if I was wrong? Then you'd have another family coming after you, putting Nora and the baby in more danger. Sorry, but I'm not putting my family at any risk unless it's necessary."

The alley goes quiet. Maybe Liam has changed. It's an action he wouldn't have taken in the past. And I can't argue what he's saying. Maksim would have made us do the same thing if we were in his shoes.

Darragh clears his throat several times then takes another drag of his pipe. He slowly exhales the smoke. "Bruno's sons will go to prison. Our men inside will kill them. But Rossi has the power of the Poles behind him now, too. And that's a problem for all of us." He steps toward Maksim. "Your family has done well. You've made a lot of enemies in the process. What I'm teaching the O'Malley men is to look at all angles where you may be vulnerable. Do not overlook anyone in the process. I've made the same mistake in the past. I will never do it again. Lead your family wisely because we are now connected."

Maksim's ice blue eyes pierce him. He says nothing, taking in every word, then finally nods. "We will need to take into consideration the power of them together. The balance will be thrown off considerably."

"Yes. And Bruno will not take it lightly that the bones have been planted on his sons. He will assume you did it. I suggest you move swiftly to handle this issue. The wrath of two men who have lost their sons becomes more powerful."

"Understood," Maksim replies.

"Are we done here?" Liam asks in an annoyed voice. "I'd rather spend my night with the sexy lass inside."

"Yeah, we're done," I reply. But we're anything but finished. His actions got me out of the mess I could have been in but created an entire set of new problems for us. And now it ties me into watching over him even more.

Instead of dwelling on my new reality, I go inside and search for Nora. Tonight should only be about her. And I haven't forgotten she's pantyless.

30

Nora

BORIS MAKES MY FAMILY HAPPY AND CONVERTS TO Catholicism. The mass is only fifteen minutes long, including the conversion process, which startles the regular parishioners and my auntie. The Ivanov brothers, Anna, and Aspen are there in the front pews with my closest family members. The priest gives us his private blessing after the mass, and we have another celebration at the pub.

Everything moves quickly over the next week. The pub is up and running again. My brothers are helping Darcey manage it so I can focus on the wedding. At the reopening party, the subject of my final dress fitting came up, and the girls all wanted to come with me. Since I don't want my auntie having any part of it, and my sisters and their kids are still barely talking to me, I happily agreed. Aspen's friends are funny, and I really like them. I even invited them to the wedding. My uncle and Boris assured me the bones are no longer an issue, but I'm not ignorant. Boris increased his security detail on me. I have two men at all times on me, and a third is a driver who could break your neck in one second. He claims he's being cautious, but it makes me nervous. My auntie is calling me every five minutes about the wedding, adding to the stress. So it's nice to laugh with Aspen's friends.

When we get to the dress fitting, the bridal boutique staff passes champagne out. I skip it and go into the dressing room. The woman helps me into the dress and zips the back. I step out and onto the wooden platform in front of the oversized three-way mirrors.

"Awww!" the ladies all exclaim.

"My auntie is going to have a heart attack for sure," I happily comment, staring at my cleavage and bare shoulders. I put my hand on my stomach. It's definitely showing. "Do you think everyone is going to stare at my belly all day?" I'm not embarrassed I'm pregnant, but I don't want it to be the focus of the day. I want it to be about Boris and me.

"No! If they do, we'll drop some booze on them or something. Then they won't be staring," Kora states.

"Yeah. I already feel your auntie might have one coming," Skylar adds.

I laugh. "Keep my auntie out of it. She means well. She'll be too distracted by my boobs. But everyone else, spill away."

"You look stunning," Hailee says.

"Agreed. And I'm so glad you removed the shoulders and got rid of the suffocating neck." Anna grimaces. She went with me during the initial fitting and kept me from strangling my auntie.

Aspen picks up my veil and hands it to the store employee. "Boris will go crazy when he sees you."

Hailee's phone rings. "Oh, sorry! Didn't know my ringer was on." She pulls it out of her purse, blushes, and sends it to voicemail.

Skylar touches her cheek. "Why do you look like a tomato?"

Hailee shrugs away from her. "Stop. I don't."

"Mmm, yeah, you do. Who called?"

"No one."

"Someone called," Aspen insists.

Skylar grabs her phone.

"Hey! Give me my phone!"

Skylar tosses it to Kora. "Six-two-eight-nine."

"How do you know my security code?"

Amusement fills Skylar's face. "I know all of yours. You don't do much to hide it."

Kora quickly types in the code. "Ohh, Liam. You should call him back."

My stomach flips. I haven't told Hailee anything about Liam. I wasn't sure what to do. I'm not sure if Anna told her he was in prison or not. But she left with Skylar. Liam was nowhere to be seen, so I thought nothing came of their meeting. But I should have known. Liam always gets what he wants, and he clearly was interested in her.

"Give me my phone back." Hailee holds out her hand.

"You didn't tell us you exchanged numbers with Mr. Please Lick Every Inch of Me," Skylar teases.

"Eww," I cry out.

She winces. "Sorry. Forgot he's your cousin."

"Oh, he just texted!" Kora sings.

Hailee lunges over Skylar and tries to grab her phone, but Kora holds her hands up.

She yells out, "Hales—ohhh, he already has a nickname for you—I was calling to see if you want to go to Nora's wedding with me. Call me."

"Give me my phone." Hailee tries to reach again, but Skylar holds her firmly on top of her, laughing.

"Text him, yes, and she's ready to get laid," Aspen says.

"Aspen!" Hailee cries out.

"What? You all made a deal with Maksim on my behalf. Paybacks are a bitch."

"That worked out well for you," Skylar claims.

Kora starts typing.

Hailee tries to grab her phone again. "Don't you dare, Kora!"

She smirks and hands the phone to Hailee. "Here. You can thank me later after your trip to O town."

Hailee snatches the phone and sits up. She reads the text. "I can't believe you did this."

"Oh, come on. Live a little for once. You were totally into him. And you gave him your phone number, so you obviously want to go out with him. All these prim and proper guys aren't doing anything for you," Kora claims.

"You shouldn't interfere with other people's business. You don't know a thing about him."

"Okay, tell us what's wrong with him."

Hailee stares at her phone.

I exchange a glance with Anna. I quietly ask, "Liam told you, didn't he?"

She glances up, and guilt fills her face. She winces. "No. I did an online search on him last night."

My heart twists. I feel bad for Liam. He's into Hailee. He wouldn't pursue her if he wasn't. I also understand and am not surprised she is conflicted. "Are you scared of him?"

She creases her forehead, opens her mouth, then closes it. Her face turns deep crimson. "Should I be?"

In my most confident voice, I state, "No. Liam is a lot of things, but he would never hurt you or any woman."

"What's going on? Why should she be scared of Liam?" Skylar asks.

I stick my chin out and stand straighter. "Liam spent the last fifteen years in prison. The state granted him parole for good behavior."

"What did he do?" Kora asks.

"He murdered my father's killer."

The room goes silent. I've never said those words out loud. Everyone always knew Liam avenged my father's death. Darragh and my father were as tight as my brothers are. Liam was just as crushed as we were when it happened. But instead of using his head, he lost it and went full-throttle on the guy in public. He told Killian what he was going to do. Killian insisted he not be stupid. But Liam went ahead with his plan all by himself.

Every one of my brothers felt guilty Liam did what they felt was their duty to do. But my brothers were still mourning when it happened. None of us could see straight at the time. It was only three days after my father's death when Liam murdered his killer.

It added another reason for us to grieve. We lost him when we lost my father. Liam was supposed to be in prison for sixteen years. My nana was heartbroken. She sat all of us down and insisted we stay out of the criminal side of our family. Uncle Darragh was at the meeting. She made him agree not to pressure my brothers to join him in his business.

Something about saying it aloud makes me feel severe remorse for my current negative thoughts about Liam. He did what he did out of love for my father. He wanted to make sure the guy never came after any more of us. Yes, he got Killian involved in shady shit a lot when they were younger, but he's not that kid anymore. Shame suddenly hits me like a brick. Liam deserves to be happy. Hell, he's earned the right more than anyone else in my family.

Anna softly says, "I really like Liam. I don't get any bad vibes from him. Maybe you should give him a chance, Hailee."

I blink back my tears and spin. I say to the lady, "Can you add my veil, please?"

She nervously nods and adds it.

"Can you give us some privacy?" I ask.

"Sure." She leaves the room and shuts the door.

"I think we should get something straight."

"What's that?" Kora says.

"Let's not pretend we all believe the O'Malleys or the Ivanovs are always law-abiding citizens. You all grew up in Chicago, minus Anna. You've undoubtedly heard of my family. And I think you understand from your run-in with Wes Petrov at the Cat's Meow, the Ivanovs aren't to be messed with."

No one denies my statement.

I point to Kora and Skylar, who I have suspicions are doing something with Sergey and Adrian. I first suspected something was up the night I met them at the fight then at my reopening party. I'm not as worried about Adrian as I am Sergey. Adrian seems to be a player and can handle Skylar. She'd be the one in trouble, not Adrian. At least, that's my impression. But I've known Sergey forever. I know his story. And I've seen him stay attached to bitchy Eloise forever. So I mostly address Kora. "If you're going to play in their sandbox, don't pretend you don't understand what they are capable of and use it as an excuse to run down the road. If you do, especially with Sergey, you'll have me to deal with, so fair warning."

"I think Sergey is a big boy and can handle himself," Kora huffs.

"Kora." Aspen shakes her head.

"What? He's a freaking animal, as alpha as they come, and I'm pretty sure emotionally unavailable. And he's made it pretty clear he isn't into relationships."

"He said that?" Anna asks in surprise.

Kora shrugs. "Not in those words, but two plus two is four."

"What does that mean?" I snap.

Kora puts her hands in the air. "Easy."

I release a big breath. "Sorry. I've known the Ivanovs and their history forever."

"What's so crazy about their history?" she asks.

Anna, Aspen, and I exchange a glance.

"What?" Kora repeats.

I shouldn't be discussing any of this.

"They didn't have it easy. It's all I'm going to say. I'm sorry. I think my hormones are messing with my pregnancy brain."

Kora hesitantly smiles. "No worries. But for the record, I'm not out to hurt Sergey."

"I know."

"So, what are you going to do, Hailee?" Skylar asks. "Are you going to tell Liam you won't go to the wedding with him?"

Hailee glares. "Kora already texted him. What would I even say? Sorry, I googled you, and now I'm judging you, so I'll be at the wedding, but I won't go with you?"

"Sorry." Kora winces.

My heart twists again. I don't want Hailee hurting Liam. "Just tell him."

She scrunches her forehead and opens her mouth.

"He's a man, not a boy. Don't lead him on and give him false hope. He's been through enough. You can't handle his past. It's understandable. He's going to have to learn to deal with it. But don't string him along. One thing Liam isn't is a player. He's like all my brothers. He fights hard and loves hard. So fess up to him and let him move on." I turn and walk into the dressing room. I wonder how much of my emotions are from my pregnancy and what isn't overreacting.

Anna comes in. She smiles. Her voice is soft. "Let me help you get out of your dress."

"Sorry. I—"

She puts her finger over my lips. "You're not wrong, Nora. If Hailee can't handle it, she should tell Liam. And if Kora hurts Sergey, she won't only have you to deal with."

I wipe a tear that escapes, and Anna pulls me into her. The rest of the day is awkward, and I breathe in relief when I'm finally by myself in the car. I pick up the phone and call Liam.

"Hey, Nora."

I smile, happy to hear his voice, and grateful I can call him whenever I want again.

"Where are you?"

"Home. My mom and dad went somewhere, thank God. My mom is driving me insane. I need to get my own place."

An idea pops into my mind. "I'm two minutes away. Can you come with me somewhere?"

"Sure. Where are we going?"

"I have a surprise for you."

He grunts. "Should I be worried?"

I smile. "No."

"Okay. I'll sit in nervous anticipation."

I pull into the driveway, and Liam comes out. He slides next to me. His eyes twinkle. "What's going on?"

"You'll see."

My driver pulls out and drives to my old house. Liam looks out the window. "Who lives here?"

"You'll see. Get out."

He chuckles. "Anyone tell you how bossy you've gotten?"

"I'm Irish and pregnant. Don't mess with me," I joke.

We go up to the house. I dig in my purse and find the keys. I haven't been here since I moved in with Boris. I sort of forgot about the house. There's been so much going on with the pub and wedding.

We step inside. Everything is empty. I turn to Liam. "This is my house I used to live in before I moved in with Boris."

"It's nice."

"It needs some work. My brothers kept bugging me to fix some things, but I kept blowing them off. I didn't know what I wanted to do with the design. It drove them nuts. I'm pretty sure you can utilize their skills and yours."

He squints. "What do you mean? Do you need to fix it up to sell it? It looks move-in ready to me unless something is going on that won't pass the inspection?"

I grab his hand and put the key in it. "This is yours. If you want it."

He opens his mouth to speak then shuts it. He slowly says, "Nora, I can't take your house."

"You aren't taking it. I'm giving it to you."

He inhales sharply. "It's very kind of you, but I'm not taking your house. This is from your blood, sweat, and tears, not mine."

"The mortgage is paid off. Taxes are due twice a year and paid for the next twelve months as well as the insurance. I'll sign a quick claim deed tomorrow."

He shakes his head. "Nora, I can't—"

"Liam, do you have somewhere else you're moving to?"

He says nothing and clenches his jaw.

I smirk. "Do you secretly love your mom nagging you all day long?"

He snorts. "Nope."

I squeeze then release my hand from his. "Good. Anna is a pretty amazing designer. I'm sure she'd whip up some awesome plans for you. My brothers will help you fix it up, and we've got an account at the furniture places. Is there anything else you need that I'm forgetting?"

"Nora, it's too much."

I tilt my head. "Do you know why I stopped calling you in prison?"

He blinks and looks at the ceiling. "I figured you were living your life."

"No. I didn't even know until today."

He looks at me and raises his eyebrows.

"I kept thinking Sean is dead whenever I thought about you, which didn't make sense because you were in prison. You didn't have anything to do with it. But I finally figured it out today."

He stays quiet.

I start to cry. "It hurt. So bad. My father, Sean, Nana... I knew they weren't coming back. But you were alive, and I couldn't see you. Every day you were in hell, and there was nothing any of us could do to get you back. You were there because you did what we should have done...what I almost did, the night you shot him."

His eyes widen. "What do you mean?"

"I heard you and Killian talking. I knew what you were going to do. I took daideó's gun. I sat in the parking lot, but I couldn't do it. I left and...it had to be only minutes before you got there. I should have been the one in prison, Liam, not you," I sob.

He pulls me into his arms. "No. You should not have done what I did. I made the wrong decision. Not killing him, but how I went about it. You used your head."

I look up. "Take my house. I want you to have it. I saved it. I didn't know why. Boris said to sell it or keep it, and something told me not to sell it. I want you to have it."

"Nora—"

"Please. Tell me you'll take it."

He hesitates.

"Please," I say again.

"Are you sure about this?"

"Yes. It will make me happy."

He smiles. "Okay. Thank you." He hugs me tighter and kisses the top of my head. He looks around and says, "You know what's going to drive my mom crazy?"

"What?"

Mischief fills his eyes. "Trying to figure out how to top this gift."

I laugh and wipe my face. "Yep."

His face turns solemn. "Seriously though. Thank you. This is beyond generous."

"There's something else I need to tell you."

"What?"

"It might hurt you."

He lowers his voice. "I'm listening."

I hesitate.

"Tell me."

"Hailee researched you online last night. Kora is the one who responded to your text."

His face hardens. "That's my fault. I wasn't sure how or when to tell her."

"I'm sorry."

"Is she scared of me?"

"I'm not sure. Things got kind of heated. I think I might have gone a little Irish on them."

His lips twitch. "Okay. Thanks for telling me."

I study him.

"Why are you staring at me?"

"You really have changed, haven't you?"

He shrugs. "There's only one thing I'm sure about anymore."

"What's that?"

"I'm never going back inside."

31

Boris

MY BROTHERS, ADRIAN, OBRECHT, AND I DECIDE HOW WE'RE going to deal with Zamir the next time he calls. But I remind them I was with him recently and it's going to be a while.

The city lot is still shut down because of the investigation. We don't know how long we'll be at a standstill, so we shifted our plans to start building on another lot first. It'll cost us an extra million, but it keeps our guys working.

Obrecht and Sergey work together and figure out who stole the steel. It was a handful of our Polish employees who had keys to our equipment. Obrecht and Sergey take them to the garage, and it doesn't take long to find out they are working for Zielinski. The problem is, they are so low on the totem pole, they don't know much more, other than they were hired to deliver our steel to Bruno's thugs. So it's no longer a hunch. The Polish mob is coming after us and we need to be prepared.

Nora and I are in the car on the way to the rehearsal dinner. I slide my hand up her dress and pull at her panties until they rip. "Oops."

She raises her eyebrow, straddles me, unbuckles my belt, unzips my pants, and frees my cock. "Oops."

I palm the back of her head and lean into her hair. "Why don't you sit your pretty little pussy on my cock one last time before you're my wife, moya dusha?"

Her green eyes sparkle. She licks her plump lips, rests her elbows on my shoulders, then hovers her wet heat over the tip of my erection. Her lips brush against mine as she says, "This hard cock?"

I clutch her hips and slide her onto me, groaning and matching her moans. She presses her hot mouth to mine, urgently flicking her tongue against mine while whimpering.

In under a minute, she unravels, her walls gripping my shaft in total bliss, her body shaking in my arms, and screaming her Jesus, Mary, and Josephs.

We pull up to the restaurant. I'm about to explode in her when my phone shrieks out Zamir's ring.

We both freeze. I lose my erection. And glance at the text.

Zamir: *Only half your annual debt was paid last time. Always be prepared.*

That mother—

"Boris, why is he texting you?"

"I wasn't even with him an hour last time. He's claiming my debt isn't paid for the year."

"He can't do that!"

I set her back in her seat, hand her some tissues, and grab one to clean myself off. She follows suit, and I cup her cheeks. "I need to speak to my brothers. Do not worry about this. I am going to end him."

She shakes her head. "How?"

"Do not worry. We need to go inside." I get out, help her out of the car, and guide her to the back room of the restaurant.

Both our families are there. I ignore the crowd of O'Malleys and beeline for my brothers. We move to the back corner, and Adrian and Obrecht join us.

"Zamir texted. He claims I still owe him for this year."

"Something isn't right," Sergey claims.

"We're ready. Everything is in motion," Obrecht claims.

"I'll move my honeymoon with Nora. I can't leave if he's going to—" The shrill ring hits my ear again. I pull my phone out. "Hello."

His cold, sinister voice hits my ear. "Twenty minutes." The line goes dead.

"Fuck!" I begin walking, and the others follow. "Twenty minutes."

The text comes across, and it's a place thirty miles away. "I'll never make this." I hand Sergey the phone, and he takes a snapshot of it.

"That's impossible."

I push through the O'Malleys and pull Nora aside. "I have to go."

"What? You can't. We just got here. It's our—"

"He called."

The blood drains from her face.

I kiss her. "Try to enjoy yourself. I'll see you tomorrow at the latest."

Killian and Liam crowd around me. They both cross their arms and raise their eyebrows.

"Make sure Nora stays with one of you at all times."

"Boris. Don't go! I have a horrible feeling," Nora cries out.

I kiss her again. "I have to. "

She tries to hold on to me. I growl. "Get her off me!"

Killian reaches for her, and Liam follows.

"Where are you going? Let us help," Liam says.

I spin and jab his chest. "Stay out of this."

He steps closer, and Maksim steps between us. "Go, Boris."

I kick my driver out of the car and race to the address Zamir sent. I'm eighteen minutes late when I arrive. His thugs pat me down. They hand the knife my father gave me to Zamir.

I didn't expect his call. I wasn't prepared. Now he's going to make me pay.

Zamir's dark eyes pierce me. A sick smile appears. He steps so close to me, I struggle not to retreat. His hand, covered in a black glove, holds my face. The scent of his personalized musk churns in my gut. In Russian, he says, "That O'Malley whore sure is a looker."

I shouldn't flinch. But my jaw clenches in anger.

He feels it and laughs. "Ah. Hit a nerve, did I?" He leans closer. "Is her pussy as red as her hair?"

I fist my hands at the side of my body.

"Tell me something."

"What?"

"Why didn't you find out the sex of your baby?"

My insides shake. He shouldn't know anything about the decisions we've made regarding the baby. But he's Zamir Petrov, the ghost who knows everything.

"You know the thing about secrets?"

I don't answer him.

He takes the blade of my knife and holds the flat part against my cheek. "Someone always knows the truth."

I don't know what he's referring to. Does he know what we've been planning? Is it about the bones?

"You're having a girl. And I know lots of men who would pay big money for her."

My heart stops beating. I struggle to maintain my composure. My insides shake, and my chest tightens.

Do not react.

Do not react.

Do not—

"They'd pay it for your whore, too."

I sniff hard, and he laughs.

He holds the point of my knife in front of my eyeball. It's so close, I'm afraid it's going to pierce me. "There it is. All these years and you still have a heart. I thought I taught you better."

I stay still, barely breathing.

He finally lowers the knife. The relief only lasts a millisecond. He repositions it next to my balls. "I've invested a lot of time into you. And we had a deal."

"I've done everything I agreed to," I growl.

Zamir tilts his head. "Have you?"

"Name one thing I haven't done."

Several minutes pass. He finally steps back and hands me my knife. "It's time." He spins and walks forward, and three shots ring on top of each other.

I lurch at Zamir, put him in a headlock so tight, his legs lift off the ground. "You know what I do to anyone who threatens my wife and unborn child?" I open my knife and hold it to his face. "I utilize the patience I've acquired over the years." I spin with him.

Maksim, Sergey, Dmitri, Adrian, and Obrecht are standing in front of me. Zamir's three thugs are on the ground, dead.

Maksim steps forward and leans into Zamir's ear. "When we killed your son, he pissed his pants. How long will it be before you do?"

Zamir struggles some more to escape my hold.

Maksim runs his black-gloved finger over Zamir's cheek. "The thing about the devil is he doesn't care who he shows up in. Right now, he chose the Ivanovs over the Petrovs. And every second, we're going to show you how we own Satan, not you."

Zamir keeps struggling, and I nod to Maksim. He holds a cloth over Zamir's face until he goes limp in my arms.

The bullets we used are untraceable. But Adrian still takes a tank of gasoline and pours it on each dead body. Sergey strikes the match and lights them on fire. Obrecht picks up Zamir's legs, Dmitri his arms, and they carry him out to the SUV.

More shots ring through the air. Adrian and Maksim get in my car, and the others go to the SUV.

"Bogden, you there?" Adrian asks on his speakerphone.

"All good. Nailed two guys." More gunfire explodes. I turn on the car and floor it. Dmitri follows me in the SUV.

For several blocks, there's more gunfire. Adrian and Maksim stay in contact with our guys, listing out Petrov casualties until we're at the garage.

"Pull back," Maksim commands our men.

We get to the garage and take Zamir inside. We undress him, then stretch his body out, so he hangs by his wrists and stands on his toes. When Viktor arrives, I wake Zamir up.

When he's fully conscious and scowling, I step forward. Viktor hands me the knife I always have to use when I'm with Zamir. I hold it in front of his face. In Russian, I say, "You think you can threaten my unborn child and wife?"

He smiles. "You mean your Irish whore?"

I stay calm, utilizing one of the most important skills he taught me. "You have whorehouses because no one wants your cock unless you force it on them. Before you die, I'm going to cut yours off and shove it in your mouth until you swallow it."

He keeps the scowl on his face, but I press my fingers to his racing pulse.

"Ah. It seems you don't like that idea."

His eyes turn colder.

I turn then spin back and punch him so hard, his cheek cracks and nose breaks. Blood bursts everywhere. He cries out in pain.

I step back and let the others have a few minutes of fun. I take off my gloves, go into the other room, and call Nora.

"Boris, are you okay?"

"I'm fine, moya dusha. We are all okay."

"Where are you?"

"Where we have full control."

She inhales sharply. "Boris—"

"Listen to me."

"Okay."

"I will not be back tonight. I want you to enjoy your family and spend the morning doing everything you planned. When you walk down the aisle, I will be there."

"What? Come back tonight. Please. You can do it later. After the wedding."

"No. I am marrying you free of him. He will no longer rule me or my family or present any risk to you."

Her nervous breath fills the line.

I close my eyes. "You are moya dusha. I need you to trust me."

"I do. I'm just worried."

"You have nothing to worry about. I am in full control," I repeat.

She finally replies, "Okay."

"Your brothers or Liam stay with you at all times until I return, understand?"

"Yes."

"Good, moya dusha. I love you."

"I love you."

"I have to go now. I'll see you at the church tomorrow."

"Boris!"

"Yes."

"You aren't going to need space, are you?"

I firmly say, "No. I will never need space again. And the only thing on earth I want is to marry you tomorrow."

She releases a breath. "Me, too."

"Goodnight."

"Goodnight."

I hang up, set the alarm two hours before the wedding, and stick my phone in my pocket. I walk back into the other room.

Sergey's behind Zamir, slicing his knife over the five-pointed star with a circle around it. It covers his entire back. Zamir is doing his best not to scream, but his breathing is labored, and his eyes are closed shut.

Sergey pauses and leans into Zamir's ear. He holds the bloody knife to his mouth. "When I'm done, I'm cutting your tongue out and clotting it, so you don't bleed to death. Remember when you taught me how to do it?"

Zamir swallows hard but stays quiet.

"You said all young boys needed the skill. Remember?"

Zamir still won't speak.

"Answer me," Sergey yells, and Zamir shakes.

Sergey takes the knife, slices the blade over his eyeball, and Zamir screams.

"You wear the symbol of the devil, but you aren't him. They say you're a ghost, but you're not that, either. When you meet Satan in Hell, make sure he knows I'm coming for you again when I get there." He steps back, takes the knife, and peels off the back tattoo as Zamir shrieks. Then he runs his blade down his naked spine.

"Fuck," Zamir screams in Russian.

Sergey's eyes blaze with a vengeance only a man who's been through what we all have can understand. He steps in front of him and holds it out. Blood drips down his arm. "Now I'm ready to show you what you taught me."

Nora

EVERYONE TRIES TO KEEP ME OCCUPIED AT THE RESTAURANT. My uncle Darragh comes up to me and takes me aside. "Nora, I heard Boris called you."

"Yes."

"He is safe, then?"

I nod. "He says he is."

"Do you know where he is?"

"Yes," I admit.

"And is it a safe place?"

"Yes."

My uncle puts his arm around me. He leans close to my ear. "When the man you love calls you from safety and tells you not to worry, you should trust him."

"I do."

He tightens his arm around my shoulder and puts his other hand on my belly. "I think you're having a girl."

I tilt my head. "Why?"

"You carry the baby the same as your mother did when she had you. Your auntie pointed it out the other day. I see it, too."

I get emotional. "I miss her."

His voice turns gravelly. "I miss all of them."

I wipe my face.

"Come and sit. You've been on your feet all night." He leads me to the table where Anna and Aspen are seated. They each grab my hand.

"Oh, jeez. I'm so sorry. I forgot to tell you they are all okay. They're at the garage," I tell them.

"With him?" Aspen asks.

I don't have to ask who she's talking about. "Yes."

Anna takes a deep breath and smiles. "When will they be back?"

"Boris said when I walk down the aisle, he'll see me."

Liam slides into the seat next to me. He pulls out a deck of cards. "I think it's time I showed all you lasses my superior euchre skills. Anna, you're my partner."

Anna winces. "I don't know how to play."

He dramatically gasps. "Aspen, please don't tell me I have to teach you as well?"

"Nope. I'm ready to kick your ass."

He laughs. "Well then, lass, show me what you've got. Anna, it's your lucky night. I'm going to show you all the tricks required to annihilate my entire family in this game."

I nudge him. "Speak for yourself."

Killian sits next to Anna. "I'll help you out a few rounds."

"Thanks."

Nolan and Declan join us and a few of my other cousins, too. More decks magically appear, and my rehearsal dinner soon becomes a big euchre tournament.

I lose track of how many games I play, and it helps keep my mind busy. When it's time to go, Anna and Aspen stay with me. Killian and Liam as well.

I change, get into bed, and Killian comes in with a bottle of water. "Thought you might want this."

"Such service," I tease.

He chuckles.

"What if he doesn't come back in time?" I fret.

"It would be an awesome way to rile up Liam's mom."

"Ha ha."

Killian stares at me for a few minutes. "You love him, right?"

"You know I do."

Killian shrugs. "Okay. He'll be there. If he's late, you'll just get married late. He's not standing you up at the altar. I mean, the guy did convert for you. That was a miracle in itself."

I cover my mouth and laugh, thinking about Boris repeating all the things the priest made him to become Catholic. "Did you have a hard time not laughing, too?"

"Especially when Father Antonio made him recite the ten commandments and vow not to break them."

Silence fills the room.

Killian rises and tucks the blankets under my chin. "Get some sleep. Tomorrow is going to be a great day."

"Promise?"

"Yes. Plus, little Killian needs you to rest up."

I don't break his hope and tell him Uncle Darragh thinks I'm having a girl. "Night."

He pats my shoulder. "Night." He turns out the light and leaves.

I close my eyes. Then I grab my phone and text Boris.

Me: *I love you. I can't wait to marry you tomorrow. And Uncle Darragh thinks we're having a girl.*

I don't get a response, not that I expect one. I slide farther under the covers and eventually fall asleep. When I wake up, it's light out. There's still no text from Boris, but I remind myself he's at the garage and in control.

I go into the kitchen. The scent of frying bacon fills my nostrils, and I see everyone is already awake.

I ask, "Has anyone heard from them?"

"No." Aspen takes a sip of her coffee.

Anna looks up from her phone and shakes her head. "Sorry."

"What do you want for breakfast," Liam calls out. He's wearing my apron with sunflowers on it and flipping pancakes.

Anna beams. "At least we have Chef-Boy-R-Liam this time."

"I'll have the pancakes," I tell him.

Killian grabs a few off the platter and sets a plate in front of me.

"Eat up. We have to leave for the church in an hour for your hair and makeup," Aspen says.

Anna jumps up and takes her phone to Liam. "Hey, this is the video on the flooring I told you about. See how it locks together?"

Liam studies it for a few minutes. "Looks simple enough."

"It's durable, too."

"Amazing what you can do with a phone these days," he says.

"Is it weird?" she asks.

"What's that?"

"So many changes?"

"Yeah, I can hardly handle phone updates. I think I'd feel like I was in the twilight zone," Aspen adds.

I don't know why Anna and Aspen are so comfortable around Liam, but I'm grateful.

Liam comes around the corner with the platter and sits next to Aspen. He looks at her with a straight face. "What's the twilight zone?"

"Oh. Umm..." She glances at us. "How do I..."

Liam starts laughing. "I'm kidding, lass. Yes, at times it does feel like the twilight zone."

"Hey, what happened with Hailee? Is she going to the wedding with you?" I ask.

Liam's smile falls. "I'm not sure yet."

"What do you mean?" I cry out.

"Calm down. I told her to think about it, and I'd call her today."

"Why did you say that?"

Liam raises his eyebrows. "Did you want me to force her to go with me if she's uncomfortable?"

"No. But why did you give her so much time? She should make a decision."

Liam snags a piece of toast off the tray. "Is this your Bridezilla moment?" He bites into the toast.

"No! I think she shouldn't string you along."

"Hailee wouldn't do that," Aspen says.

"Sorry, I know she's your friend and all, but—"

"It's a lot of information for someone like her to deal with, Nora. Give the lass a break. If I'm cool with it, you should be, too."

"You must really like her to deal with that," I mumble.

Killian takes a piece of toast and shoves it in my mouth.

"Killian!"

"Eat and stop talking."

We finish breakfast. I shower, get dressed, and we leave for the church. I text Boris again.

Me: *I'm leaving for the church to get my hair and makeup done. I hope you're okay. I can't wait to see you in a few hours.*

Like last night, I don't hear back from him. The longer it goes and I don't hear from him, the antsier I get. My hair is curled and put in an updo. My makeup is flawless. I step into my dress, and Anna zips me up.

"Wow! You look—"

"Jesus, Mary, and Joseph! What did you do to your dress?" My auntie shrieks in horror.

Anna bites her smile.

"I think she looks stunning," Aspen says.

"Me, too," Anna agrees.

My auntie steps forward and gapes at my chest. "You have way too much cleavage for church."

"It could be a lot worse," a woman's voice chimes in.

I spin. Kora and Skylar are both here.

"Did you ever look at the tabloids? The women on there have much more hanging out than Nora," Skylar adds.

"What about my sleeves? They look great, don't they?" I ask, trying to keep a straight face.

My auntie glances at them. "Yes, they are beautiful. Let me try and find you a shawl."

"No. She's not wearing a shawl," Kora says.

My auntie slowly turns and glares. "Who are you, exactly?"

Kora steps in and holds out her hand. "I'm sorry to be rude. I'm Kora Kilborn."

You can see the wheels turning in my auntie's head. She takes Kora's hand. "I'm sorry, your name sounds familiar. Have we met before?"

"No. I would remember you," Kora sweetly says with a smile.

"She's Chicago's top divorce attorney," Skylar blurts out.

My auntie's eyes widen. She snaps her fingers. "You were Mary Kelly's attorney, weren't you?"

"Sorry, I can't discuss my clients."

"You were. You took her husband to the cleaners."

Kora gives her a tight-lipped smile.

"Did any of you see Boris?" I ask.

"No," my auntie says.

Kora and Skylar shake their heads.

My auntie continues, "You did an excellent job. Her ex-husband is a rat. She said you found assets she didn't even know they had. He was begging for her to take him back."

"Tell me she didn't go back," Skylar says.

"Do you know Mary, too?" my auntie asks.

"No. But he sounds like an ass."

"Oh, he is."

I roll my eyes at Anna and Aspen as my auntie continues raving about what a great job Kora did on her friend's divorce. I recheck my phone.

Twenty minutes until the wedding and no Boris.

I pace the room, and more people come in. I ask each one if they've seen Boris or his brothers, but no one has.

At noon, the moment I'm supposed to be walking down the aisle, they still aren't at the church.

I try to call him, but his phone goes straight to voicemail. Aspen and Anna attempt his brothers, but it's the same.

At twelve thirty, I begin to panic. "What if something happened?"

Anna and Aspen try to assure me they are okay, but I see the worry in their eyes as well. Anna says, "Maybe you should sit down. You've been on your feet for a long time."

I ignore her suggestion. "Boris told me he would be here. Something is wrong."

Then it hits me. *What if he needs space?*

The all-consuming panic I felt the last time he dealt with Zamir returns. I clutch my stomach and bend over.

Aspen guides me to the couch. "Nora, take some deep breaths."

My chest tightens, and I get dizzy. I'm trying to breathe when Uncle Darragh comes in. "Nora, what's wrong?"

A tear drips down my cheek. "He's not coming, is he?"

"No, he's here. I came to get you."

I gasp. "He is?"

"Yes. He's been here since 11:30. His brothers have been outside waiting for him to come back out."

"Dmitri nor Maksim came to tell us they are here?" Aspen cries out.

"Dmitri's in trouble," Anna mutters.

Darragh shrugs. "We've had business to discuss with them. There wasn't time."

I rise. "Boris is okay?"

"Yes. They all are."

"Then why didn't you come get me at noon?"

Darragh raises his eyebrows. "Boris was in the confession box for a long time. Father Antonio looked sick when he walked out. He said he needed a ten-minute extra prayer break. But they are both standing in front of the altar waiting for you now."

I put my shaking hand over my mouth, not sure if I should cry in relief or laugh. I don't know what Boris told the priest, but I can only imagine. And I didn't expect him to take confession seriously.

Uncle Darragh embraces me. "Stop crying, lass. It's time to get you married. Lord knows the man paid enough to the church."

I laugh through my tears.

Anna and Aspen fix my makeup, and Uncle Darragh leads me through the building. When I get to the back of the church, the doors are shut. The organ begins playing "Here Comes the Bride," and when the doors open, I don't notice all the people. All I see is Boris, his eyes full of fire, looking sexy as sin in his tux, and a smoldering expression on his face. Before Uncle Darragh gives me away to him, he mumbles to Boris loud enough for me to hear, "You're an O'Malley now."

Boris pulls me to him. The humming in my skin begins. He leans into my ear, and murmurs, "Sorry I'm late, moya dusha."

I cry again and cup his face. The priest hasn't given us permission, but I pull his lips to mine and kiss him.

He puts his hand on my ass, tugs me closer, and firmly holds my head, kissing me deeper and deeper until my knees buckle. My auntie gasps in horror, and the priest loudly clears his throat.

Boris pulls back and murmurs in my ear, "You look stunning, moya dusha. Please tell me you didn't wear any panties."

I laugh, wink at him, and reply, "I guess you'll have to find out."

EPILOGUE

MC

Boris

3 Months Later

"Push," the doctor instructs.

"Come on, moya dusha!" I growl, holding her hand and pushing the hair off her face.

"I can't anymore," Nora cries out.

She's been in labor going on twenty hours, and the doctor warned us if it goes any longer, they will take Nora for a C-section.

I kiss her forehead. "Yes, you can. You're an O'Malley and an Ivanov. And you're doing so good. One more."

"I'm going to count to three, and I need you to push as hard as you can," the doctor instructs.

"Give me one more," I tell her.

She nods, crying, and takes a deep breath.

"One...two...three...push!" the doctor yells.

"Argh," Nora screams and squeezes my hand so hard, I think she might break it.

"That's it!" The doctor pulls the baby out, and everyone goes silent for a moment.

Why isn't she crying? My blood rushes to my face and pounds between my ears.

"Waaa!" the baby shrieks, and relief hits me.

"Congratulations, it's a girl," the doctor says.

I kiss Nora. "You did it, moya dusha."

She keeps crying, but now they're happy tears.

The nurse quickly cleans the baby off and hands her to Nora. The baby instantly latches on to Nora's breast.

I stare in awe at Nora and our little girl. "Shannon has your hair." We decided to name her Shannon O'Malley Ivanov after Nora's nana and to keep our promise to Darragh to have O'Malley as the middle name.

"And a lot of it," Nora laughs, stroking her cheek.

I kiss the baby's head then Nora's. "I love you. You did so good. You're a true champion, Nora Ivanov."

Nora beams. "I love you, too."

When I finally hold Shannon, she's well-fed and asleep. I'm in awe at how tiny she is and that I'm a real father now.

We stay overnight at the hospital. The O'Malleys and Ivanovs arrive to see the baby. The next day, we go home. I get a text.

Sergey: *We need to meet. Now.*

Maksim: *What's wrong?*

Sergey: *Not over text.*

Me: *Come to mine. I don't want to leave Nora and Shannon.*

Dmitri: *Give me thirty minutes.*

Sergey arrives first. He paces and is fidgety.

Nora asks, "Are you okay?"

His coloring in his face is off. "Yeah."

It's a lie, I can tell. "Nora, why don't you and Shannon go rest in the bedroom."

She meets my eyes. "Okay." She pats Sergey on the shoulder and takes Shannon with her.

"What's going on," I demand in Russian.

He steps up and points in my face. "I told you we needed to get in the Petrov organization and destroy it piece by piece until nothing was left."

My blood chills. I firmly ask, "What happened?"

Dmitri and Maksim walk in.

"We have a problem," Sergey says.

"What?"

"I had a visitor in my house today." He continues to pace.

My stomach flips.

Maksim steps in front of him and puts his hands on his shoulders. "What is going on?"

"Kora stayed over last night. She walked out of the bedroom to get something out of the kitchen. I heard her yell. When I got to the living room, Boyra Petrov had a knife to her throat and a hand on her naked chest."

"Boyra, Zamir's brother from Russia?" Dmitri barks.

"Shh. I have a baby in the house," I remind him.

We all step closer and drop our voices.

"Is Kora okay?" Maksim asks.

Sergey scowls. "She's shaken up. Adrian and Skylar are with her right now. He slit her arm."

"Shit. Was it deep?" Dmitri asks.

"No. But she bled and it hurts."

I scrub my face. "Why was Boyra in your home?"

Sergey's face turns green. "He said since his brother is dead, our debt carries over to him. And I'm the one who's going to pay it off."

READ CRUEL ENFORCER - FREE ON KINDLE UNLIMITED

A tormented soul on the verge of breaking...

The night we met, I joked about being his cougar. He said it depended on how much I could handle. Nothing prepared me for how Sergey Ivanov turned my world upside down.

Borderline scandalous describes the things he introduces me to. Every limit I reach, he knows to back off or keep pushing. Each sinful touch is a catalyst for greedy desire I never knew existed within me.

Once I step into his world, it's impossible to get out. There's no retreating from him. It's a magnetic pull swirling with pain and kindness unable to be defined.

The world views him as strong and intimidating. I see love and demons he never should have been exposed to but can't escape. Even when he thinks it's safe, it never really is.

He's my cruel enforcer...

READ CRUEL ENFORCER - FREE ON KINDLE UNLIMITED

SERGEY

CRUEL ENFORCER PROLOGUE

Sergey Ivanov

BEFORE ZAMIR DESTROYED OUR LIVES, MY MOTHER ALWAYS claimed when one door closes, another one opens. She would say it when we were down on our luck and barely had enough food or the lights would flicker off from an unpaid bill.

Somehow, she and my father always found a way to open the next door. Things in our home would get good again until the subsequent chain of events, so I always took new doors opening as a positive scenario.

Until Zamir showed me reality.

Ever since my father's death, I've seen how the door swings open but isn't full of light or ways to solve problems. All the new entryway represents is another path into some new situation, which seems to create more issues swirling with deeper pain.

Tonight, a new door opens. The feeling of dread washes over me when my phone rings. "Eloise, are you almost through security?" I've been in the airport waiting for her for over an hour. My driver parked in the car lot. According to the arrival screen, her flight landed, but she hasn't responded to my messages. It's not the first time she forgot to notify me when she got off the plane. And it's not always easy for her to get through the terminal, but this is the longest I've ever waited for her.

Over the last few months, Eloise's modeling career has significantly taken off. People recognize her wherever she goes and ask for autographs. While she won't admit it, she loves the attention. She will stop whatever she's doing and sign. I wanted to add a bodyguard to keep her safe, but she refused.

Her thick, French accent comes through the line. "Darling, I'm so sorry. I forgot to call you earlier today. I'm not coming to Chicago this weekend."

The pit in my stomach grows. "Is this a joke?"

Her voice turns to annoyance. "No. There's a new nightclub opening my agency wants me to attend."

I move to the side of the airport, toward the corner where there aren't any people. My delivery is calm, but I'm boiling inside. "I'm in the airport right now."

"Sorry. I got swamped, and it slipped my mind," she snaps.

Meaning, she wasn't thinking about me.

Does she ever?

"My brother's rehearsal dinner starts in an hour. The wedding is tomorrow," I bark.

Eloise groans. "Don't be dramatic. I'll see you next weekend."

My jaw twitches. I run my hand through my hair. "Don't bother coming. We're finished."

"What? Don't be silly. I'll fly in next weekend," she states, as if missing my brother's wedding weekend isn't a big deal.

I've said a lot of things to Eloise over the years. Never once have I told her I'm through with her. I breathe through my nose and close my eyes. "I told you months ago to plan on being here this weekend. It's a big event for my family. You've bailed the last two times, and this time, you didn't even bother to tell me you aren't coming."

"I flew in and surprised you to make up for it."

"Yeah, because you were horny as fuck, and only stayed four hours to get off," I spit out.

She rattles off something in French then says in English, "Stop being a baby. I'll see you next weekend."

"No. You won't. Have a nice life, Eloise." I hang up, text my driver to pull up, and storm outside into the snow. Out of all the nasty things Eloise has ever done, this I'm taking personally.

She's never committed to me. We only see each other when she's in Chicago. But she knows what my brothers mean to me.

I'm already agitated enough. My brothers and I intentionally created a war between the two most powerful crime families. The evidence we planted to set up one of Zamir Petrov's thugs was finally discovered. It linked him to the death of Lorenzo Rossi.

For months, we waited for the evidence to show up. It took all the patience I had to not obsess over it. If anything went wrong, the deal Boris made with Zamir for our freedom would be in jeopardy.

My mother created a debt with Zamir when my father died. My brothers and I were ignorant of it. Then Boris found out. I was twelve when Zamir kidnapped her. He made us learn to torture and kill men in order to save her. I don't remember which night with Zamir it was when my mother could no longer look at me. When he allowed her to return home, she couldn't bear to be in the same room as me.

We didn't get my mother back. We saved the shell of the woman who used to be her. The woman who returned to our home barely spoke to my brothers, but she completely ignored me. Shortly after, she killed herself. I came home and water was seeping under the bathroom door. I broke it down and found my mother in a bloody tub.

For five years, I barely slept. I never knew when Zamir would call. Nightmares haunted me. Men's voices, the smell of their decay, and visions of their agonizing faces filled my every thought day and night. None of it ever went away. Anxiety plagued me. If I fell asleep and missed his call, there would be consequences to pay. I learned the night of my mother's funeral what happens when you don't act on Zamir's wishes. My brothers got a front-row seat to watch.

Then, when I was seventeen, Boris negotiated a deal for our freedom. We aren't really free. Once a year, Zamir still owns Boris. That means he still owns us. Part of the deal is all Ivanovs are off-limits. So far, Zamir has held up his end of the bargain. I don't believe it will last forever. You can't mix with the devil and expect him to keep his word.

I'm always waiting for the other shoe to drop. Whenever Boris gets the text from him, warning he's going to require him to do whatever sadistic thing he has planned, my fixation on killing Zamir and destroying everything he's a part of intensifies. My insomnia can last weeks. Sometimes it'll stretch past a month. Screwing Eloise was the one thing to calm me. Except for the last few months. The few times I've seen her, the spark I usually feel for her isn't there. She begs me for my dick as she always has when we're together. In some ways, she's more desperate than ever for what I give her.

The problem is, her confidence, which I usually admire, has morphed into ego and snobbery. The remarks she usually reserves for others have found their way to me. While I control her in the bedroom, I would never want her to be a doormat in public or private. Somehow, she's under the impression it's okay to treat me like one. I'm not sure when it changed. So much is going on, I didn't notice it until recently.

When Boris called a meeting and told us the war had started, a calm went through me. You would think a war would do the opposite, but I could have just had a mind-blowing orgasm and smoked a joint after, I felt so much peace. Then he dropped another bomb. And the ticking in my jaw and tightening of my chest started all over again.

The head of the Polish mafia, Bruno Zielinski, visited Giovanni Rossi in prison. Giovanni is Lorenzo's father and the head of the Italian mafia. It makes me uneasy. If they form an alliance against the Petrovs, it will be harder to keep things in equilibrium between each side. The war could backfire on us.

My mother's words, "When one door closes, another opens," ring in my ears, but I'm not sure I like what I see on the other side. One thing I've learned is you need to choose your door wisely. Eloise standing me up for an hour at the airport during my brother's wedding weekend is just the icing on the cake.

Selfish woman.

Everything about our relationship is about her. I should have ended things with her a long time ago. I kept thinking we were too good together for her not to eventually drop her *I don't do relationships* act and commit to me.

All she wants is my cock.

Sure, everyone close to me thinks she's a bitch. She's a strong woman. I like that about her. She can stand up for herself and doesn't let others take advantage of her. In public, she's a piranha. She'll eat you up and spit you out just for looking at her the wrong way. It's a quality I wish my mother would have had. Maybe then she wouldn't have fallen prey to Zamir.

I never reprimand Eloise for her actions. It turns me on watching her alpha attitude with others. Not the times she is nasty for no reason but the ones where others underestimate her. One time, someone commented on us being together since she's black and I'm white. It was a woman, so I couldn't show her my wrath like I would have had she been a man, but Eloise put her right in her place.

Alone in the bedroom, she can't do anything without asking for my permission. Usually, it's while she begs. She's submissive. I'm the opposite and demand full control. Experiencing her morph from the powerful, take-charge woman she shows the world to one who fully trusts me to determine her every move is something I get off on. The first time I showed her who was in charge confused her. She wasn't used to it. No one had made her succumb to their every wish or made her give up her control. She didn't understand how she could love it so much. It created an addiction within her for more. I saw it. It's a side of her no one else gets to see.

Well, not many.

I know she dates other men when she's not in Chicago. I'm free to see other women, too. I rarely take advantage of my freedom and don't ask Eloise details about the times we aren't together. I did once, and it ruined our weekend. So I stay away from the topic, pretending it's not happening.

But it is. She admitted it to me drunk one night. She also confessed she loves me, how I'm the only man who truly gives her what she needs, and how she wanted to only be with me.

Then she woke up sober the next morning and conveniently forgot everything she blurted out. She hopped on the first plane out of Chicago, and when I tried to discuss getting serious again, she told me she was drunk and didn't mean a word she said.

Things were tense between us for a while. I decided to stay away from her and tell her we were through. Then Boris pursued Nora in secret, we started getting pulled into the O'Malley's issues with the Rossis, and Zamir texted him. When he disappeared, I felt like my skin was crawling. Then Eloise showed up at my door. So I spent twelve hours controlling and fucking her until it was time for my workout with my brothers. I went to it, came home, then woke her up. I repeated tormenting her until she lost her voice from all the pleasure I gave her.

She left for her flight, and I felt calm again. It's then I decided to once more overlook her inability to commit to me.

The next time I saw her, I took her to a grand opening for a restaurant my brothers and I invested in. At first, I couldn't put my finger on it. Then it hit me. She was annoyed to be with my family. She didn't want me to take her out to a nice dinner or spend the evening with people in my life. She was only here for my cock.

Her bitchy attitude was getting to me when an altercation with Lorenzo Rossi occurred. So she got her wish. I took her home and gave her what she wanted. But it didn't calm me how it usually did. That was the last time I saw her.

Now I get to be at all the events on my own this weekend.

I get in the car and light up a bowl. I need to calm down. I can't go into Anna and Dmitri's rehearsal dinner anything but happy for them. This is one of the rare times my brothers and I get to celebrate. I'll be damned if I let Eloise spoil it.

The ride to the restaurant isn't long. I pop a mint, rub lemon hand sanitizer on my palms, and try to cover up the scent of my weed as best as possible. My insides are still in turmoil but not as bad as at the airport.

I arrive and go through the motions. When Maksim turns up by himself, I'm surprised. I don't ask him where Aspen is, and I'm grateful no one asks me why Eloise isn't with me.

They're probably relieved.

It's not a secret my brothers don't like her. They've never said anything, but I'm not stupid.

I do my best to forget about Eloise and enjoy my family. At the end of the night, Maksim swiftly comes over to me and growls, "I need you to come with me."

"Where to?"

"Cat's Meow."

I raise my eyebrows. "Seriously?" The Cat's Meow is a co-ed stripper nightclub. It has everything you could ever want for a night of trouble.

"Yep."

"This your way of trying to get over whatever is going on with you and Aspen?"

"Not funny," he barks.

I hold up my hands. "Easy there. All right. I'm not doing anything exciting. Guess it's a night at the Cat's Meow. But do you want to tell me why we are going there?"

He scowls. "To get my woman."

My anxiety only gets higher when he tells me Aspen and her friends are in Wes Petrov's VIP suite.

When we bust through the door, Zamir's son, Wes, and his three thug friends each have a woman on their laps. Adrian headlocks their guy on the door right away. I only glance at Aspen and can see she's drunk and not overly excited to be on Wes's lap. Her fear from the current scenario of us barging in with guns and knives pulled is evident in her expression.

I ignore the other women. All I see are a room full of Petrovs I want to slice and dice and toss to the lions to enjoy.

After throwing out some threats, we get the women out of the room. Adrian and I are left. We slowly back out and hightail it out of the club. Maksim is standing outside his car, and relief fills his face. Adrian and I get into the back of the other vehicle with three of Aspen's friends.

Like Aspen, they're all beautiful women. One has magenta hair and slides on top of Adrian the minute he sits. "Thanks for saving us," she says.

He stares at her.

The blonde woman twists her fingers and winces. "Thank you. Sorry about that."

I'm about to respond to her when the woman next to me slides her hand on my thigh. Electricity races straight to my cock. I turn and remind myself to breathe.

She's stunning. Her dark skin glows against the dim light in the car. Her hazel eyes pierce me. They swirl with confidence, but it's different than Eloise's. Hers has a warmth and coldness to them. It's a polarity I've never seen before. Her lips are lush and pouty. I think of a dozen different things I want to do with her mouth.

She puts her face right next to mine. "You're the youngest Ivanov brother?"

"Yes."

"Thirty-three, right?"

"Last time I checked."

She looks me up and down, and a stirring in my belly ignites. She tousles the top of my hair. "So you're a young silver fox?"

"Kora!" her blonde friend mutters.

I don't respond. Out of all my brothers, I started getting gray hair the soonest. I only have a little mixing into my black locks. Maksim's hair is the closest to mine out of all my brothers. Boris has only a few strands of silver. Dmitri shaves his head. When I made a comment about my hair, Maksim told me not to worry about it, claiming it's made women even more attracted to him.

Kora ignores her friends and leans even closer. The scents of tequila and flowers mix in my nostrils and send heat down my spine. Her eyes focus on my lips then she slyly drills her eyes into mine. "What do you think of cougars?"

"Kora!" the woman reprimands again while putting her hand over her mouth and laughing.

I lick my lips, studying her, and she inches her hand closer to my groin. I reach for her hair. I almost groan at how soft it is with just a hint of coarseness to it. I twirl it tight around my fist. I grip her hand on my thigh, move it to her other hand and secure my fingers around her wrists. "It depends on what the cougar can handle."

READ CRUEL ENFORCER - FREE ON KINDLE UNLIMITED

ALL IN BOXSET

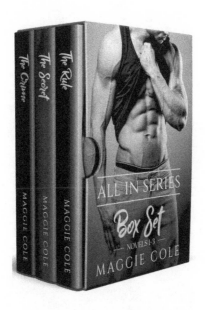

Three page-turning, interconnected stand-alone romance novels with HEA's!! Get ready to fall in love with the characters. Billionaires. Professional athletes. New York City. Twist, turns, and danger lurking everywhere. The only option for these couples is to go ALL IN...with a little help from their friends. EXTRA STEAM INCLUDED!

Grab it now! READ FREE IN KINDLE UNLIMITED!

CAN I ASK YOU A HUGE FAVOR?

Would you be willing to leave me a review?

I would be forever grateful as one positive review on Amazon is like buying the book a hundred times! Reader support is the lifeblood for Indie authors and provides us the feedback we need to give readers what they want in future stories!

Your positive review means the world to me! So thank you from the bottom of my heart!

CLICK TO REVIEW

MORE BY MAGGIE COLE

Mafia Wars - A Dark Mafia Series (Series Five)

The Ivanovs

Ruthless Stranger (Maksim's Story) - Book One

Broken Fighter (Boris's Story) - Book Two

Cruel Enforcer (Sergey's Story) - Book Three

Vicious Protector (Adrian's Story) - Book Four

Savage Tracker (Obrecht's Story) - Book Five

The O'Malleys

Unchosen Ruler (Liam's Story) - Book Six

Behind Closed Doors (Series Four - Former Military Now International Rescue Alpha Studs)

Depths of Destruction - Book One

Marks of Rebellion - Book Two

Haze of Obedience - Book Three

Cavern of Silence - Book Four

Stains of Desire - Book Five

Risks of Temptation - Book Six

Together We Stand Series (Series Three - Family Saga)

Kiss of Redemption- Book One

Sins of Justice - Book Two

Acts of Manipulation - Book Three

Web of Betrayal - Book Four

Masks of Devotion - Book Five

Roots of Vengeance - Book Six

It's Complicated Series (Series Two - Chicago Billionaires)

Crossing the Line - Book One

Don't Forget Me - Book Two

Committed to You - Book Three

More Than Paper - Book Four

Sins of the Father - Book Five

Wrapped In Perfection - Book Six

All In Series (Series One - New York Billionaires)

The Rule - Book One

The Secret - Book Two

The Crime - Book Three

The Lie - Book Four

The Trap - Book Five

The Gamble - Book Six

STAND ALONE NOVELLA

JUDGE ME NOT - A Billionaire Single Mom Christmas Novella

ABOUT THE AUTHOR

Amazon Bestselling Author

Maggie Cole is committed to bringing her readers alphalicious book boyfriends. She's been called the "literary master of steamy romance." Her books are full of raw emotion, suspense, and will always keep you wanting more. She is a masterful storyteller of contemporary romance and loves writing about broken people who rise above the ashes.

She lives in Florida near the Gulf of Mexico with her husband, son, and dog. She loves sunshine, wine, and hanging out with friends.

Her current series were written in the order below:

- All In (Stand alones with entwined characters)
- It's Complicated (Stand alones with entwined characters)
- Together We Stand (Brooks Family Saga - read in order)
- Behind Closed Doors (Read in order)
- Mafia Wars (Coming April 1st 2021)

Maggie Cole's Newsletter
Sign up here!

Hang Out with Maggie in Her Reader Group
Maggie Cole's Romance Addicts

Follow for Giveaways
Facebook Maggie Cole

Instagram
@maggiecoleauthor

Complete Works on Amazon
Follow Maggie's Amazon Author Page

Book Trailers
Follow Maggie on YouTube

Are you a Blogger and want to join my ARC team?
Signup now!

Feedback or suggestions?
Email: authormaggiecole@gmail.com

9 781792 347757